Wolf Tales VII

Also by Kate Douglas:

Wolf Tales

"Chanku Rising" in *Sexy Beast*

Wolf Tales II

"Camille's Dawn" in *Wild Nights*

Wolf Tales III

"Chanku Fallen" in *Sexy Beast II*

Wolf Tales IV

"Chanku Journey" in *Sexy Beast III*

Wolf Tales V

"Chanku Destiny" in *Sexy Beast IV*

Wolf Tales VI

"Chanku Wild" in *Sexy Beast V*

Wolf Tales VII

KATE DOUGLAS

APHRODISIA
KENSINGTON PUBLISHING CORP.
http://www.kensingtonbooks.com

APHRODISIA BOOKS are published by

Kensington Publishing Corp.
850 Third Avenue
New York, NY 10022

ISBN-13: 978-0-7582-2693-8
ISBN-10: 0-7582-2693-4

First Kensington Trade Paperback Printing: January 2009

10   9   8   7   6   5   4   3   2   1

Printed in the United States of America

One thing I never expected when the first *Wolf Tales* was released was the amount of contact I would have with readers. Now, three years after the series debut I can honestly say I have the best readers in the world—wonderfully generous individuals who are so supportive and open that they continue to amaze me with their kindness. This one's dedicated to you, for taking the time to drop me a note, for your encouraging words and, when needed, for your prayers and kind, supportive thoughts. You restore my faith in the basic goodness of the human race and make this sometimes frustrating career more fun and more emotionally rewarding than I ever expected.

Thanks again to my terrific beta readers: Karen Woods, Ann Jacobs, Devin Quinn, and Sheri Fogarty. You truly help me see the forest in spite of all the trees. As I've said before, this wouldn't be nearly as much fun without you.

Chapter 1

Rocky Mountains, Montana

Night was all around him, and the darkness complete, but he sensed he wasn't alone. It was unbelievably dark, considering his terrific night vision. He wondered, for a moment only, if he might be in one of the many limestone caverns nearby, but that didn't feel right. He thought of turning around, to see if he could see who or what waited behind him, but he couldn't move.

He tried to scream. His lungs expanded and his vocal chords strained, but he made no sound.

Why?

Impossible.

The voice in his head sounded smug. His own voice. *Well, of course. Anton Cheval knows everything.*

Bastard.

Well, crap. Was it possible to curse oneself?

Okay . . . so if I know it all, why the fuck are my arms trapped? Why is my heart pounding? Why can't I move. Why?

He fought whatever held him but fear exploded. Alive, a twisting, clutching thing, and it made its own horrible sound. His sounds. Heart pounding, blood rushing in his

2 / *Kate Douglas*

ears, the loud *whoosh, whoosh, whoosh* drowning everything.

Telling him nothing.

Keisha screamed.

My love! I can't move! His heart thundered, muscles
strained. *Nothing. Not a damned thing. I'm sorry . . . so
damned sorry. I can't help you. . . .*

Scalding tears filled his eyes. They slid down his face.
Hot, wet trails of frustration.

Lily cried. The terrifying sound ripped through him.
The heartrending cries of an infant, of *his* child! He fought
harder, battled through the cloying darkness, struggled to
reach out with arms like lead, tried to run with feet trapped
in thick, grasping mud.

The screams grew louder, more frantic. He ran blindly,
free now, but the very air surrounding him was impenetrable. Gelatinous, thick, clinging stuff. Someone had his
family. Someone was stealing his mate, taking his child,
taking everything that mattered.

Everyone he loved.

Gasping, Anton struggled harder, cried frantically for
Keisha. Called out to Lily, but he couldn't run and he
couldn't see and his world was ending.

It . . . was . . . all . . . ending. . . .

"Anton? Wake up! You're dreaming. You're having a
nightmare."

He blinked, shocked into awareness, surprised out of
cloying madness by the gentle glow of sunlight filtering
through the window blinds. It seemed so much at odds
with the frantic pounding of his heart. He took a deep
breath, relieved yet unbelieving, to see the lovely face of
his mate peering down at him.

He reached for her, ran trembling fingers along her
silken cheek. "You're okay? Lily's okay?"

Keisha laughed. "We're fine. I was already awake or

you would have scared me half to death, shouting like that. What were you dreaming?"

He shook his head. His body sagged back against the mattress as he realized his loved ones were safe. For now.

"It was nothing. I don't remember what it was."

But he did remember and he blocked his thoughts, hiding them away from Keisha. He remembered all too clearly the dream that had awakened him, and it was much too threatening.

It was the same dream he'd had, in one form or another, all this past week.

Someone wanted his mate and his child. Someone evil.

He was used to being a target. As the most powerful of the Chanku shapeshifters of the three known packs in existence, Anton was well aware of the risk of capture. There were those in the medical world who wanted his kind for study. Others in the government had hoped to create a secret army, breeding more Chanku to train and use for some unknown yet nefarious purpose. His race maintained secrecy as best they could, but enough humans knew the Chanku existed to make the threat of disclosure all too real.

It was one thing to worry about his own safety. Another altogether to worry about those he loved. He'd been entirely alone for so long. Then, in such a short span of time he, Stefan, and Alexandra had formed a pack. His life mate, Keisha Rialto, had joined them, and Keisha had given him the ultimate gift of love, their daughter Lily Milina. Just as Stefan and Xandi had produced little Alex.

Anton had never understood the strength of the family bond. Now he knew it all too well. Knew how powerful it was, how all consuming.

Finally, he understood the meaning of unconditional love. Even more, he understood the fear of losing what he'd not had before—that deep, immeasurable love of family. It weakened him, made him vulnerable. At the same time, the love of his packmates, of his child and his one true mate, made him more powerful than he'd ever been.

His abilities as a wizard had grown exponentially. He'd developed skills over the past couple of years beyond anything he'd dreamed of, among them a more powerful sense of foreknowledge, an ability to sense what was to come.

The problem was figuring out if he was merely projecting his own neurotic fears into what should have been restful sleep, or if he was having a valid premonition?

His premonitions had been frighteningly accurate, yet he'd had dreams just as frightening that were nothing more than dreams.

The secret lay in determining which was which.

His thoughts slipped back to the trip they'd all taken to Tia Mason and Lucien Stone's wedding in San Francisco, and the hijacking that had almost succeeded in ending their lives.

He'd worried about that flight for days. Had put his unease aside, assuming the graphic dreams were merely those of an overly concerned mate and Keisha's advanced pregnancy.

Then he'd come so close to losing her. So close to never knowing Lily, to never again holding his beloved Keisha in his arms.

Anton wrapped his fingers loosely around the back of Keisha's neck. He wondered if she felt his tremors. It took only a small amount of pressure to bring her close, to touch his lips to hers.

Lily slept on. The morning sun caressed Keisha's dark skin with golden fire as Anton slowly kissed her full lips, nuzzled the tender skin beneath her right ear. He twisted his fingers in the silken strands curling against her throat and drew her close.

She arched against him, her body supple and sleek in spite of the extra pounds she carried since giving birth.

Her full breasts, heavy with milk for their daughter, drew Anton. He ran his tongue across one turgid nipple, tracing the taut edge of darkened areola.

Keisha moaned and lifted her hips, pressed her mound against his burgeoning erection. The sleek brush of her pubic hair tickled the underside of his penis where he was most sensitive and forced his shaft up against his belly.

He reared back and slipped his cock down between her slick folds, sliding over her clit with his entire length. Raising up again, he dragged himself slowly back and then surged forth at the same measured pace, sensing her growing arousal with the increased heat and friction.

Keisha moaned. She spread her thighs and arched against him. With his hips maintaining a slow but steady rhythm, Anton's tongue lightly circled the darker edge at the base of her nipple. He pressed his lips around the swollen tip and flicked the sensitive nub with his tongue.

"Ah," she breathed, laughing softly. "Be careful, my love. I'm really sensitive and my breasts are so full they ache. Lily's not fed for almost four hours. We could end up with a very big mess."

He chuckled and gently ran his tongue around the taut curve beneath her right breast, then the left, careful now to avoid her tender nipples. Keisha's fingers clutched at the tangled bedding beside her hips and he felt the rush of slick fluids between her legs. The knowledge that she was so ready for him sent a new surge of blood through his loins. His engorged cock, already aching and hard, grew even harder, stretched even longer.

Her desire was a potent aphrodisiac; the evidence that she needed him every bit as much as he needed her. Raising his buttocks, Anton carefully positioned the sensitive head of his cock between her slick folds. He held still for a moment, savoring the heat and moisture, the soft clasp that teased him. Then he thrust forward, slowly entering her tight passage.

Amazing, he thought, how this rippling channel that clasped him so warmly could be the same passage their daughter had taken when she entered their lives. The same passage his seed had traveled almost a year ago.

Keisha enclosed him within her heat and sheathed him like a warm, wet glove, holding him tightly, drawing him forward.

Anton sighed. Nothing in his world felt better than this. *Nothing.*

Keisha raised her hips, inviting him deeper. Tiny whimpers escaped her parted lips when the head of Anton's shaft touched the hard mouth of her cervix. He held himself there, immobile, relishing the enduring warmth of his beloved mate, the tiny sounds she made that told him she was lost in desire, caught completely in sensation.

He was caught as well, preternaturally aware of her halting breaths, her beating heart, her desperately needy cries.

Then she shuddered beneath him and her thoughts grabbed his, sharing the pressure of his cock deep inside, sharing the ache in her breasts and the urgent yearning of her body for the friction that would take her so quickly over the edge.

She wanted. She needed. She must have more of him. More of his heat, more of the fullness, the thick girth and filling length of his cock. She wanted the pain that so quickly leapt into pleasure when the flared crown of his glans pressed against her cervix. The pressure inside when he filled her, then slowly retreated, only to fill her once again.

Anton began to move, thrusting deep and slow, driving the solid length of his cock over her swollen clitoris with each deliberate penetration. Her growing arousal fed him, her need increased his own. He felt the rhythmic clenching of her powerful vaginal muscles as Keisha reached for her climax. She arched her back, pressing him even deeper and he drove into her harder, faster.

Keisha cried out. Her fingers clutched his sides and her nails scored his back while Anton raced her to the next orgasm.

She won, shuddering beneath him once more. Her long legs wrapped tightly around his hips. Her heels dug into the hard muscles at the backs of his thighs and she strained against his lean torso.

Clinging to him, Keisha met him thrust for thrust. Anton wrapped his arms around her and reared back, carrying her with him. When he sat on his heels and felt the tight clasp of her vaginal walls holding him close, pulling him deep, their minds and bodies linked. Their thoughts blended into a single tortured flash of fire and light, and still he held on, still his hips thrust hard and fast against his mate . . . and his arousal grew, hot and demanding.

Anton groaned, caught on the precipice of climax. He buried his face in the silken curve of Keisha's throat. He was enveloped in her scent, her warmth, the salty dampness of her skin. He existed only in the firm clasp of her rippling sheath, the rhythmic plunge of his hips as he drove into her warmth.

Then Keisha nipped his shoulder. The stinging pain from her sharp teeth sent him flying over the edge.

A white-hot flash of pure, indefinable power rolled from spine to balls to rock-hard cock. Burning a trail of pleasure so closely linked to pain, it coiled and struck him like a bolt of lightning. His body surged forward. He felt the hot blast of his seed and the familiar touch of Keisha's mind to his.

Lungs bursting, lights flashing behind his tightly closed eyes, he cried out with his release. Still holding his mate in his arms, Anton's hips continued their steady thrusting into her welcoming body. His heart opened to her love.

His mind, all his thoughts and fears, were now an open book.

He could never hold a secret from his mate. No matter how hard he tried, in this she would always have power over him. Taking his seed into her body, she took his fears and his love into her heart. They fell together, collapsing against the thick comforter and tumbled sheets, their bodies still linked, their thoughts as one.

Keisha brushed the sweat-tangled hair away from Anton's face and kissed him softly on the mouth. Her tongue circled his lips and tangled with his for a brief moment, easing him down from such a mind-blowing climax. Her taste was ambrosia to him, the food of the gods, and it was his alone this morning.

Just as his thoughts, his dreams and all his fears, were hers.

Keisha's lips moved once more against his mouth. She sighed, a soft sound of exasperation and love. "It was a dream, my love. When will you learn to share your worries? You have to learn to tell me your concerns, not hide them from me. We're mates. You're not meant to carry these unnecessary burdens alone. No one will ever take me from you. No one will take Lily. We are yours and you will always keep us safe." Her fingers combed through his long hair. Her beautiful amber eyes glistened with tears. "We will keep each other safe," she said, and kissed him once again.

That she would try to shoulder his fears made him feel small and vulnerable, but her thoughts laughed at his foolish notion. Keisha shook her head. Once again she kissed his mouth. Lily stirred in her crib. Keisha raised her head and smiled at their daughter. "I'm going to miss her being so close to us at night."

He'd heard this argument before. "I know, but it's time she moved to her own room."

"I know, but she's so tiny."

"She's Chanku. She has an old soul."

Keisha laughed, and he knew he'd won this battle, at least for now. Anton rolled to his back, carrying Keisha with him. She raised up with her forearms crossed on his chest and her heavy breasts warm and damp against him.

He felt her turgid nipples where they met his chest, the press of her large breasts, solid with the weight of milk for her daughter. She kissed the end of his nose, teasing.

"I feel you getting hard inside me again, but Lily is waking up and my breasts are about to burst. Worry about that, not about something that's merely a bad dream."

He kissed her lips and smiled. The mental link had quietly slipped away. He could worry in peace, now that Keisha was out of his head. "Yes, ma'am. Now take care of our daughter before I decide you've not been loved nearly enough this morning."

Laughing quietly, Keisha slipped her body free of his and headed to the bathroom to wash away the remnants of their lovemaking. He watched her walk, lost in the slow sway of her rounded hips and the deep indentation tracing the sensual curve of her spine. She was so perfect, so trusting. So unwilling to admit to danger, even though she had once endured the worst possible abuse.

He would never let anyone harm her again. Not ever.

She was his world. There was no life without her, and once again, he worried.

Days later, in the still darkness of the late summer night, Anton stood on the back deck, alone but for his sleeping daughter in his arms. He was naked. The warm night air brushed his skin with a soft caress. The darkness felt personal, almost sentient as it surrounded him, as if it purposefully hid a lover.

Which, of course, was exactly what it did. Anton sighed and wondered how far his mate had run in her quest for a moment of silent communion with her own soul.

She'd carried the weight of his worry with her for almost a week now. While he couldn't stop the nagging sense of something evil in their future, he could at least release his dictatorial grasp on Keisha so she could enjoy a few hours of time to herself.

He held tiny Lily Milina's warm little body against his bare chest. He loved the feel of her soft skin next to his, the rhythmic puffs of her warm breath touching his chest, right over his heart. She slept the pure sleep of innocence, her body warmed by his embrace and a fresh diaper, her rosy lips puckered in a sleepy kiss that swelled with each little snore.

Keisha was entirely devoted to their little one, giving one hundred percent of herself, twenty-four hours a day, seven days a week. Somehow, tonight, Anton had managed to convince her to take time for herself. She'd fought him at first, but when he reminded Keisha that if she fell ill, there was no one as capable to care for Lily, she'd finally acquiesced.

Laughing at his persuasive turn of phrase, she'd allowed herself the luxury of a few precious moments alone. With only a small sigh of regret, Keisha'd managed to deposit their tiny daughter in Anton's arms and slip away, shifting into a beautiful dark brown bitch. Light shimmered across the tips of her fur in rich, russet patterns as she turned once toward Anton and her daughter, growling. Anton waved her off, ignoring her repeated instructions of how to take care of Lily.

As if he didn't know already? Now it was Keisha's turn to worry. He'd been laughing when she flipped her beautiful plume of a tail and ran into the forest alone, but he sobered as soon as she was out of sight.

He hadn't told her details of the dreams, but he knew she'd seen them in his thoughts. Knew she respected his worry, even though she felt it was merely his own need to find danger in everything she did. Still, as Anton stared into the dark forest, he almost wished he'd openly shared the vivid images that bedeviled his nights, the fears that gnawed at him during the day. He wanted her to understand the need to take care. Wanted her to watch her surroundings even as she raced alone through the dark forest.

As he let the worry take form once again, Anton caught himself. *No.* Keisha was right. He needed to learn to let go, to keep his compulsive need to control and protect under restraint.

It was a good thing he'd kept his worry to himself.

Keisha deserved this time alone. She needed to touch base with her feral half without the encumbrance of Anton's all-too-human fears.

A sound behind him caught his attention and he spun around. Stefan slipped quietly through the sliding glass door wearing nothing but a tired smile on his face. He carried a crystal goblet of amber liquid in each hand.

Anton immediately relaxed. "Hey, Stef. How's it going?"

Stefan handed one of the glasses to Anton and slipped his arm around his waist. He peered down at Lily. "I wish Alex was as relaxed as this little princess. Takes me forever to get him to sleep."

"Where's Xandi?" Anton lifted the glass to his lips. The smooth liquid left a warm and very welcome trail down his throat.

"She saw Keisha take off and decided to join her. Alex woke up the minute she put him in his crib. I've been trying to get him back down ever since."

Anton chuckled as memories flooded his mind. "Remember that morning when you told me Xandi was expecting? We shared a glass of this same cognac that day."

"Yeah. We were both bare ass that morning, too. What's that tell ya?" Stefan bumped his bare hip against Anton's and took a sip. "As I recall, we wondered how much things were going to change once the babies were born." He shook his head and laughed softly. "I had no idea."

"I imagine no new parent ever does." Anton cuddled Lily in the crook of his left arm and peered into the darkness once more. He promised himself, again, not to let his worries rule his life . . . or Keisha's. "Keisha shifts so rarely, anymore. It's been at least a week. I almost had to threaten her before she agreed to go run tonight."

"Hoping she'll come back horny?" Stefan grinned around the rim of the goblet.

"There is that."

But even as he made jokes, Anton worried and watched the dark forest, his thoughts following his mate through the night.

I'm really glad you came with me. Keisha crossed a small creek, sniffed a burrow on the far side, and waited for Xandi.

You should have told me you were going to run tonight. I almost missed you. Xandi lifted her paw and placed it carefully on a flat stone as she crossed behind Keisha.

I wasn't sure. Anton has been concerned. He worries that I don't take the time to shift and run, and then he worries even more when I'm not with him. In fact, he's driving me batty with his worry.

He worries because he loves you.

Keisha sighed. *I know. Still, he makes me feel trapped, even more than caring for Lily ever does.*

Xandi paused and cocked her wolven head. *Do you regret having Lily?*

Never. I miss the freedom Anton and I once had, but I can't imagine life without her.

I know. I feel the same way about Alex. Xandi turned her head to one side. *Did you hear that?* She moved closer to Keisha. *Ahead of us. Something rustling in the bram-bles.*

You, too? You're as bad as Anton. I haven't said any-thing, but he's been having these stupid dreams. . . . Laughing quietly, Keisha followed Xandi's steely glance and listened for whatever sound her packmate thought she'd heard.

It wasn't sound, but scent that came to her sensitive wolven nose. The acrid, sour smell of fear, of adrenaline and sweat. Someone waited beyond them. A stranger, pos-sibly two. Holding perfectly still, Keisha inhaled once again. Without turning to her friend, she sent a silent message.

Maybe his dreams aren't as stupid as I thought. There's definitely someone up ahead, one, maybe two men, near the base of the cliff by the waterfall. Fade into the brush. You go left, I'll go right. See if your mindtalking can reach Stefan. I'll try for Anton. Whoever is there is up to no good. I don't want them to get away.

Keisha hoped whoever was watching the trail had missed their swift disappearance into the heavy growth alongside. Creeping low to the ground, she slowly and silently worked her way through the brambles and thick undergrowth before she contacted Anton. Immediately, she felt the warmth of his mental touch and the sharp slice of his fear.

And, his typical, autocratic orders. *Stay away from them. Wait for Stefan and me.*

It's too late. I'm near their hiding place now and their scent is clear.

Keisha! Don't . . .

She immediately set her mental barriers, blocking Anton from her thoughts, knowing full well she'd hear about it later. Right now she needed to concentrate, and listening to orders she had no intention of following wasn't going to help.

There were two men. Definitely two. Keisha raised her nose and sniffed again. She scented Xandi on the opposite side of the trail before she caught the light of her glowing eyes, high up on a cairn of tumbled rock. Xandi crouched low with only the top of her head showing above the ledge where she waited.

I see them. Xandi's voice was a quiet whisper in Keisha's thoughts. *Two men, armed with rifles and what looks like lots of rope and a couple of leather muzzles. They're still looking down the trail, waiting on us. How could they know we'd come this way? That we'd run tonight? I don't understand it.* She paused, obviously frustrated, and then added, *They probably have tranquilizer guns if they're planning to take us alive.*

Did you reach Stefan?

Yes. He's on his way. Anton?

He's coming. Mei and Oliver stayed with the babies.

Good. I suggest we just wait and keep an eye on things.

Probably a good idea. Anton started giving orders about staying out of trouble and I blocked him.

You blocked Anton? Oh, shit. He is going to be so pissed. Xandi's silent laughter skated across Keisha's mind.

Let's hope he takes it out on our two visitors instead of me. With that dry comment, Keisha settled back on her haunches to wait.

Xandi's quiet chuckle echoed in her mind. *He'll need more than just these two. I bet he's furious. He's never even raised his voice to you!*

I know. And between you and me, I'd like to keep it that way. I'd hate to be the focus of his anger. Keisha's soft comment was met by Xandi's silent agreement.

Chapter 2

Mei Chen prowled the long dark hallway in Anton's sprawling home, her broad, padded paws soundless on the wood floors. Oliver guarded the grounds. He'd chosen his snow leopard form with its camouflaged coat of dark rosettes scattered across a pale background.

Mei rarely chose otherwise. She preferred the cat . . . and the company. In leopard form, her newly acquired spirit guide, Igmutaka, was a powerful presence within her. Their relationship had been more adversarial in the beginning, but over the past few weeks they'd reached an understanding, at times an almost affectionate cohabitation of the powerful snow leopard's form.

When she ran as the wolf, Igmutaka was an unhappy cat in the wolf's body. When she was Mei Chen, the woman, he was but a shadow of himself, present, though not overwhelmingly so.

Except when she made love. Igmutaka enjoyed sex, no matter what form Mei took.

In the snow leopard's body, the spirit guide shared an equal part with Mei, something she'd at first questioned and resented. Now, she welcomed him. His strength had become hers, his cunning, even his ancient knowledge.

More importantly, Oliver accepted him. Accepted what

was essentially a secondary male presence connected most intimately with his mate. He acknowledged Igmutaka's right to exist within Mei without any sign of jealousy or resentment.

She'd known Oliver was special when they first met. She'd never dreamed just how special.

The babies slept, their home protected by Oliver on the outside, Mei and her guide on the inside. She'd left the ever-present baby monitors near the front door in case she went out, and found a spot in the hallway where she could see both babies' cribs through their open doors. Silently she lowered herself into a crouching position, alert yet restful.

Minutes passed. The babies were stilll quiet. Igmutaka was a silent presence in her mind. At least until Oliver's voice brought her head up, her tufted ears forward.

Mei?

What is it?

I think I hear a car coming up the drive. Lights must be out. The engine is fairly quiet, but they're not all that far away.

I'm ready.

I'm shifting to wolf so I can contact Anton and let him know.

The lack of communication between the leopard and the wolf was the only drawback to this form. Mei stood and walked a few paces down the hall to a room that faced the driveway. She shifted and her human hands opened the window to the night breezes. She shifted again. The leopard's sensitive ears caught the sound of tires on crushed rock and the low hum of an engine. Oliver was right. A vehicle moved slowly up the long, tree-shrouded driveway.

Her heart hammered in her chest. Not from fear. The adrenaline rush merely prepared her for whatever was to come. Mei's large, sinewy body was tense. She and Igmutaka were ready for anything.

The babies would be safe in their care.

She felt Igmutaka stirring, his spirit gathering strength,

his power spreading from head to heart, to lungs and limbs. She opened her mouth in a silent snarl and waited, watching for their intruders to arrive.

Frustrated anger fueled his journey through the dark forest, propelling him onward every bit as much as fear for his mate. Anton ran alone, taking the trail directly toward their quarry, his dark wolven body a quickly moving target. Ebony claws grabbed the turf. Mud and grass flew behind him. As fast as he moved, Anton knew that Stefan kept pace, racing through the thick undergrowth on hidden pathways, his silence a direct counterpart to Anton's purposefully noisy run.

Anton reached once again for Keisha. He fought his outrage, furious with her for blocking his mental voice. He knew how she resented his attempts to control her, but he had no choice. Didn't she realize the danger she was in?

Oliver's voice slammed into him and Anton's heart thudded even harder in his chest.

We have visitors. Someone's coming up the drive. SUV. Lights out. They should be here in a few minutes. I don't want you to worry, but you need to know this looks like something that's fairly well planned. An assault in the woods timed with one at the house isn't accidental.

We'll take care of these two and get back there ASAP. Protect our young.

As if they were our own.

Oliver's voice snapped out of his thoughts so quickly, Anton knew he must have shifted directly from wolf to leopard. Thank the Goddess he and Mei were protecting the babies.

Stefan, we have more trouble. Oliver just contacted me.

I know. I heard him. I see Xandi. She's in position in the rocks above the two men. Keisha's in the forest to your right. Once you round the corner ahead, the men will see you.

They're just going to get a glimpse. Anton raced around the corner. He didn't give himself time to locate his adversaries. Instead he immediately leapt to his right, disappearing into the thick undergrowth just ahead of a dart that whistled past his flank.

It made a loud *thunk* when it struck the thick trunk of a pine tree behind him.

One of the men quietly cursed.

Anton tucked low and rolled when he hit the ground. A second dart buried itself in the trunk of a fir tree just above his head. Anton raced toward Keisha's scent. With his body stretched low to the ground he followed a narrow trail through the brambles, careful not to make a sound.

He knew immediately it was the same trail Keisha had used. Her rich scent filled his nostrils. *Where are you?*

Here. Behind the twisted oak. I've got a good view of both of them. Are you okay?

I'm fine. Other than the fact he wanted to throttle her for shutting him out earlier. He had more to worry about right now than his headstrong, independent mate.

Anton rounded the oak and found Keisha hidden in a thick patch of grass beside the twisted tree. The moment she saw him, her head pressed to the turf and her tail tucked between her legs.

Submission was not typical behavior of his alpha bitch.

Anton's anger melted away into the night. He slipped into the brush beside her and touched his nose to her muzzle. *What happened?*

Xandi and I were running, sniffing for game when she heard something. I scented the men almost immediately and we split up before they saw us.

They know now that at least one wolf is nearby.

I saw him shoot. Thank the Goddess he missed. What do you think they want? Your dreams . . .

I wish I understood my visions better. Frustration boiled through him. There'd been ample warning of all this. He hadn't trusted his nightmares any more than Keisha had. *I don't know what these two are after, but Oliver and Mei have unwanted visitors coming up the drive. They have to be acting together. We need to deal with these two as quickly as possible.*

Lily! Keisha's beautiful wolven head snapped around and her ears flattened to her skull.

She'll be okay. Mei and Oliver will protect both the babies. He hated the look of fear in Keisha's eyes, but she had to know the danger facing them.

Stefan's voice slipped into Anton's mind, linking both females as well. *Okay. I'm in position. Xandi and I are going for the guy on the right. Can you take the one closest to you?*

Yes. Give me a few seconds to get in position. Make it clean and fast and final. We don't have time to toy with them. We'll get our answers from the ones at the house. Go now.

The intruders hardly knew what hit them. Stefan leapt down from his place in the rocks beside Xandi. His powerful jaws locked on the back of his target's neck, the weight of his solid wolven body snapped the man's spine.

Anton's kill was every bit as fast, though not as clean.

His target must have heard something just before Stefan grabbed the first man. He cried out and raised his gun, but Anton's teeth clamped onto his throat and ripped through his carotid artery. The gun fired, but the dart flew uselessly into the forest. Blood spurted high, spraying a wide arc as the man went down with Anton's jaws still locked around his throat.

He struggled for a moment. His mouth opened in a gurgling scream. Anton reset his jaws and choked off the sound. Finally the man's body went still. Anton held tightly to his throat until the blood stopped pumping and slowed to a trickle, the pressure no longer governed by a beating heart.

Stefan and Xandi had already shifted. Xandi quickly looked through the supplies the two men had brought while Stefan searched the pockets of the one he'd killed. Keisha sat off to one side, ears still flat against her broad skull, and silently watched her mate.

Anton released his victim and shifted.

Only then did Keisha shift. She found the man's wallet in his hip pocket and handed it to Anton. They'd still not exchanged a single word. Anton took the wallet and touched his mate's hand with his.

"I'm sorry. You did the right thing. I should not have given you orders you couldn't follow."

Keisha's shoulders slumped and she lowered her head. "I'm sorry I blocked you. I want you to know I absolutely hate going against your directions, but I will when I feel I have to." She raised her head then, and looked at him directly, without any sense of her earlier submissiveness. "I'm also sorry I didn't credit your dreams for the warnings they were."

"I know. I wish I understood them better myself." As far as Anton was concerned, the issue was closed. He glanced inside the wallet. Credit cards, a California driver's license and the name of a business located somewhere south of San Francisco. It sounded like a lab of some kind. He quickly handed the wallet back to Keisha. "Stefan and I are going back to the house to help Mei and Oliver. Can you and Xandi take care of these two?"

He saw Keisha glance in Xandi's direction. Xandi took the second man's wallet from Stefan and nodded. "We'll drag them into the cave." She gestured to the rocky terrace where she'd been hiding. "Their injuries are consistent with a wild animal attack, should anyone ever find them. The odds they'll ever be discovered are fairly slim." She took the wallet from Keisha and stuck both of them in the low cleft of a tree to retrieve later.

Anton leaned over and kissed Keisha. "Good idea. Bring the wallets back with you. We need to figure out who the hell these two were, what's going on, who sent them. I'll get the info to Luc Stone. C'mon, Stef."

Anton shifted. Stefan followed him. With a final backward glance at their women, both wolves raced back down the trail and headed toward the house.

The black SUV rolled slowly into the shadows and stopped in darkness just beyond the glow of lights ringing the driveway near the main house. Oliver waited close by. His mottled leopard coat made him nearly invisible.

Mei remained on the porch, tucked down low beside the porch swing. She'd slipped through the open window and moved closer in case Oliver needed her, but first she'd turned all the house lights off. The porch was completely dark. The lights along the drive were solar powered, so she'd not been able to extinguish them, but their light might work to her advantage.

The intruders would be going from bright light to the darkened house, should they get that far.

Igmutaka's presence was strong within her tonight. She sensed his excitement and his coiled strength. Mei knew that, were she in human form, she might have laughed out loud. Who would have thought that Mik Fuentes's Sioux grandfather's spirit guide would end up inhabiting a mongrel Asian shapeshifter from Florida?

Of course, who would have thought little Mei Chen would grow up to be a Chanku shapeshifter in the first place? The many turns her life had taken since Eve Reynolds caught her shoplifting in a little mini-mart in Tampa still boggled her mind.

Mei heard the sound of car doors opening and raised her head, once again fully alert to her surroundings. There was no interior light in the vehicle, but with her powerful night vision Mei picked out at least three shadows moving near the side closest to her. She wasn't sure if there was a fourth one.

She wished Eve and Adam were here, but they'd gone south to San Francisco to see Mik, Tala, and AJ. A few extra bodies would come in handy about now.

The soft scrape of nails on the far side of the deck caught her attention. Mei jerked her head in the direction of the sound, and recognized the dark wolf as Anton Cheval the moment he rounded the corner. Another wolf, this one with silver-tipped fur, followed close behind him. *Stefan Aragat.*

Mei growled quietly, alerting both wolves to her presence. They couldn't communicate while she was in leopard form.

She closed her eyes, thought *wolf*, and shifted. It always took her a moment to get her bearings, going from leopard to wolf, and she felt Igmutaka's ire. He did not like this form at all.

I'm here. Silently she spoke to the two wolves, mind-talking in the way of their kind. *By the swing. Be very quiet. At least three, maybe four guys just got out of an SUV parked under the big fir tree at the end of the drive. There, just beyond the lights. Oliver's near them, in leopard form. Are you guys okay? Where are Keisha and Xandi?*

Hiding the bodies. Anton's terse reply told her nothing, yet explained everything.

Mei shifted back to leopard before more of Anton's thoughts slipped into her head. She'd been reading him much too clearly lately, and his anger at this moment was a living, breathing thing. Right now, she definitely didn't need the distraction.

Igmutaka filled her with power once again as she settled back to wait, watch, and protect. Anton and Stefan slipped quietly over the wooden railing and landed without sound in the soft grass below the deck.

Oliver? Anton and Stefan are moving toward your position.

Got it. I see them. Thanks.

Mei stayed put. She would guard the babies with her

life. Besides, she had a terrific view of the action from her spot here on the wide deck. If the men needed her, she was close by. She watched Stefan and Anton race across the front lawn, two silent, deadly shadows drawing closer to the three men standing beside the SUV. There was no moon, but her leopard eyes saw everything with perfect clarity.

Two of the intruders carried rifles. The third slung a large bag over his shoulder. They moved silently toward the house, walking single file, close to the dark perimeter where landscaping met forest.

There was a swirl of light and dark and the third man, the one at the rear holding the bag over his shoulder, disappeared. The two walking ahead, paused. For a brief moment it appeared they weren't certain they'd lost their partner.

Suddenly, two dark wolves charged out of the forest, moving so quickly even Mei was startled. Each one took down his target. Mei heard a deep grunt, a sharp snap that could only have been bone, and then silence. She reached out for Oliver. *Are you all right?*

Yes. We got three of them. I thought I saw a fourth guy get out on the opposite side of the car, but there are just three here.

One of the baby monitors near the door crackled with static. A baby cried out. *Alex!* The sound ended so quickly the silence shivered. Mei whirled around and leapt through the open window. She raced down the hallway. A dark shape hovered over Alex's crib.

Oliver! There was *a fourth man. He's here. In the house!*

She caught the intruder's scent, the acrid odor of fear and unwashed human. How had he gotten past her defenses? She was alone, the only one here now, to guard the babies.

Igmutaka roared within. Mei's powerful haunches bunched beneath her and she covered the distance from doorway to crib in less than a heartbeat.

She locked her jaws on the intruder's throat, heard a sharp *snap*. Her weight bore him to the floor. He landed in a heap. She figured he was dead by the limp sprawl of his body, the awkward twist of his head in relation to his shoulder, but she kept her jaws clamped tightly around his throat. Her breath huffed loudly through her nostrils. Saliva and blood soaked the man's shirt.

She felt the power of the spirit guide lending her strength, giving her the knowledge she needed to kill.

She was not nearly so alone as she'd feared.

When Mei was certain the intruder was dead, she shifted and checked on Alex. He lay in his crib, silent and unmoving. His eyes were open and he was awake, though he seemed groggy. His rosy lips were tightly clenched around a strange pacifier. Mei pulled it out of his mouth. It was sticky, covered with some kind of syrup and it had a strong medicinal odor.

Alex whimpered, a small, thin wail so unlike his usual rowdy cry. Mei set the pacifier on the table beside Alex's crib and raced across the hall to Lily's room.

If one intruder had gotten past her, there might have been another.

Anton's daughter slept on, unaware of the drama playing out around her. Mei ran back to Alex and carefully lifted him out of his crib. Silently she cried out again to Anton, to Stefan and Oliver, sending her mental voice in a commanding shout.

Within seconds she heard the sound of nails scrabbling on wood as three wolves raced up the stairs to the deck. The noise changed to pounding feet, and she knew they had shifted to get through the front door.

Mei held Alex's warm little body against her shoulder with one arm and ran back into Lily's room. Anton's baby girl slept on, but her sleep was the typical relaxed sleep of a tired baby. Alex, though, felt limp and unresponsive.

He had to have been drugged.

Mei glanced up as Stefan raced toward Alex's room. Anton and Oliver reached Lily's room at the same time. Oliver followed Anton through the open doorway. Anton went directly to Lily's crib. The light went on across the hall. Mei called out, "Stefan! Over here. I'm in Lily's room. I've got Alex."

Oliver stopped beside Mei and put his arm protectively around her waist. Before she could explain what had happened, Stefan called out her name.

"Mei?" Stefan burst through the door. He sounded frantic and she knew he'd seen the body of the dead intruder beside his son's crib. "Where's Alex? What the fuck happened?"

"I've got him." Mei carefully handed the baby over to his father.

"Thank the Goddess." Stefan let out a relieved sigh, cuddled Alex against his bare chest and gently rocked the sleepy infant in his arms. Tears rolled silently down Stefan's cheeks as he murmured quiet words of encouragement, as much to himself as his son.

"I think he's okay," Mei said, peeking around Stefan's shoulder, "but he's really groggy. The guy in there stuck a pacifier in his mouth to keep him quiet. It's sticky and smells familiar, like it had cough syrup on it. Something to keep him quiet, I guess. I don't think it was poison, but he's awfully sleepy."

"I'll go call the doctor." Anton took one last glance at Lily and raced back out the door.

Oliver slipped away from Mei and went into Alex's room, but returned to her within seconds. He put his arm around her waist again and held her close. She turned and wrapped both her arms around his neck and burst into tears.

Oliver held her tightly and soothed her with soft words of encouragement. "It's okay, sweetheart. You did great. He's dead. Neck's broken and he won't hurt anyone again. The babies are fine. Alex will be fine. Don't cry."

Oliver brushed Mei's tangled hair back from her eyes and held her tightly against his chest. He looked over Mei's shoulder and caught Stefan's eyes. "How's the baby?"

"I think he'll be okay. He's beginning to stir, so he's not completely knocked out. His breathing sounds normal. I wish Xandi was here. She always knows what to do."

"Can you reach her?" Mei raised her head from Oliver's shoulder and sniffed. "Does she know someone tried to kidnap your son?"

Stefan nodded. "She knows. She and Keisha should be here any minute."

Anton stepped back into the room. He'd slipped a pair of flannel pants on but his chest was still bare. "Here. Give this to him if he'll take it. It's Xandi's breast milk, some she had in the freezer. I nuked it in the microwave. It should be warm enough." He handed a small baby bottle to Stefan. "The doctor said to wake him up and watch him, make sure he's just sleepy and not acting sluggish or getting worse. Get some fluids into him to dilute whatever he was given. This should work until Xandi gets back."

Stefan took the bottle from Anton and placed the soft nipple against the baby's lips. Alex opened his eyes and stared at his father. Finally he sucked on the rubber nipple. From the indignant look on his face, it was obvious he knew this was not Mom, but he was hungry enough not to fight it.

He was also completely awake now, and definitely more alert.

"He's taking it," Stefan said. He glanced sideways at Anton, who now held Lily in his arms. "Thank you. Mei, Oliver, I can't thank you two enough. If anything happened to this little guy . . ."

"The same from me." Anton raised his head, but his eyes were on Stefan. "I never realized . . ."

"How vulnerable they would make us?" Stefan smiled and shook his head. "My, how things change."

Mei hung her head. Shame engulfed her. Tears flowed

without any control. "I'm so sorry. He never should have gotten in the house. I failed you, all of you. I . . ."

"No you didn't, Mei. We owe you more than we can ever repay. You did exactly as you should have." Anton's warm words were heartfelt. He sounded as if he meant exactly what he said.

Without meaning to, Mei searched his thoughts and found nothing but appreciation, and a sense of compassion for a young woman forced to kill. She sniffed and took the tissue Oliver offered her.

She still couldn't meet Anton's eyes. He had no idea she saw his thoughts so clearly.

Oliver squeezed her waist. Then he tilted his head and gazed steadily at his packmates. "Does either one of you have any idea what the hell is going on?"

Anton shook his head. When he spoke, his voice vibrated with a depth of anger Mei'd never heard from him before. He was usually so calm, so unaffected by the world around him. Unless, of course, it had something to do with his mate . . . or his child.

"Not yet," he said. "But don't worry. We will. Stefan, can you give Alex to Mei?" Anton carefully put his sleeping daughter back in her crib and led the others out into the hallway. He stood for a moment, staring at the floor as if gathering his thoughts.

When he raised his head, his amber eyes glowed. Anger created an almost palpable aura around him. "We have a busy night ahead of us. There are four more bodies to dispose of. We need to figure out who the hell these bastards are, and why they're after us. And then we have to notify the other packs."

He took a deep breath and let it out, as if forcing himself to remain calm. "Until we know more, we have to assume this isn't merely an attack against our group. It might be aimed at all of us."

Chapter 3

San Francisco, California

Tianna Mason walked slowly between Eve Reynolds and Lisa Quinn, her arms filled with a lavish bouquet of red and white roses, her amber eyes filled with tears. Tala Quinn followed behind, her head bowed.

Lisa, both packmate and lover, slipped an arm around Tia's waist in silent support. Eve glanced at Lisa and frowned. She and Adam had met most of the members of the San Francisco pack only a couple mornings ago. They'd been invited down from Anton's Montana home by Tala, Mik, and AJ, who hoped to recruit them to work for Pack Dynamics, the secretive Chanku agency based in San Francisco.

This solemn trip to Golden Gate Park had been unexpected. Eve still wasn't certain why she'd been asked to come along, nor did she know why they were here.

Their somber procession passed by the Japanese Tea Gardens and crossed an open stretch of green grass. Trees swayed in the gentle breeze and Eve heard the sound of laughter from children playing near a small lake.

They stopped at the edge of the grass where a tangle of shrubs grew thick and green. The morning fog had burned away, but the air was cool. Eve shivered and wrapped her arms around herself. She'd expected warmer temperatures this late in the summer, but it was actually cooler here in San Francisco than it had been up north in Montana.

She stayed to the back of the small group, curious, wondering if anyone would explain the reason they were here. Tia knelt down and plucked some wild clover away from what appeared to be a small slab of white marble. There was nothing written on it, though the symbol of a wolf had been etched into the stone.

Tia carefully set her bouquet on top of the stone, touched the petals with her fingers, and then stood up. Tears coursed down her cheeks. Eve dug into her pocket and found a clean tissue. Tia took it from her with a grateful smile.

"Thank you." She wiped her eyes and sighed. "Thank you for coming with me. Eve, I'm sorry. I realized just now that you probably have no idea why we're even here. What significance this place has."

Eve shook her head and shrugged. "No, but it obviously means a lot to you. I appreciate your including me. Can you tell me what happened?"

"My mother died here, right on this spot, when I was six years old." Tia knelt once again and ran her fingers over the white marble and the beautiful bouquet of roses. The other women sat with her, forming a close ring around the marker.

"What happened?" Feeling oddly out of sync, Eve settled her fanny in the cool grass. That was the last thing she'd expected to hear from Tia.

"She was shot and killed by a young rookie cop. He saw a wolf in the park and thought it was after a group of children, so he shot it. He had no idea it was my mother. No idea he was shooting a woman, a wife. Someone's mom."

"Oh my God." Eve touched Tia's hand. "You poor thing. I'm so sorry." She gazed at the mass of roses. Then she looked around her, at the beautiful, peaceful surroundings. It was hard to imagine violence in such a tranquil setting.

She turned back to Tia. "What about the cop? I can't help but think of him, too. He must have felt terrible. Whatever happened to him?"

Tia's chest rose and fell with her deep breath. "I married him."

"Luc? You mean your husband killed your mother?"

Tia nodded. "It was a long time ago. He's lived with the pain of what he did for all these years, but that horrible event led him to my father. Dad realized right away that Luc was one of us. That was the beginning of Pack Dynamics. Finding Luc was the catalyst for Dad to retire from the police force and go in search of more Chanku. He found Mik and AJ next, then Tinker and Jacob Trent."

Once again, Tia stroked the white marble. "You haven't met Jake, yet. He's settled in Maine with Baylor Quinn and Manda, your mate's sister. I know you've met them."

Tala leaned close and gave Tia a hug. "Mik and AJ told me what happened. I had no idea. It's hard to lose your mom, especially when you're so young."

"At least I had my father." Tia hugged Tala back.

Before Eve could ask, Tala answered her unspoken question. "My father caught my mother with another man. He shot and killed both of them." She said it so matter-of-factly, but there were tears in her eyes when she glanced over at her sister, Lisa, and added in a bare whisper, "Baylor and I testified against him at the trial, but it was Lisa's testimony that really put him in jail. She was there when it happened. It was pretty ugly."

Lisa reached out and took Tala's hand in hers. "We were old enough to be on our own," she said, "but it was really tough for a lot of years."

"How awful." Eve touched Lisa's free hand.

Lisa nodded and actually smiled. "You'll find most of us have had pretty unsettled childhoods. All of us who are shapeshifters now had mothers who carried the Chanku gene, but they never knew. Only Camille, Tia's mom, understood why she was the way she was, but she died before she could pass on her knowledge to Tia."

Lisa shook her head slowly from side to side, as if the memories were too painful to dwell upon. "Just think about your mom, our mom. Remember how unhappy you were before you found out you were Chanku? How unsettled? The drives and the unmet needs our mothers lived with must have been devastating for them. The knowledge there was something powerful missing in their lives."

She glanced away, beyond the four of them, and stared into the distance. Then she turned her attention back to Eve. "What's your mother like?"

Eve glanced down and studied her bare toes through her sandals "I have no idea. I was orphaned as an infant and raised in foster care. I don't remember my mother." She'd always felt so alone. Who was the woman who had borne her and then died? What had she been like? What would Eve's life have been like if her mother had survived?

She rarely told anyone her story, but Lisa's simple explanation made so much sense. "I never thought of what her life might have been like. Never even wondered what kind of pain my mother lived with. She was totally alone. She had no one. My father's name isn't even on the birth certificate. I always just figured she was a drug addict or a prostitute. I never knew what she died from. There's probably a record somewhere, but I've never checked."

"Still, that's really tough." Lisa rubbed Eve's shoulder.

"At least I survived. I was a few months old when she died. I went directly into foster care. Mei Chen, Oliver's mate had it really rough. She was abandoned in a public park. A little boy found her, umbilical cord and placenta still attached, all of it wrapped in bloody newspapers. Authorities never were able to locate her mother and she was raised in foster home care, too. That's how we met."

"Where was that?" Tala leaned against her sister.

"Tampa, Florida."

"You're kidding." Lisa glanced at Tala, then back at Eve. "That's where we're from. We were raised in a little town east of Tampa."

"Small world," Eve said. "You guys, me . . . Mei Chen, all of us from the same place." They sat there quietly for a moment. Eve figured they were all lost in their own childhood memories. She found herself studying the two women much closer. How come so many of this small group had come from that one community?

Tala's voice dragged her back to the present. "What's the significance of today's flowers, Tia? Is it your mom's birthday."

"Nope." Tia grinned and shook her head. Her long, dark blond hair curled in every direction and her beautiful amber eyes glittered with laughter and emotion.

"Well?" Exasperated, Lisa leaned forward as if she might be able to squeeze the secret out of her packmate.

"Well. Hmm . . . deep subject." Tia giggled and slapped her hand over her mouth.

Tala pretended to swat her.

"Okay. I'll tell. I wanted my very best friends . . ." she touched Lisa and Tala's hands, "and my newest friend here when I told Mom my news." She smiled at Eve. "Luc and I are expecting a baby. Sometime at the end of April, maybe early May. I can't believe it happened the first time we tried to conceive."

She was covered in hugs and kisses from Tala and Lisa. Eve grabbed Tia's hands and squeezed. "Congratulations. You must be absolutely thrilled."

"Well, yes and no." Tia laughed, but at the same time, she ran her fingers lovingly over the marble stone. "My dad got a message from my mom, after she died. She said I'd have two daughters. Two little girls with her sass and attitude. Dad's always interpreted her message as meaning I'd have twins. I'm hoping like hell he's wrong!"

"How many eggs did you pop out?" Tala leaned forward as if Tia's answer meant a lot to her. Of course, Eve thought, with two hunky males making love to her at the same time, Tala might be more concerned about that sort of thing.

"I think just one, but I'm new at this." Tia patted Tala's hand. "Why? Are you planning two at a time to keep the boys happy?"

Tala laughed. "That, my love, is my worst nightmare. Can you imagine short little me pregnant with twins? Especially from those two bruisers?"

Lisa hugged her sister. "You're all of five feet nothing and Mik and AJ both over six and a half feet? You'd be preggers from your toes to your nose."

"Thank you for that image." Tala glared at her sister, then burst into giggles.

Laughing along with the others, Eve suddenly felt her skin prickle. She glanced over her left shoulder. Two men seemed to be watching them. She looked at Tia, Lisa, and Tala and realized they'd not noticed anything.

When Eve glanced back again, she saw that the men had moved closer. They were now barely twenty feet away. She smiled brightly and turned back to the others, silently mindtalking. *Don't be obvious. Keep talking or laughing, but you need to know we're being watched. Two men to my left. They're slowly getting closer to us.*

You're right. Tia smiled and giggled, as if she'd just heard a funny joke. *They're acting like they're not watching us, but they're definitely moving our way. Stand up, girls. It's time to leave.*

Lisa and Tala hopped to their feet. Eve stood as well and held out a hand to Tia. The four of them stood together as if meditating over the small marble plaque covered in red and white roses.

Start walking back toward the lake. We'll cut around it to Nineteenth Ave. See if they follow. Tia led the way, chattering about the weather as if there were nothing at all on her mind.

They've changed direction and they're following us. We need to let the guys know. Tala walked at Tia's right, Lisa was on her left. Eve took the rear with the realization they were all subtly protecting the one among them who carried young. She wondered if that was typical wolven behavior.

There was so much to learn of this new reality, especially how to stay safe. She hadn't been a shapeshifter for all that long, but she knew she would protect Tia and her unborn child with her life.

Eve sensed the men drawing closer without even looking their way. She opened her mind and called out to Adam. He answered immediately.

I'm coming, he answered. *Luc's with me. AJ, Mik, and Tinker are already at the park boundary near Nineteenth. Watch for them.*

Tala noticed a group of three men ahead, blocking the trail. *It looks like our guys have friends up ahead, or am I just being a total neurotic?*

I think I'm sharing your neurosis. Lisa drew closer to Tia.

We're sisters. We're supposed to share things. They're watching us. Tala laughed, but Eve noticed a distinct lack of humor.

Do you want to cut through the bushes? Tia smiled at the others and nodded her head toward the thick undergrowth to her left. The two men behind them were only about thirty feet away and the women were drawing much too close to the group ahead.

Aren't we better off here in public, where people can see us? Eve's heart hammered in her throat. Fear seemed to clamp down on her windpipe until she could barely breathe.

Suddenly the three men up ahead turned and came at them. The sound of pounding feet behind made the decision to run an easy one. The four women ducked into the thick shrubs along the trail and took off, twisting and dodging through the tangled bushes.

I see them! Adam's voice echoed in Eve's head. *Run, Eve. They're right behind you. We're coming!*

Tala stumbled. Lisa grabbed her left arm and Eve caught the right. They practically carried her through the thick shrubbery, following close behind Tia. She ran like a rabbit, cutting back and forth along unseen trails, finding clear spots in the thick greenery where no one else could see. Behind them, Eve heard cursing and the crash of branches.

A cacophony of snarling and growling, punctuated by angry shouts and the loud thrashing of someone fighting in the thick brush ended in a scream of pain. The women stopped their headlong rush and crouched down, breathing hard. They were hidden from their pursuers by the thick bushes, though not that far away.

Two loud reports. Gunfire! Tala grabbed Eve's hand.

The noise and commotion moved beyond them, and away, until all Eve heard was the rush of their labored breathing and the cry of seagulls overhead.

Lisa grabbed her temples and cried out. "Tinker's down. He's been hit." She turned away from them and raced back the way they'd come, in search of her wounded mate. Tala, Tia, and Eve followed.

He wasn't far away, and thankfully, didn't appear to be hurt too badly. Their attackers were nowhere to be seen. Tinker, AJ, and Mik were huddled together in a tiny gap between the shrubs, totally hidden from anyone in the park. The three of them were naked.

Eve realized they'd just shifted from their wolf to human forms. Tinker lay calmly on the ground, leaning against AJ's muscular chest while Mik inspected a bloody slash running across the top of Tink's right shoulder. Blood dripped from the deep slice, shining brilliant crimson against Tinker's dark skin.

Lisa reached him first. Tinker caught her with his left hand and pulled her close against his chest. "I'm fine, sweetie. Don't you worry. It looks worse than it is."

Lisa burst into tears.

Luc and Adam arrived, their arms filled with the guys' clothing. Luc dropped his bundle and pulled Tia into a protective hug. Adam handed his bundle to AJ. "Didn't want you guys arrested for indecent exposure," Adam said. He leaned close and kissed Eve. *Are you okay?*

I'm okay . . . but I'm so glad you're here. Kissing Adam immediately settled her nerves. She tangled her fingers in his long, dark blond hair and inhaled his familiar scent. A sense of calm flowed over her, soothing her racing heart and taking away her worry.

Adam slowly pulled away from her and smiled. Then he knelt in the dirt next to Tinker.

AJ stayed where he was, supporting Tink's broad back against his chest. Mik moved aside and got out of the way with a nod to Adam. "He's all yours, bro."

Adam flashed a grin at Mik and placed his big, scarred hands over the bleeding gash on Tinker's shoulder. He bowed his head and closed his eyes as blood poured from the wound and dripped around and beneath his fingers.

While Mik slipped into his clothes, the others watched Adam. Eve practically glowed with pride. Her mate was the new guy on the block, still proving himself among the members of the pack. This was a chance for him to show what he could do. Just looking at him, no one would ever suspect the extent of his amazing abilities.

Adam looked like the quintessential man of the west— tall and lean with rangy muscles and work-roughened hands. He appeared to be exactly what he was—a mechanic, a farmer, a cowboy. A man used to working with his hands.

Someone who fixed things.

He might still be learning the extent of his Chanku abilities, but one thing Eve knew for certain—Adam Wolf was the guy to have around when something needed repair. It didn't matter if it was a broken toaster, a broken leg, or a bad carburetor.

Or, as in her own case, a massive head injury.

She heard the quiet gasps of disbelief and a soft, awestruck curse from Luc, who held Tia cradled against him. Both his hands protectively covered her flat belly.

The deep gash on Tinker's shoulder had already stopped bleeding. Lisa bit back an audible sob and clutched Tinker's left hand with both of hers. As all of them watched, the flesh beneath Adam's fingers began to knit. Within a couple of minutes, there was a pale pink seam almost hidden beneath dried blood.

Adam took a deep breath, dropped his hands away from Tinker's healed shoulder and sat back on his heels in the dirt. Sweat poured off his forehead, but he was grinning like a kid.

"Shit, man." Tinker turned his head as far as he could to see what Adam had done. "It doesn't even hurt anymore. I can tell it's fixed because all I can think about right now is getting Lisa naked, not how bad my shoulder hurts. What kind of mojo are you working?"

"Later, Tink. Now is not the time for getting naked." Lisa hugged him, laughing and crying at the same time.

Adam shook his head. "Damned if I know. I've always been able to fix things. Anton's the one who suggested it would work on people."

Luc laughed. "That's amazing, Adam." He shook his head. "Ya know, it used to bug me when everyone acted as if Anton Cheval knew everything there was to know. Believe me, I learned my lesson. Don't question Cheval. He's always right."

"What took you so long?" Adam stood up and stretched. "I figured that out the first time I met him."

Luc just laughed and hugged Tia closer.

"Get your clothes on, Tink." AJ slipped out from behind Tinker and divided up the clothes and shoes Adam
had given him. "No more of this lying around, looking for
sympathy. Besides, I get nervous when you guys start making jokes about Anton. He could be listening to us right
now."

Everyone fell silent. Eve was sure they wondered if AJ
was teasing or not. Anton Cheval was definitely a step beyond the rest of them. None of them really understood
most of his powers. Of course, no one, including Anton,
really understood Adam's either.

AJ slipped on his boots. "We better hurry. We need to
get back to our cars before they get towed. I think we're
all parked illegally."

"Great." Tala laughed, and the sound broke the building tension. "Whose going to bail those suckers out of im-
pound?"

"Won't be necessary if we get our butts in gear," Tia
said. "Luc and I can take my car. I, of course, am legally
parked." Tia smiled, but she was obviously upset. Obviously, the day had not gone as planned. "I don't think any
of us have been here long enough to get towed," she added
softly. "We haven't been here very long at all."

But long enough to change everything. Eve squeezed
Adam's fingers. His soft *I love you* filled her mind, followed just as quickly by, *I need you.*

As I love and need you. She smiled up at him and held
tightly to his hand, trembling now, in the aftermath of
danger. It wasn't entirely fear she felt, and she wondered if
she'd ever completely understand this new reality.

Her body pulsed with arousal, with the rush of adrenaline and the yearning sense of desire. Would she ever grow
used to this constant state of lust, the powerful libido that
seemed to overpower every other need?

I hope not.

Adam's wry comment made her smile. She realized she

was wet and swollen, her body anticipating the offer in his gorgeous eyes. They crossed the street to the rental car and he opened the door for her. Eve climbed in and buckled the seat belt while Tala, Mik, and AJ filled the broad backseat.

Eve couldn't wait to get to the rambling Victorian mansion Pack Dynamics owned nearby in the Sunset District. Lisa and Tinker spent most nights with Luc and Tia in Ulrich's home in the Marina District, but Adam and Eve had been given one of the individual apartments reserved for other Chanku, as well as their visitors. Right now, Mik, AJ, and Tala were the only others in residence, but the converted mansion offered privacy along with the sense of community the pack members craved.

They'd been offered a room, should they choose to stay here in San Francisco as members of Pack Dynamics. It was a beautiful city and a wonderful apartment, but it wasn't Montana. Eve already missed the towering trees and rugged Rocky Mountains, as much as she missed the sense of privacy there and the feeling of safety on Anton Cheval's huge estate.

Today had been a terrifying reality check. Why had those men been after them? Why, when she'd finally found the life and the man she wanted forever, was someone threatening to take it all away?

When she gazed at Adam, he squeezed her hand. *I'll keep you safe,* he said. *No one will ever harm you. I promise.*

She felt his words in her head and in her heart. Earlier, she'd only known abuse from men, but then she'd not known Adam Wolf. She leaned close to him and whispered, "Hurry. I want you now."

Adam didn't answer, but the tires squealed as he pulled out into traffic.

Chapter 4

Northern Maine

Some of the trees were already beginning to turn, this far north in Maine. The sky was a brilliant cerulean blue and the air so crisp and clear it felt as if you could see forever. Manda Smith stood on the wide front porch, naked as the day she was born, and reveled in the perfection of the day. She spread her arms, took a deep breath and laughed out loud for the pure joy of living.

"What's so funny?" Baylor Quinn stepped up behind her and wrapped his arms around Manda's waist. She leaned into his warmth, pressing back into the thick mat of hair on his chest until it tickled her spine. He nuzzled the sensitive skin just below her ear and made her giggle. She felt him quicken.

In mere seconds he was hard and ready, though they'd made love most of the morning. With Jake and Shannon away on business for a few days, she and Baylor had felt no need to do more than eat, sleep, and make love.

"Everything. Nothing. It's just so beautiful here, Bay. So perfect."

"So are you." He turned her in his arms and rested his hands on the curve of her buttocks. Then he kissed her.

His lips moved over her mouth, his tongue finding each point more sensitive than the last. He sipped at her mouth, gently drawing her lips between his, using his tongue to test the seam between them.

Manda groaned into his mouth as their tongues tangled. She pressed her hips close, catching his suddenly rigid cock between her belly and his before she finally broke away, laughing even harder. "You're right, big guy. I am perfect, and it's all because of you."

The days when she'd been a deformed, misshapen creature, half wolf and half woman, were not so far behind Manda that the memory had begun to fade.

Not even close. "Are you going to stand out here and tease me, or make love to me the way you should?"

Bay brushed a strand of her long blond hair out of the way and nipped the lobe of her ear. "And how might that be?"

Manda stepped away from him and looked out at the forest. She glanced back at Bay, winked one eye and shifted. With a little yip, the gray wolf turned, waved her long plume of a tail like a challenge and jumped off the deck.

She cleared the railing and landed lightly in the thick grass below. Manda knew it wouldn't take Bay long to catch her. She made it as far as the first line of trees where the forest met the cleared land surrounding the house before he finally got close. He caught her there, both of them running full out, and the weight of his body sent her tumbling and rolling through the bushes and beyond into a small clearing out of sight of the house.

Growling, feinting and snapping, Manda scrambled to her feet, but Bay was waiting. He crouched back with most of his weight on his hind legs, one paw raised, ears flat on his skull.

Manda shuddered. She reacted immediately to his aggressive pose, responding with an amazing rush of desire.

Her body turned pliant and submissive before her brain had a chance to consider any other alternative. She growled softly, then whined and crouched low. Her ears lay flat. She curled her lip in a soundless snarl.

Bay growled and stalked closer with raised hackles. He looked huge and ferocious, almost menacing—a totally dominant male wolf. The musky scent of his arousal filled the air, and all the fight went out of Manda. She rolled over and displayed her soft belly. The wolf leaned close, sniffed her sex and licked her there, dragging his long tongue across her vulva. Once and then again.

Her body shivered in response.

He sniffed again and Manda heard him whine. The needy sound seemed to come from deep in his throat. He snorted loudly, and then he backed away, raised his nose in the air and howled.

Manda scrambled to her feet and turned as if to flee, but Bay stopped her with a single paw to her shoulder. His sharp claws raked through her thick coat and held her. Whimpering, humanity momentarily submerged in the pure sensual response of the pliant bitch, Manda turned her back to him and planted all four legs to steady herself.

Bay mounted her, his powerful forelegs grasping her shoulders, his sharp cock probing the sensitive tissues around her vulva. She adjusted her stance and he finally slipped easily into her sex.

She whimpered again, but it was a sound of pure, un-equaled pleasure. This was what her body had been de-signed for, this ultimate connection between herself and her mate. Manda opened her thoughts, caught Bay's pure, animalistic arousal and more, his love for her as a man for his woman, his amazing sense of pride in all that Manda was, all she had become.

Manda knew she owed him her life.

From the pathetic, feral creature held prisoner by a body neither human nor wolf, to this—a confident alpha bitch in one world, a tall, graceful woman with a perfect body and brilliant mind in another. She had grown out of despair to become a combination of beings unequaled by any other species.

All of it due to Baylor's love, his patience, his amazing devotion to a woman who had once been so hideously formed, no one could bear to look at her.

Finally confident and whole, Manda knew she was now true to her dual nature—woman and wolf. She was Chanku, a creature both intelligent and strong, yet ruled by an unrelenting sex drive, a libido equally matched against her other strengths.

A sexual need only Baylor Quinn could ease.

Manda's body quivered with the first stirrings of climax. She opened her thoughts even more, crawled deeper into Bay's mind at its most basic until she became the air rushing in and out of his lungs, the strength of his cock thrusting hard and deep into his bitch. She was muscle and sinew, lust and desire, love and overwhelming need.

Manda growled, lost in sensation, caught in the mental and physical loop between herself and Baylor. She was both of them, feeling everything each of them shared and unable to contain all that she felt, all that she was.

Manda's climax hit with amazing force at the same moment Bay's wolven cock swelled and locked her body tightly to his. Her vaginal muscles stretched and adjusted and then clamped down on the hard masculine knot deep inside.

Clenching and rippling over his length, aware of the rhythmic pulse of his ejaculation, the sharp scrape of his claws on her shoulders, Manda rolled with the powerful sensations. She whined when his teeth caught the sensitive skin behind her ear in a painful nip.

Her nostrils flared with the musk of their mating. She drew the scent in deeply, filling her lungs full of its rich perfume. Her body trembled, shuddering over and over with the powerful jolts of orgasm. Caught up in the myriad sensations of their joining, Manda melded even more completely with Bay.

Merging totally into the synapses within his mind, sensing his thoughts on an almost cellular level, she became one with her mate. Her body's organs matched the pulsing rythm of his. The beat of his heart and the rush of his blood were hers. She felt the hard thrust of his cock from his perspective, her own rippling muscles holding him deep inside. She moaned with the pleasurable ache in his balls as if she were the one thrusting, the one aching . . . and then she shifted.

Lying there in the sun-warmed grass, blond hair tangled about her shoulders and eyes half-closed, Manda hovered in that near perfect bliss after climax. Bay remained a wolf, his large body tied intimately to hers, his breath hot against her neck. Manda's long hair tangled in his paws and his thoughts slipped easily into her mind.

Human or wolf, you are mine. Always mine. I love you.

"I know." She turned her head and looked into his amazing amber eyes. Baylor's eyes in the broad skull of the wolf. "As I love you."

His long tongue caressed her cheek. He shifted then, and they lay there in the warm sunshine, their bodies lax in the aftermath of another amazing orgasm.

Manda stirred, but before she could sit up, Bay shifted once again and she lay beside the wolf. He scooted down between her legs and ran his long tongue over her sensitive tissues.

Much more effective than a bath, don't you think?

She giggled with the sound of laughter in his silent voice, then stretched her long legs wide to give him better access. His tongue lapped at their combined fluids, and while he'd said his intention was merely to cleanse her from their lovemaking, his amazingly dexterous tongue managed to find her clit on every pass.

Manda covered her mouth with her hand and clamped her teeth down on her palm, though she wasn't sure if she was hiding giggles or screams. Already sensitive to his touch, her sex responded to his almost painful ministrations.

Her entire being centered on the slow lick and sweep between her legs, on the wet, squishy sounds of his mobile tongue as he found every crease and licked every crevice of her wet and swollen sex.

If he intended to cleanse her, it wasn't going to be easy. She was wet again and growing wetter.

The soft rasp of his hot tongue had her moaning and writhing with each amazing sweep. He held her down with his front paws and worked his broad, wolven shoulders closer. Feasting now, nipping lightly at her inner thighs to hold her still, his long tongue speared deep inside her sex, curled against her sensitive channel and managed to find her swollen clit with every sweep and lick.

Suddenly he was human once again. Manda hung there on the edge, aware that one more long, hot sweep of wolven tongue would take her over. Her body quivered and her vaginal muscles pulsed in time to the rapid beating of her heart.

I like this part too much because I know it makes you crazy. Bay's warm breath tickled her throbbing sex.

Manda whimpered, hanging by a single thread, hovering over her impending climax.

Bay's fingers thrust deep inside her vagina just as his lips compressed her clitoris. He suckled her, squeezing the tiny bundle of nerves between warm, wet lips and moist, soft, tongue.

Screaming, Manda arched against his mouth. Her inner muscles grabbed his fingers, her entire body clenched in a powerful spasm and held it forever. Finally she tumbled headlong into another screaming orgasm.

Bay's silent laughter followed her into oblivion.

She opened her eyes and watched as he licked his fingers clean of her cream. Her sex still pulsed and her nipples tingled. Her toes and fingers felt numb. When Bay finally stretched out beside her, Manda closed her eyes and wallowed in the magnificent afterglow of yet another mind-blowing orgasm.

She awoke some time later to a sense of something not right, as if things were out of sync or a little off kilter. Still wrapped in Bay's arms, Manda nuzzled her cheek against the dark mat of hair on his chest and filled her nostrils with his familiar scent. Then she turned her head, sniffed the air, and caught the slightest whiff of something that didn't belong.

Bay, do you smell something different? Out of place? Is there someone else here?

Bay rolled over slowly and rose up on his elbows as if to kiss her, but he took a deep breath and tested the air currents. *Get up slowly, like nothing's wrong. We're going back to the house.*

Should we shift?

No. There are intruders. In the woods near the rocks. I smell two, maybe three men.

She forced a smile when Bay stood up and grabbed her hand. She gazed up at him a moment, at the perfect body of the man who was her mate. Powerful and dark with the lean muscles of an athlete, he might have been a professional model except for the feral gleam in his eyes. Looking at him, standing so tall and powerful in front of her, so perfect, it was hard to believe anyone would be foolish enough to threaten them.

Bay pulled her to her feet. He wrapped an arm about her waist, holding her close. Then he took her hand. His long fingers tangled with hers and she squeezed him tight.

Together, they walked back to the house, two naked lovers holding hands and gazing into one another's eyes as if nothing but the two of them existed in all the world.

And while it might appear to anyone watching that nothing was wrong, Manda felt the heat of strange eyes on her and knew someone watched them walk away.

She wondered if the intruders had watched them making love. A cold chill coursed through her, thinking of their lovemaking, so personal and perfect, and the fact it might have been observed. She didn't want to consider an even worse scenario. What if the intruders had been there long enough, hiding close enough to see everything?

Had they been there, watching, when she and Baylor shifted?

When they reached the front porch, Bay pulled Manda in through the door as if he intended to make love to her again. Damn, he couldn't believe they'd been so careless, but the property was posted and fenced, and his senses so sharp he thought he'd have known there were intruders.

But no, it had been Manda who'd saved his sorry ass. Manda's sharper senses and awareness.

Thank the Goddess.

He grabbed his jeans from the living room floor where they'd ended up a couple days ago. Manda had already slipped into a pair of sweats. She was using Jake's powerful binoculars to study the area where they'd both scented the intruders.

Baylor loaded the rifle and stuck extra shells in his pants pocket. Neither of them said a word, yet they worked together as a perfect unit.

Until Manda gasped and the binoculars dropped from her hands. He heard them clatter on the wood floor.

"What the hell? Manda? Sweetie, what's wrong?"

"I know them. Two of them, anyway." She was shaking like a leaf. "I saw a third man, but I don't recognize him." She turned to Baylor, looking as if she'd seen a ghost . . . or worse.

"Who . . . ?" Bay touched her shoulder and tried to

touch her thoughts as well, but her mind was blocked and the walls she'd thrown up were impenetrable.

When she finally spoke, her voice was barely above a whisper. Bay grasped her hand to steady her.

"One of them is the man who raped me. The other helped tie me for him. He put the muzzle on me so I couldn't bite." Manda turned and stared at Bay, trembling so hard she could barely talk. "They're from the lab. The one where I was held the longest. Where I was tested and examined and experimented on for all those years."

Her voice was rising, her eyes blinking rapidly. Bay touched Manda's shoulder. She had to stay in control, no matter how frightened she was. "Sweetheart, I won't let them get—"

She interrupted him. Her voice trembled. "What are they doing here, Bay? Why are they coming after me?"

"Shit." Bay leaned down and grabbed the binoculars off the floor, but when he straightened up, he realized he didn't need them. The three men walked across the yard, evenly spaced and watchful, as if they had military training. They came directly toward the house, and while there were no guns visible, Bay had no doubt they were armed.

He grabbed the rifle and cradled it against his chest. At the same time, he sent out a silent call to Jake. He and Shannon were due home later today. With any luck they might be close enough to hear.

Nothing. *Shit.*

"Manda, you answer the door if they knock. Don't open it for anything. Remember, even if they saw you, they can't possibly recognize you. You don't look anything like you used to. You're not half wolf and they've never seen you as a woman. Your voice is completely different." He touched her cheek with his fingertips and gently kissed her mouth. "You're different. And you're mine. I won't let anyone hurt you."

She nodded, a sharp jerk of her head that couldn't hide

the way her body was shaking. Her thoughts were still blocked and Bay could only imagine what she was thinking.

What she remembered.

He knew exactly what had happened to her so long ago.

He'd been there, in those dark recesses of her memories when they'd finally mated as wolves for the first time, when they'd bonded as life mates. He'd seen more ugliness than any one person should have to endure. Manda had not only lived it, she'd persevered and survived it with bravery and grace—and she'd come out stronger.

There was a sharp rap on the door. Manda jumped. She glanced at Bay and took a deep breath. Then she called out, "Who's there?"

"Name's Ted, ma'am. Me'n my buddies need to use the phone."

Wide-eyed, Manda glanced at Bay and shook her head. *His name is Allen. I recognize his voice.* "I'm sorry," she said, glancing toward the telephone on the table. "We don't have a phone. You'll have to go somewhere else."

Bay heard quiet footsteps as if someone moved carefully across the deck and along the side of the house. He aimed the gun at the back door.

"That won't work, ma'am. Ya see, we're looking for someone. A friend of ours. She's lost. Name's Manda. You know her? We heard she might be out this way."

"There's no one here by that name. You're trespassing on private property. It's posted. Now please go."

"She'd be real easy to spot. She's different."

"She's not here. I said I want you to leave. Now, please." There was a long silence. Manda wrapped her arms around her waist. She was breathing hard, as if she'd run a mile.

"Sorry to bother ya, ma'am."

Bay heard the sound of departing footsteps, but he shook his head, nodding toward the back door. *Get down. Now!*

There was a loud crash. Glass shattered and flew as the back door slammed open. Two men rushed into the kitchen, handguns ready. The third man waited on the deck.

Bay dropped the first with a single shot. The second man spun around when a slug caught his left shoulder. He dropped down behind the kitchen counter, cursing.

The third man took off running, and something primitive clicked in Manda's brain. She stopped shaking, ripped off her sweats and shifted. Bay reached behind him and opened the front door. With a mighty leap Manda cleared the deck railing and hit the ground at full stride. Bay watched her circle the house and take off after the third intruder.

He hoped it was the one who raped her. Manda deserved her revenge.

He had to trust in Manda's strength, no matter how much he worried. This was Manda's battle, one she needed to fight on her own. Besides, Bay still had a wounded and very unwelcome guest bleeding all over his kitchen floor.

They had come looking for a woman who was half human, half wolf. It seemed apropos that a wolf would be the last thing this bastard saw. Slipping out of his clothes, Bay shifted and closed in on his wounded prey.

It was almost too simple to find him. Her heightened senses recognized the man's scent the moment she entered the woods. Manda wrinkled her nose against the familiar stench. Instead of fear, she felt nothing but anger. This man had raped her. He'd thought her so ugly, he'd gotten drunk first. She'd never forgotten the pain, the humiliation she'd suffered at his hands.

She'd been a helpless creature. Still a child, half wolf, half scared kid, convinced she'd been punished by a vengeful god for committing a hideous sin. She'd accepted the horrible things the men and even some of the women had done to her because she truly believed she deserved a living hell.

What else could she believe? Before he died, her father

had caught her masturbating. He'd told her then she would burn in hell, that God would punish her unless she stopped such disgusting behavior.

She hadn't stopped. And both her parents had died.

When she awakened after the attack that killed them, she'd become a horrible freak, half wolf, half human.

It wasn't until Baylor showed up on her doorstep and convinced her she was not some deviant, cursed creature, but instead a woman of value, that Manda finally realized none of what happened had been her fault.

She hadn't deserved their cruelty. Not then, not now. She was Chanku. Trapped in the process of shifting she'd lived as a feral outcast instead of what she really was—a woman deserving of love and compassion, an alpha bitch ripe with power.

Now she herded the man who had once tormented her. Herded him like a stupid sheep, forcing him from trail to trail until he finally entered a blind canyon. She knew the moment he realized he was trapped. Heard him curse and beg as he tried to scramble up the sheer rock face.

She growled and ducked low behind a boulder. He fired his handgun, shooting wildly. Bullets ricocheted off the rock walls of the canyon on both sides of her.

Manda moved closer. The stench of fear and unwashed male assaulted her nostrils. A rabbit jumped from behind a nearby bush and scampered back down the trail. Gunfire followed its path but the bullets pinged harmlessly off rocks and buried themselves in tree trunks.

Finally Manda heard the sound she'd been waiting for—the sharp *click* as the hammer came down on an empty chamber.

Before he had time to reload, Manda cleared the low barrier of rocks separating them. She caught the man in the middle of his chest and drove him back against the stone wall. Her snapping jaws missed his throat, but the handgun flew from his grasp.

With a panicked scream, he grabbed for Manda's throat. She twisted free. Snarling, she faced him. Paced back and forth directly in front of him, remembering.

He'd been one of the worst. Quick to cause pain, to embarrass and humiliate her. He'd known she had the mind of an intelligent young woman, but he'd treated her like an animal.

Worse than an animal.

The question was, could she kill in cold blood? His pistol lay on the ground. He was terrified, but unarmed.

She thought.

Suddenly he reached into his boot and pulled out a knife. The six-inch blade gleamed in the sunlight. He rushed forward, swinging wildly.

She went for his wrist first. Her teeth closed around his forearm and she clamped her jaws shut. The satisfying crunch of breaking bone was followed by a harsh scream of pain. The knife clattered to the ground. Manda twisted in midair, hit the ground and jumped again.

This time, she aimed for his throat.

She didn't miss. He went down without a sound. She ripped into the soft flesh beneath his jaw and then backed away from the spurting blood. His eyes were open, his mouth gasping like a fish out of water.

Manda shifted. Standing tall and proud, naked and perfect, she stared down at the dying man and felt nothing but disgust. "Sorry, Allen. I bet that hurts. Remember me? The little freak you loved to torture?"

He blinked and stared at her, dying but still aware.

"That's right. I'm Manda. Hard to imagine, isn't it? Not a helpless, deformed little creature now, am I?" She squatted down and looked directly into his eyes. "I want to be the last thing you see before you reach hell, Allen."

He blinked and Manda rose to her full height. She waited and watched while he bled out, until his chest no longer heaved in search of breath, until the shimmer in his dead eyes turned dull.

It took much longer than she'd expected.

It took hardly any time at all.

Bay's voice in her mind brought her back. His concern. His love. His need for her. Sighing, Manda turned away from the body lying in a pool of warm blood at the base of the cliff. Feeling somewhat dazed, she shifted once more and headed back to the house at a slow trot.

She needed a shower, badly. Needed to wash away the stench of death, the ugly feeling in her soul. She'd long dreamed of vengeance. Wanted the visceral satisfaction of seeing her tormentors dead.

Unfortunately, she'd never realized how empty it would make her feel. How sad. She had the crazy thought that she was thankful wolves couldn't cry.

Baylor met her at the back door. He'd slipped on a clean pair of faded blue jeans. His feet were bare, his chest covered only in the thick mat of dark hair. Manda shifted and flowed into his embrace. She burst into tears, sobbing, unable to catch her breath or form any coherent thought.

Blood covered the kitchen floor. There was more on the back deck, spatters on the walls, but the bodies were nowhere to be seen. Bay walked Manda through the house to the front deck where everything seemed perfectly all right. Where the only things she could smell were the rich, clean scents of forest and fresh air.

Bay sat on the old porch swing and pulled Manda into his lap, holding her, soothing her. Long minutes later, she managed to catch both her breath and her composure.

"He's dead, Bay. I killed him."

"I know. I sensed his death through you. I know it wasn't an easy decision, but it was the right one." He sighed and pressed his forehead against hers. "There's something you need to know."

Manda raised her head. "What's wrong?"

Baylor sighed, as if he'd rather not say anything. He brushed her hair back from her face and kissed her very gently on the mouth. "Anton called a few minutes before you got back. Someone tried to kidnap Xandi and Keisha's babies last night. The intruders are dead and the babies are perfectly safe, but it was a close call. This morning, five men went after the women from the San Francisco pack while they were in Golden Gate Park. They wounded Tinker in the attack but everyone else is okay. Unfortunately, so are the bad guys. They all escaped."

Manda pushed herself away so she could focus on Bay's eyes. "What else?"

He gazed out across the meadow in front of the house. "The ones up in Montana? The guys that went after the babies and their mothers? They're all from the South Bay. They worked for a bio-engineering lab. Not the same name as the one where you were held, but the way these places change names and ownership . . ."

"They know about us. They know about the Chanku." Manda covered her mouth with her fingertips.

"It appears that way. I checked the IDs from the two I killed here. Nothing to tell you where they worked, but one was from Belmont, the other from Oakland, both cities in the San Francisco Bay Area. It's too great a coincidence, especially since you ID'd two of the three."

"Have you told Anton?" Manda felt a chill run up her spine when he nodded, and along with that, a huge dose of guilt. They were all in danger because of her.

"When Jake and Shannon get back, we need to find the men's car. I've stashed the bodies of the two guys I killed here, but I want to run the car into one of the old quarry ponds. They won't be found in our lifetime. We need to see if there's any evidence in their car, any hint of why they're after us."

Manda nodded. She looked absolutely numb. "Bay, we need to do something about Allen's body. I just left him there in the woods."

"Don't worry. He'll go in the car with the others. We've got time. We'll take care of things once Jake and Shannon are here. I don't want to leave you alone. Are you okay?" He touched her chin with his fingertips and turned her to face him.

She loved him so much. He'd sacrificed for her. Killed for her. She'd never before realized how difficult that was . . . killing. But in so doing, Bay had saved her from the worst kind of hell. She felt like such a failure. Manda bowed her head, unwilling to make eye contact. "I didn't think it would feel this bad."

"What, sweetheart?" Bay wrapped his fingers lightly around her upper arms and softly rubbed her skin.

"Killing. I feel terrible for killing Allen. Even though he . . ."

"I'm glad. Killing should make you feel horrible."

"What?" His grasp on her arms tightened. She raised her head and frowned. "I don't understand."

He slid his hands down her arms and wrapped his long fingers around hers. "I don't kill easily. When I worked for the government, that was pretty much my job, but it's not something I ever did lightly. There are times . . . to save my life, to save the life of someone I love or have sworn to protect, that I've had to." His voice dropped even lower. He shook his head slowly, but he smiled at her. "Never for pleasure. Not for sport. Wolves kill to eat or to protect the pack. If you had not killed him, he would have found a way to capture you. You had no choice, but you should feel badly for taking a life, even one as foul as his."

Manda leaned back against Baylor's chest and thought about what he'd said. She wondered if Allen had a family, if he had children he'd loved. She finally decided she couldn't go there and survive intact. He was dead. That ugly part of her childhood was over. It was time to consign him to the past.

Bay's arms tightened around her waist and she snuggled against his chest while he held her in his lap like a child. They were still sitting there when Jake and Shannon arrived with some very unsettling news. Still there when the phone rang.

It was Anton Cheval. He wanted all of them to come to Montana. Another attempt had been made, this time against Keisha and Xandi when they'd gone to town for groceries. It looked like an all-out attack. Someone wanted the Chanku badly enough to kill for the chance to make a capture.

Wanted them badly enough to die. The question was, who? And why?

It wasn't until Baylor and Jake retrieved the body of Manda's rapist that they got their first bit of solid evidence. Allen carried a mobile phone in a small leather holster fastened to his belt.

One loaded with names, phone numbers, and dates. Baylor slipped the phone into his pocket and helped Jake carry the body back to the car.

Chapter 5

High Mountain Wolf Sanctuary, Colorado

Ulrich Mason rolled over and pulled his mate into his arms. She snuggled against his bare chest and made the sleepy little sounds of a woman well pleasured. Life was good.

He'd grown more comfortable living here in Colorado. After so many years on the edge, he felt as if he could finally relax and enjoy life.

After spending his entire life in San Francisco, this move to northern Colorado and the rural life Millie West had always known had been a major change for him. Much to his surprise, Ulrich loved Colorado. Even more important, he loved Millie. He would do anything for her.

Even leave his city, his daughter, his people. He'd founded Pack Dynamics so many years ago, it was like his own child. Now, though, his daughter and her mate were running the business even better than he had.

Damn, he missed Tia. Missed her husband, Luc, just as much. Lucien Stone had become the son Ulrich had never had, a young man who'd grown into someone absolutely spectacular. Luc was now an alpha male capable of running Pack Dynamics while loving and protecting Ulrich's beautiful, headstrong daughter.

Odd thing, that, to love the man who'd killed his wife so many years ago. But that tragic accident had brought much positive change to Ulrich's life, in spite of the years of sadness and the irreplaceable loss.

Camille's life had been cut short and he and his daughter had suffered, yet out of the tragedy had come a future for the fine young men he'd drawn together when he'd built Pack Dynamics.

Overall, the ensuing years had been good. He'd made his peace with Camille's spirit, raised his daughter as best he could, and brought together an amazing group of shapeshifters in an even more amazing agency that still managed to save lives and solve crimes no one else could handle. And now, at a point in his life when he'd never expected to find love again, he had Millie.

"Are you awake?" Millie's soft voice broke into his memories. "It's the middle of the night."

He kissed her, lingering on the taste of her lips, the curve of her jaw, the soft swell of her breasts. "Actually, it's almost five. We have to get up soon."

"I was afraid of that, but you're right. We need to move some of the animals into their winter pens. Hard to believe the summer is ending."

"Nothing wrong with long, cold nights." Ulrich ran his fingers along her side, tracing each rib until he reached the gentle swell of her belly. Lower, then down through the soft curls between her thighs and into the damp heat below.

Millie arched her hips and groaned. "Ah . . . Ric! This is not how I go back to sleep."

"I hope not." Chuckling quietly, Ulrich slipped his fingers between the moist lips of her sex. Moving them slowly in and out, he managed to find her clit on each downward stroke.

"You fight dirty." She groaned and arched into his touch.

Ulrich laughed. "I'm old. I know more tricks."

Millie whimpered when he stroked her deeper. "Ah . . . we just did this an hour ago. Oh . . . there. Yes!" She arched her back higher and sighed and he knew he'd found the perfect spot with his probing fingers. "I have to admit," she whispered, "I love your tricks."

"I know. You love me as well. In fact, you love me so much you'll let me take you now, when it's not quite five in the morning."

Millie raised up on one elbow and squinted at the bedside clock. "Beast. It's only a quarter after four." She flopped back down beside him.

"See? Almost five." He leaned close and kissed her mouth, running his tongue along the seam between her lips. Millie opened to him. Opened her mouth, opened her thoughts . . . opened her heart.

Groaning, Ulrich rolled her away from him and spooned her closely from behind. He found her breasts with both hands and plucked at her stiff nipples until she groaned her acquiescence.

"Are you ready for me, Millie, m'love?" Ulrich nuzzled the line of vertebrae along the curve of her neck and nipped her shoulder.

"Always." Millie rolled a bit more and raised up on her forearms and knees, presenting herself like the receptive bitch she was. Ulrich knelt behind her and took his cock in his hand, swept it along her moist sex and then surged forward. He buried himself to the balls in one long thrust. Then he held still for a moment, savoring the tight clasp of Millie's rippling muscles and the hot gush of her fluids. His lungs expanded as he breathed in her warm, morning scent. Pressing his thighs against Millie's, he felt the sensitive crown of his cock slide against the hard mouth of her womb.

This was perfection. Holding her. Loving her.

Just loving her for all she was worth.

"I am a very lucky man, m'love. Very lucky." Ulrich thrust deep and withdrew, then again, setting up the rhythm that he knew would take her over the top.

"Not as lucky as I am." Millie turned to watch him over her shoulder. Outside, a wolf howled, and then another, joining its packmate as night drifted into dawn.

The mournful sound sent shivers along Ulrich's spine and he battled a need to join them. Then Millie growled, a feral sound deep in her throat and Ulrich no longer fought his nature. He shifted, changing from man to wolf in a heartbeat. His cock was longer, sharper. He penetrated deeper and faster, his forelegs grasping Millie's shoulders, his cock surging deep, hitting her cervix on every thrust.

She cried out, a cry of pain that morphed into a long, low howl of glorious pleasure. Her muscles clasped him tightly, and Millie shifted. The change was instantaneous and the woman became the wolf, the alpha bitch, Chanku.

Two wolves mated, hips thrusting, tails aloft, held stiffly behind them amid the twisted sheets and tumbled blankets on the bed.

When Ulrich's wolven cock swelled within his mate and locked him tightly to her sex, he shuddered and clung to her. His black nails dug deep furrows into her reddish-brown coat and his heart pounded out a beat in perfect rhythm with hers.

He collapsed to the bed, taking Millie with him. They lay there together, his midnight fur melding with her brown, his grizzled muzzle resting on Millie's soft shoulder, their sex tightly linked—as tight as their thoughts, as once again they found the deepest connection known to their kind.

Nothing compared to the mental bond of mated Chanku. Ulrich's thoughts were Millie's and her memories and dreams were his. Shared, dissected, accepted, and understood.

Millie knew his love for his late wife. She felt a kindred affection for the woman and a powerful love for the man who had proved to be her own salvation. Ulrich knew Millie's loneliness, her steadfast desire to know her children, her love for those babies she had lost at birth, and the adults they had become.

Adults who now, finally, knew Millie as their mother.

Most of all, he felt her love. Boundless, unchanging, a powerful emotion complete and unadorned. She loved. That was all Ulrich needed. Pure and powerful love.

Millie shifted first, still bound to the wolf, her body clenching around him in the final moments of her climax. He knew she loved this feeling, this amazing moment with her humanity linked to his beast. It epitomized the power of their devotion, the fact that nothing would come between them so long as they had this connection.

They dozed, the two of them, woman and wolf. The swelling that held Ulrich inside Millie had long ago subsided, but he had no reason to pull himself free of her moist and welcoming heat.

Until the phone rang. With a deep groan, Ulrich roused himself, morphed into man and reached for the phone. When, after a terse conversation, he placed it back in the cradle, Millie raised up on one elbow.

"There's trouble, isn't there? What's happened?"

Ulrich lay back beside her and cradled Millie in his arms. She lay her head on his chest, just over his beating heart. "That was Anton. Someone tried to kidnap his daughter and Stefan's son a couple nights ago, while at the same time another couple of bastards made an attempt to grab Keisha and Xandi. Both failed. The next morning, an attempt was made on the women of the San Francisco pack, including Tia. I can't believe she didn't tell me." He shook his head. Tia tried so hard to protect him from worry . . . as if he needed protection!

"Is Tia okay?"

He nodded. "She's fine, thank the Goddess. At least she is until I get hold of her." He laughed without humor, and then ran his fingers down Millie's smooth cheek, loving her more every time he touched her. "There's more. About the time Tia and her friends were being pursued, someone went after Bay and Manda up in Maine. Yesterday evening, a second attempt was made on Keisha and Xandi when they went into town to shop."

"Manda . . . is she . . . ?" Millie touched her fingers to his face. Ulrich covered her hand with his.

"Everyone is fine and there are a number of bodies that will never see the light of day, but obviously there's a damned good reason for concern. It sounds like an all-out assault. Anton wants us to meet at his place in Montana as soon as we can be there. He thinks if we're all together, we might be able to figure out what's going on. Can you get someone to cover the sanctuary so we can go?"

"Of course." Millie sat up and swung her legs over the side of the bed. "You make the travel arrangements, I'll take care of the sanctuary. There's nothing pressing right now and it's a good chance to see if the folks we've hired can handle things without me. We should probably leave as soon as we're able."

Ulrich grinned. "That's one of the things I love about you Millie. You never ask why or how. You just get things done."

She leaned over and kissed him. "I was single for a lot of years, Ulrich Mason. If I didn't get things done, there was no one else to do them. Besides, this means I'll get to see Adam and Manda again. I missed way too many years with my babies. Now get that fine butt of yours out of bed. We have work to do."

"Yes ma'am," he said. Then he saluted and did exactly as Millie requested.

* * *

Keisha made one last inspection of their walk-in freezer and then checked the goods in the pantry. With seventeen more hungry mouths to feed around the dinner table expected by tomorrow evening, she needed plenty of food on hand.

She set her lists on the kitchen table, thankful to have such a tedious job. It took her mind off the reason for this unprecedented gathering of all they knew among the Chanku.

If she let herself think about the danger they were in, she'd never step outside again.

Last night's attack while she and Xandi were on a quick run to the grocery store, had left her badly shaken. Thank goodness Anton and Stefan had insisted Oliver go with them, or they might not have gotten away.

This all seemed like a horrible nightmare. Keisha brushed her hand across her forehead.

It's too much like Anton's nightmare. She never should have doubted him.

Something just outside her peripheral vision moved. Keisha spun around and covered her mouth to hold back a scream. Then she lowered her head, body shaking with fear as Mei wandered into the kitchen.

She was not like this! Not this frightened, jumpy coward who . . .

"Are you okay?" Mei touched Keisha's shoulder. "I didn't mean to startle you."

Keisha nodded. "I know. I've got to get past this. Anton would be so ashamed of me."

Mei shook her head. "No, Anton would understand. No way could he ever be ashamed of you. It's been a horrible time for you and Xandi. I think I'd be jumpy, too, if someone had tried to kidnap me not just once, but twice."

Keisha raised her head. "It's not me I worry about. It's Lily. I can't believe they could go after my baby." She glanced at the portable crib in a corner of the kitchen where Lily slept. "I'm afraid to be away from her at all. I actually suggested to Anton that we move into the wine cellar for more protection, but he just laughed at me."

"It's too darned cold down there for babies. You know that!" Mei wrapped her arms around Keisha in a quick hug. "We'll keep her safe. Alex, too. No one will get through us, now we know there's a threat. Before, it was all so unexpected."

"I know. I'll be okay, though Anton must have taken some of my fears seriously. He's had Stefan working on something down there," she nodded at the wine cellar door. "He just started a few days ago. He's been really noisy, pounding away on whatever it is. I don't know for sure what he's up to. At least he's not working on it today. It's so hard to get Lily to sleep with all the noise."

"Whatever he's doing, you know it's to make all of us safer."

Mei's soft voice made Keisha's fears seem so silly. She took a deep breath. Let it out. Felt her heart rate begin to slow down to normal. At the same time, she felt Anton's gentle touch inside her thoughts. He must have sensed her fear and was checking on her. Letting her know he was with her.

The trembling in her hands stilled. She was able to smile finally, when she looked at Mei. "So, what's up?"

Mei grinned and stepped back. "That's more like it. I hate seeing you so worried. Okay, Xandi and I got all six guest rooms made up with clean sheets on the beds and fresh towels in the bathrooms. That'll take care of just about everyone, but before he took off, Oliver said he'd like to ask Mik, AJ, and Tala if they wanted to stay with us in the cottage. That way, every mated pair, or triple, in their case," she said, laughing, "has their own bed."

Keisha managed to flash her a quick grin. "Any reason for choosing those three in particular?"

Mei laughed and flopped down in one of the kitchen chairs. "You mean beside the fact they're all sexy as hell?" She waved her fingers in front of her face. "Nope."

Keisha laughed. Mei could always make her laugh—if only she could help her relax, because right now her nerves were officially shredded. Consciously forcing her fears to the back of her thoughts, Keisha pulled out a chair and sat across from Mei.

Of course, all she could think to talk about was the current situation. "Have you heard anything from Oliver or Stefan? It feels so weird, knowing we've got to have someone patrolling this place."

Mei shook her head. "No, but that's good news, isn't it? Of course, knowing how Oliver and Stefan are when they get together, I can only imagine what they're up to." She grinned. "Oliver said they'd check in regularly with Anton. Which reminds me. Where is Anton? I haven't seen him all morning."

"He's in the study, glued to his computer." Keisha shuffled her lists. Anything to keep her hands busy. "Between business matters and the crappy stock market, and researching these attacks on us, I've hardly seen him."

Keisha glanced at her hands and realized she'd completely shredded the lists she'd spent all morning writing.

Mei reached across the table and covered both her hands. "You need to relax. Everything will be okay. There's so much power in this group. When we all get together and use our minds and bodies collectively to accomplish something, stuff happens. Good stuff."

Keisha bowed her head and stared at Mei's long, golden fingers covering her own dark hands. The contrast in their colors wavered and dissolved as her eyes filled with tears.

What they faced felt like a bad movie, not reality, not the reality she'd known since meeting Anton Cheval, since finding her true birthright as Chanku. Keisha took a deep breath, but it did little to calm her. "Nine men have died so far, trying to kidnap one of us, Mei. They've marked us, for some reason. Targeted the Chanku. They're after our babies and our women, which means they must know how we breed, how the woman is the one who carries the Chanku genes."

She paused and took a moment to calm herself. Damn, this was no way to live! "What's so awful is they won't hesitate to try and kill our men, and our men will always be out in front, trying to protect us. I can't imagine life without Anton, without Stefan or Oliver. There'd be no point in living without them. I've always felt safe in this house, safe with Anton and Stefan and Xandi, with you and Oliver . . . now I don't. I'm frightened all the time. How many more of them are out there? Why are we so important that their lives are so cheap? They're dead, and no one has even come looking for them. It doesn't make sense."

Keisha's tears fell once again. She, who so rarely cried, had done little more than weep for the past two days. She'd hardly slept. She now moved Lily's portable crib to whatever room she was in, afraid of being separated by more than a few inches from her only child. Even now, the baby slept here in the kitchen, within sight and touch.

To think it was just a couple days ago she'd been thrilled to have Lily moved into the big crib in her own room. It would be a long time before she could relax enough to be that far from her daughter again.

It felt like years ago when she'd last been safe. Another life. A good life, before all the ugliness began. Anton, with help from Xandi and Stefan, had helped her heal after the horrible assault she'd suffered before she knew any of them. Because of Anton, her nightmares had finally been dealt with and relegated to her past.

Until now. Now the memories followed her, fresh and alive once again. The memory of the horrendous acts she had endured at the hands of men was now reawakened by new threats and new terrors.

She'd endured, but she had also won. How could she forget? Unbidden, another memory filtered into her thoughts. A memory she'd tried so hard for so long to block, but one that now gave her a renewed sense of strength.

She'd killed before, to save herself. She would kill again, if she had to, to save the ones she loved. Her daughter. Her mate. Her packmates. There was no doubt in Keisha's mind. Not of her physical ability. Not of her emotional and mental strength.

She could, and would, kill if she had to.

Keisha took a deep breath. She felt the strength of her resolve flow through her veins. She would not live in fear. Never again. She flipped her hands beneath Mei's fingers and squeezed. Mei squeezed back, and they sat there, two strong women holding hands in silence for a long, long time.

Anton stared at the array of identification papers spread out on his desk and thought of the bodies he prayed to the Goddess would never be found, hidden as they were, deep underground in a bottomless pool in one of the many limestone caves beneath his land. He tried not to think of the questions their deaths might have raised.

He ran his hand across his eyes, and once again went over his conversation with Baylor Quinn. Thank goodness Bay and Manda were safe. The fact Manda actually recognized one of the men who attacked them provided an invaluable clue. The cell phone Bay had found should lead to even more names and more clues. Once Luc got hold of it, there wouldn't be a secret left—he hoped.

At least now he had an idea who their assailants were by their common link—the experimental labs where Manda had been held.

But why the current attacks? What was their motivation, and who was behind them?

Were the attacks tied to Jake's discovery? He and Shannon had met with a man who claimed to know of shapeshifters living in northern Maine as well as Montana and California. They'd discovered him while monitoring babble on the Internet, in a chat room where he bragged about his knowledge of amazing shapeshifters who lived among the human population. He actually appeared to have a slice of real information to back up his rumors.

He'd been after money, which Jake had not paid. Instead he'd told the man he must be nuts, especially when the guy admitted that he had no proof to back up his claims.

Only rumors.

But why had he made those claims in the first place? Where had he gotten his information, some of which was perilously close to the truth?

Anton sat back in his chair and allowed his mind freedom to wander through his memories. Somehow, the key to the present attacks had to be linked to events of the recent past. Staring at the neat row of books shelved across the room, he sifted through his tangled thoughts.

The ex-Secretary of Homeland Security Milton Bosworth immediately came to mind—the only man who had successfully kidnapped a Chanku shapeshifter when he orchestrated the capture of Ulrich Mason. Bosworth had him drugged and moved across the country where Ulrich was finally rescued through the combined efforts of Anton's Montana pack and the members of Ulrich's San Francisco Chanku.

Ulrich's rescue was the first time the two packs had worked together. It had been more than successful, cementing a link between Ulrich's Chanku and Anton's that had only grown stronger with time.

Bosworth was dead, but he had to be the link to what

was occurring now. Anton ticked the various points off on his fingers. One, Bosworth knew about the Chanku. He also had unsavory links to both the east and west coasts. At one time there had been rumors of a secret camp prepared to house his captives, though Anton had never been able to find anything concrete behind that rumor.

It was known by some members within the government that he'd had plans of breeding shapeshifters and creating his own secret army, though Anton hadn't been able to find out what the man's ultimate goal was with that, either. Luckily, those who'd heard the rumor had mostly discounted it as the ravings of a lunatic.

Unfortunately, Anton knew that, before his death, Bosworth had no scruples in doing what he could to learn more about the Chanku. He allowed nothing to stand in his way, and there was no such thing as honor or integrity in his search for information.

He'd shown that lack of character before his death.

Milton Bosworth had been the one to find Manda, a child caught halfway between human and wolf. The tragedy of Manda's twenty-five years in hell because of one man's obsession would forever weigh on Anton's mind. Even now, just thinking of what she'd been through made him physically ill.

Living in Tibet with her adoptive missionary parents, she must have unwittingly been exposed to some of the nutrients needed for the shift from human to Chanku, though obviously not enough. When she witnessed her parents' brutal murder, her Chanku instincts had forced her body to shift, but she'd only been twelve years old, not yet sexually mature.

Whether she lacked the physical maturity to allow the physical changes from human to Chanku, or just hadn't eaten enough of the native plants and grasses when she first shifted, was a mystery. One Anton would never have answers to.

Trapped in the midst of shifting, incapable of completing the process, she'd been imprisoned in a feral hell, a hideous combination of animal and human. Caught halfway between girl and wolf, Manda had spent the next twenty-five years as a misshapen, deformed freak of nature.

But the hell she'd endured had gone far beyond the mere effects of her mutated appearance. Much, much further.

She'd told Anton how a man she knew only as Papa B had rescued her. Anton wanted to weep, thinking of the abuse and depravity the girl had endured after her so-called rescue. Papa B and Milton Bosworth were one and the same, and his motives for saving the feral child had been anything but altruistic.

Baylor Quinn, Manda's mate, had explained to Anton how Bosworth kept Manda prisoner. She'd lived in various laboratories throughout the country, though most of her years were spent on the West Coast in the San Francisco Bay Area. She'd been subjected to abuse above and beyond Bosworth's horrible experiments that would have killed a lesser woman. Raped by both human and beast, she'd managed to come through it all with her mind and spirit intact.

Thanks to Baylor Quinn's patience and amazing love.

Bosworth had never known exactly what he had with Manda, but he'd obviously realized she represented something he could use to further his own career. Playing the kindly savior to the young woman, he'd actually been the one to order her abuse, the one directing the unimaginable tortures disguised as scientific and medical experiments.

All those years Manda had endured. She'd believed the terrible things being done to her were to help her look normal, yet it appeared Bosworth's goal had been to try and breed more creatures just like her.

But for what reason?

Anton wiped his fingers across his cheeks and they came away damp. No wonder he wept. The stories Baylor had shared with him after bonding with Manda were tales of unimaginable horror and pain. How anyone could possibly survive such terrible treatment amazed Anton, but she'd not only survived, she'd finally become both a beautiful woman and a whole and self-confident alpha bitch.

He knew what had helped her survive, of course—Adam Wolf, Manda's fraternal twin, a brother she'd not known in person until just this summer.

However, she'd had his thoughts, both his mental and emotional support for most of the years she'd been imprisoned. Thank the Goddess for Adam, and the amazing mental connection he and Manda were able to share.

They'd been separated at birth by adoption, and lived until recently completely unaware of both their feral birthright and their familial connection. Thank the Goddess, their mental connection had given Manda the strength she needed to endure years of Bosworth's *experiments*.

Adam's power as a healer was only now beginning to emerge, but he'd obviously saved his sister's life. *Amazing thing,* Anton thought, *the power of love.*

And he was still no closer to a solution than he'd been before. What in the hell was going on? Why were he and his people targets, and who was ordering the attacks?

Frustrated, he buried his head in his hands. There were no answers to his questions, and all he did by trying to sort things out was come up with more questions.

Chapter 6

"Anton? Hey! Are you okay?"

Anton raised his head and blinked. Mei Chen stood in the doorway with a pensive smile on her face. "Hi, Mei. I'm fine. Just frustrated."

"I know. I can feel it." She moved slowly into the room with the sinewy grace of a lean jungle cat, more specifically, the snow leopard she was. She stood about six feet from his desk in what appeared to be an unnaturally submissive pose.

There was rarely anything submissive about Mei. She'd been a tough kid before her first shift. When she finally changed, she'd surprised everyone, but the snow leopard she'd become instead of a wolf like all the rest had added to her confidence and her attitude.

Throwing a powerful Sioux spirit guide into the mix had turned Mei into a unique member of the pack, one with whom Anton would always feel a special bond. Now, her amber eyes glittered and Anton felt the presence of more than one consciousness behind those lovely eyes.

Igmutaka was not a spirit to remain in the background. It was unsettling, to say the least.

Mei shuffled uncomfortably before she finally straightened her shoulders, looked directly at Anton and spoke.

"There's something I have to tell you. That special bond you're thinking about? Well, it's more than you realize. It's embarrassing, but I can sense you, Anton. Even when you think you're blocked, like now. Your mind is an open book to me."

Shocked beyond speech, Anton sat back in his chair and steepled his hands in front of his face. This was certainly unexpected! It took him a moment to begin to organize his thoughts. Having his every thought broadcast, if only to this one woman, could be damned uncomfortable. Even Keisha couldn't read him all the time.

"You're right, it is uncomfortable." Mei sighed. "I've been trying to ignore you, but I can't, so I wanted you to know. It started after we had sex, before I could shift. Almost as if we bonded on some level, but I feel as if I'm intruding where I don't belong. It's getting stronger, this ability to read your every thought. It's such a horrible invasion of your privacy, but I don't know how to stop it."

She blinked and looked warily at him. Again, there was that disconcerting sense of a dual presence. Anton realized he was trying to reach out for it, but Mei's soft words brought him back.

"When you think of things, private things, I hear you. I know how much you worry about the attacks, how frightened you are for Lily's sake. I know about the cave, the one you . . ."

"Have you told anyone else? About the cavern?" He sat up and realized his heart pounded in his chest. He wasn't ready to share the location of this particular one, not yet. Stefan knew, and Xandi and Keisha, of course, but he hadn't said a word to Oliver or Adam. Not until it had been fully explored, until he had time to make it truly accessible to all of them. There was still so much to . . .

Mei shook her head. "I never tell anyone what I hear from your mind, though I imagine Oliver is aware of most of what I know. When we have sex, we share our thoughts so openly. . . ." She shrugged. "We've been pretending the things I hear from you don't exist."

Anton sighed. He would have to tell Oliver about the work he and Stefan had done in the wine cellar. He nodded his thanks.

Mei looked insulted. "It's bad enough that I hear it! I'm certainly not about to discuss anything so private as another's thoughts. Goddess, Anton . . . when you make love to Keisha, I'm in your head, and because of you, I'm in Keisha's head as well. That's just wrong! Is there any way to stop this connection? I feel like I'm violating both of you, as if I am intruding where I have no right to be. I had no idea, when we had sex, that . . ."

Anton smiled and shook his head. "Calm down, Mei. It's okay. Remember when we made love? You got upset with me because I was reading everything you thought. Now I can't read your thoughts at all, yet mine are open to you. Curious, don't you think?"

"I remember. You were answering questions I hadn't asked yet. It was freaky, but it's even worse, me seeing inside your head when I'm not expecting it. It's getting stronger. I want it to stop."

She looked even more disgruntled and irate than she had a moment ago.

Anton concentrated on blocking his thoughts, on rebuilding barriers he'd allowed to lapse. At the same time he held his hands up and out in a helpless gesture. "I apologize. I'll work harder at keeping my private projects, self-recriminations, and worries—and my libido—to myself. I've gotten sloppy with so much going on, and that's a dangerous mistake to make."

Mei frowned. "That's good. What you just did. Just now, you sort of *winked out*. Whatever you're doing, keep doing it, okay?"

Damn but he enjoyed this young woman. She said exactly what she thought without any regrets or pretense at all. Anton laughed and gestured toward the chair beside his desk. "Well, that's good to know. Have a seat, Mei. I've been wanting to talk to you. As far as your emerging voyeuristic talents, I don't think you're entirely to blame."

Mei sat, but she kept her hands folded in her lap and the wary look in her eyes. "What do you mean?"

Anton sat back in his chair. "We need to talk about your companion."

"Oliver?" Mei frowned.

Anton laughed and shook his head. She looked so serious sitting there, hands folded primly in her lap. He knew what Mei was like when she totally let go, when her climax was building and her arousal ruled every thought. There was nothing at all prim about her then. "No," he said. "I probably know Oliver better than you do, in spite of your mating bond. I want to know about Igmutaka. You are the only one of us who carries a spirit guide within your soul. None of us really knows him, yet he's a part of our pack, for better or worse. Could he be using you to read my thoughts? Are you comfortable with his presence? I guess what I want to know is, does he interfere with your life? Is he in any way a threat?"

Mei laughed and shook her head. "I was connecting with your thoughts even before Igmutaka joined me." She tilted her head then, and studied Anton with an almost ferocious intensity. "I don't know. He might have made the connection stronger. It's hard to tell. As far as having my very own spirit guide . . . at first I was really pissed that this, this *entity* had moved into my space like he belonged there, but now we've actually developed a sort of truce. When I'm Mei, like now, he's quiet and leaves me alone." She chuckled. "Except during sex. He really likes sex, no matter what form I'm in."

She laughed and once again looked like a carefree young woman when she shook her head. "Yeah, he does enjoy sex, but that's okay, because I do, too. When he pops up and makes himself known, it seems to make everything a lot more intense."

Anton smiled. Sometimes Mei seemed so young to carry so much responsibility. At others, she was more adult than most. "I guess that's a plus. Where is he in your other forms?"

Mei studied him now with the eyes of a much older person. "When I'm the snow leopard," she said, "Igmutaka is very powerful. He's a strong ally as well. He's also very sensual, curious about my desires as well as his own." Again she laughed and her dark hair swung across her shoulders.

There was such a freshness about Mei. An openness to life, an innocence unusual to one who was Chanku. It amazed him, how well she'd managed to adapt to the unusual changes that had come so suddenly into her life.

She'd touched him deeply when they made love, even though it had been more a business proposition than anything, a chance to learn what he could from her at a deeper level, more than she was able to convey in words. He'd been willing to try anything to help Mei and Oliver find a way to bond, impossible when she was a leopard and Oliver a wolf.

Thank goodness, with Igmutaka's help, the problem had been solved, but the sex with Mei had been a fascinating experience for Anton. He knew she'd enjoyed it, but not nearly as much as he had . . . of course, she'd been very new to the Chanku way of life.

They'd had sex before the spirit guide took up residence in her mind, thank goodness, as her powers were so much more complex now. It was disconcerting to realize how well she knew him after their intimate connection. Almost as thoroughly as his mate—and Keisha knew him very well.

Anton felt himself stir, remembering their one time alone together. They'd been intimate since, but always

with others present. It usually happened at Oliver and
Mei's cottage, so he'd been on her home territory, and the
impact hadn't been anything out of the ordinary. That first
time, though, had been an unusual experience, to say the
least.

More than he'd realized if she could read him as easily
as she said.

Was she reading him now? He hoped his blocks were
holding. "I imagine Igmutaka enjoys the sex most when
you're in your leopard form, right?" Anton rested his chin
on his fingertips.

Mei shook her head, still giggling. "He's male. I'm not.
He's having trouble adjusting to penetration and he wants
to be on top, to be the aggressor, which is great when I tie
Oliver up and play the dom with him. Igmutaka loves to
be in control."

Anton raised his eyebrows and tried to picture his personal assistant tied to the bed. Obviously Oliver wasn't
wasting any time discovering all the attributes of his newly
won sexuality. He had to bite back a grin when he asked
Mei about Igmutaka. It wasn't easy with the visual of
Oliver tied to that great big bed for Mei's pleasure. "Is that
a worry," he finally asked, "when Igmutaka wants control?"

"Not really." Mei shook her head. "He's dealing with it
fairly well when I'm in my human form, but when I'm a
leopard, I think he and Oliver have issues. He feels what I
feel. That barbed cock of Oliver's infuriates him, though
he does make it less painful for me."

Anton didn't even try and control his chuckle. "Ah, I
imagine it does. I've heard about Oliver's cock, though I
must admit I've not actually experienced it, thank the
Goddess. What do you think of it?"

Mei actually blushed. "I love it. It takes me to a perfect
level of pain that makes the pleasure stronger." She nodded her head. "It's definitely a good thing. Igmutaka's just

going to have to get used to it. To be honest, he does help lessen the pain and turn it toward pleasure. At least he's not acting like he does when I'm the wolf. Then he's almost powerless. I sense his presence like a spoiled little kid who's not getting his way."

"I imagine he's not too fond of that perception. You're saying he's aware of what you think all the time?"

Sobering now, Mei nodded. "At first he wasn't, but now, always. I'm getting used to him, but he is constantly there, a presence in my mind."

"I didn't realize . . . now? Even as we speak?"

Again Mei nodded. "Yes. He's curious, I think, of the connection I have with you. He's really curious about our world. Curious about Chanku. He's interested in the tunnel you've found. I'm not really certain why, but when you're working on the gateway or talking to Stefan about it, your thoughts are crystal clear to me. He must be doing something then to make me hear you better. I sense his curiosity. I don't get an actual voice or words from him or anything, but I can feel his questions. He wants to know more about everything. Even so, I do feel as if I control him. He doesn't control me."

For now Anton decided he would ignore Mei's curiosity about their work on the tunnel. He wondered, though, at Igmutaka's interest. Switching the subject he asked, "Does he take an active role in sex? Do you feel as if he's a third party when you're with Oliver? What about when you're with more than one partner?"

Mei frowned. "No," she said. Her long, black hair swung across her shoulders when she shook her head. "I hadn't thought of him that way. Like I said, he seems to make the sex more intense. It's like everything I feel is amplified. I sense him as being totally heterosexual. I think he's adjusting to the fact his host is a woman, but I'm not sure how happy he is. I've only had sex with Oliver since Igmutaka moved in, but AJ, Mik, and Tala will be staying with us when they arrive." Mei shrugged and seemed to think about that a moment. Then she smiled. "If I am with Tala, I wonder how Igmutaka will react to her?"

"It could get interesting," Anton mused, "with AJ and Mik, too. Especially Mik, since he's the reason you've got Igmutaka in the first place."

"Yeah, but Tala's the one who had him in her head first, even though it was my body." Mei's grin was pure deviltry. "I'm wondering what Igmutaka will think when he realizes he's making love to the woman who held him under control."

Anton leaned back in his chair and let his mind wander a moment with the possibilities. "It's a good question, Mei, and something I think we need to pursue, given the current situation. I want you to think about your spirit guide. I sense his power in you and I believe he has tremendous strength. Untapped strength. Right now, we need everyone we can get on our side if we're going to figure out what's behind these attacks."

"That's another reason why I wanted to talk to you." Mei fiddled with the arm of the chair for a moment, then once again raised her head. Anton sensed the young woman's power, her own strength of purpose.

She was every bit as strong as her Sioux spirit guide. Stronger than Anton had realized.

"I sensed your worry," she said. "I felt it in Keisha and that led my mind to yours. Everyone assumes you're so powerful, but I know you're just as worried as the rest of us. It made me feel bad, the fact I can feel things, private fears you probably don't want to share."

Appreciating her concerns more than he wanted to admit, Anton shook his head and smiled. "I'm not perfect, Mei. Far from it. I think the others realize I'm just as prone to fear as they are. I'm not embarrassed for you to know it, or anyone else, for that matter. The point is, we may need Igmutaka. I'm thinking that if he wants to share in your lovemaking with the members of the San Francisco pack, you should encourage him. Give him whatever freedom he wants to take part. He needs to know that for you to be safe, we all have to be safe. He may actually offer something we need to stop this assault on our people."

Anton looked down at his hands and felt even more helpless. At the same time, he wondered if Mei sensed the shame pouring through him. He couldn't believe what he was asking of Mei, that she essentially prostitute herself, but when he glanced up, she was smiling.

"There's no need for shame, Anton."

Anton sighed. "You really do sense my deepest thoughts, don't you?"

Mei nodded. "Yeah, but now it's not as persistent. I felt what you just thought, but you've been a blank screen for the past few minutes. That's good. Besides, I like your idea. I hadn't thought of that, of actually using Igmutaka to help us. I'm still not sure how he can, but I've been with Tala before and the sex was amazing. With Igmutaka along for the ride, it could be even better. Sort of like killing two birds with one stone, right? Make the guy happy, keep him happy, then see how we can use him?"

She stood up and held her hand out to Anton. "Thank you. I always feel better after I talk to you, even when you don't have answers." Shrugging her shoulders, Mei slipped her fingers free of his and stared at him for a moment with a pensive smile on her face. "Ya know, I used to be so scared of you. Oliver was right. You're a really good guy."

Mei grinned and once again Anton sensed her dual personality. "Everything will be fine," she said. Then she turned to walk away, paused and looked back at him. "I think it will be even better if you go now and find your mate. Keisha needs you."

With a flip of her long black hair, Mei turned again and left his study. Anton sat for a moment. She was so young,

he'd once made the mistake of thinking of her as a child,
Now he found himself thinking instead of all she'd said.

Then he laughed out loud, shut down his computer, and
went in search of Keisha.

Mei headed back to the cottage she and Oliver shared.
By tomorrow, the whole compound would be overrun
with more Chanku than she'd ever seen in her life, but for
now the place was quiet and peaceful.

It was hard to believe someone was out to do any of
them harm, not on a gorgeous late summer day like today.
She opened the door and stepped into the cool, still air inside. The cottage felt so empty and neglected without
Oliver there! Mei sent out a silent call for her mate. He'd
been gone most of the day, patrolling the northwestern
edges of Anton's huge estate.

She missed him.

His voice came back to her. She recognized the deep
growl of the leopard, and knew Oliver paced silently along
the perimeter, hidden in the speckled guise of the big cat.

When are you coming back? I miss you.

Not for a few hours, he said. *It's quiet, though. No sign
of trouble. Why don't you come join me?*

Mei smiled and leaned against the front door. *Won't
that interfere with your job?*

Two can observe as well as one.

I'm coming. Mei cast her thoughts and found Anton.
She smiled when she realized he was on his way to Keisha.
I'm going to meet up with Oliver, she said. *I wanted to let
someone know where I was going.*

Good idea. Be very careful.

His voice in her mind was serious, but she sensed the
smile on his lips. *You too, Anton. And tell Keisha hello
for me.*

She heard his laughter as she stripped off her clothing

and shifted. She would meet Oliver as a leopard, but he was a couple miles away. The wolf traveled much faster and enjoyed the run more.

She left through an open rear window. They'd all become careful about changing shape outside where an observer might see.

One more freedom denied.

Igmutaka grumbled in the background of her mind, irritated she'd chosen the wolf and not the leopard for her shift. He was definitely stronger, but she didn't feel any threat from him. His presence had grown so familiar she actually felt stronger and more confident, knowing he was close.

Even if he was grumbling.

Mei sensed Oliver's presence the moment she crossed the small hill that dropped down into a long, narrow valley cut by an even narrower stream. Halting beneath a thick stand of pines, she shifted from wolf to leopard.

Igmutaka's satisfaction poured through her veins as Mei trotted across the grassy stretch of meadow into deep shadows beneath a granite cliff. Oliver waited near the base, lying on a flat rock where he had a commanding view of the long valley and the service road that crossed it far below.

He stood when she approached, unfolding his speckled body in a long, slow stretch that showed off his powerful shoulders and sleek flanks.

Mei snarled and sat back on her haunches, surprised by the immediate rush of arousal, the sense of need that filled her. They'd made love this morning, mere hours ago.

She wanted him again.

Now.

Igmutaka stirred within. Mei's desire grew. She leapt across the small stream and stood directly in front of Oliver. His eyes narrowed at the same time his nostrils flared.

Mei curled her lip, exposing sharp canines. Oliver growled and his ears went flat against his broad skull. He positioned himself as if to jump, and his powerful haunches quivered as he watched Mei.

She stretched, uncoiling her sinuous length in front of Oliver, teasing him with her feline beauty. Dipping her right shoulder, she flopped to the ground and rolled over, pointing all four legs in the air. When she righted herself, her tail pointed straight behind her, increasing her overall length and presence.

Mei heard a deep *chuff, chuff, chuff*. She turned her head. Oliver had crept closer. His nose wrinkled as he sniffed her, moving from shoulder to rib cage, to rear leg. His stiff whiskers ruffled her fur and raised shivers along her spine.

Mei reached for his thoughts and found nothing beyond a solid barrier of need, proof Oliver was ruled now by his libido, caught in the mind of the leopard. Enthralled by her scent and her shape, his body was driven by his need to take her and once again claim Mei as his mate.

Empowered by the strength of his desire, Mei turned and rubbed her head under his chin. She nipped at his ear. His purr was a deep rumble rolling up from his chest. She rubbed him again, pressing the side of her head against his neck, butting his shoulder.

One large paw swept over her shoulders and his hind leg slipped across her hips. He held her tightly, his big front paws wrapped around her upper body, his belly tight against her back. She lowered her back legs and at the same time, arched into the stiff, probing thrusts of his cock as he jabbed beneath her tail in search of her sex.

Growling, Mei cocked her long, thick tail to one side and gave Oliver clear passage. His slick penis speared her deep and she felt the sharp sting of the barbed tip as he planted himself against her womb.

Pain blossomed, intense and focused deep inside with the first short, sharp jab. She yowled, raising her head and crying out until her screech echoed off the hills.

Igmutaka stirred and filled her with his presence. Mei felt an answering rush of sensual heat. It overwhelmed the pain, reduced the agony of Oliver's penetration to pure unadulterated pleasure.

Oliver's weight bore her to the ground and his body was a hot and heavy blanket over hers. His hips jerked against her backside, his cock hooked her cervix. She worked the pain now. Turned it, with Igmutaka's silent assistance, into pure sensation. The pain built as did her pleasure, one amplifying the other, growing more intense with each sharp thrust.

In the wild, were she a true leopard, Oliver's barbed entry would force ovulation. As Chanku, Mei controlled the release of her eggs. There would be no young from this mating.

No young, no pain.

Only pleasure with the powerful stimulation of this perfect body. With her spirit guide's assistance, she turned the pain into something wonderful, and as her climax neared, she opened her thoughts to her mate.

Oliver was there, waiting for her. Aroused to a pinnacle of mindless need, he was a seething stew of emotions and sensations, all of it powered by love and sexual desire.

Igmutaka hovered just beyond Mei's consciousness.

She recognized the spirit guide's question, his desire to experience sex from Oliver's point of view.

Will you let him in? The request slipped from Mei's thoughts. She feared Oliver's reaction.

Would Oliver be jealous of her constant companion? Their relationship was still new and they'd never discussed Igmutaka's role between them. He had been thrust into Mei's life purely by accident. The spirit guide was linked forever

to the cat family—a panther in this hemisphere, guardian
of the Sioux, locked now in the body of a Tibetan snow
leopard, tied to the mind of an Asian shapeshifter.

Mei sensed the startled reaction in Oliver. Felt him question, then acquiesce. There was a sense of pleased surprise
from Igmutaka as well. Then she felt his presence slip from
hers, felt Oliver's cock swell as the new entity energized him.

Pain ripped through her womb and Mei yowled again.
Just as suddenly the pain shifted and she knew her spirit
guide had not abandoned her completely.

The dynamic changed. She'd been in complete control
with Igmutaka inside her. Now Oliver plunged deeper,
harder. His front legs grasped tighter, his heart beat louder.
She felt it thundering against her spine, and reached for
the orgasm that hovered just out of her grasp.

Somehow, she knew her spirit guide delayed the final
climax. Split into two, experiencing both Mei and Oliver's
arousal, Igmutaka seemed to swell within her, his own
level of sexual excitement building upon itself as Oliver
and Mei climbed to an ever higher peak.

Then Oliver caught the back of Mei's neck in his sharp
teeth. He bit down hard. Pain blossomed and Mei's world
exploded.

The delayed climax ripped through her. Stronger,
deeper, more powerful than anything she'd experienced.
Her body shuddered as Oliver's seed filled her. Her mind
blanked for a moment, overwhelmed by sensation, by desire, by the connection to the man she loved . . . and the
one who guided them both.

Igmutaka?

It was Oliver's voice in Mei's head. Oliver who asked
what the spirit guide had done.

A strange voice entered Mei's mind. She sensed him in
Oliver as well, and he was speaking clearly in the language
of the leopard.

I am here. I will guide both of you. The female is a new experience, the male a more comfortable abode. I need you both. I will serve you both . . . as you will serve me.

Unbelievable. Mei lay still beneath Oliver's warm body. His chest heaved against her back with each deep breath he took. With the heady rush of climax ebbing, she felt the pain from his penetration.

Oliver rolled away from her body and his cock pulled free of her womb. Mei howled with the sudden pain as the small barbs at the tip of Oliver's penis jerked out of her flesh.

Mei shifted. Naked and shivering in the warm grass, she grabbed her painful crotch with one hand. "Son of a bitch! Next time, shift first. Then when you pull out, it doesn't hurt." Looking contrite, even for a huge leopard, Oliver nudged her fingers aside with his broad nose and sniffed her swollen tissues. Mei lay back with a sigh as his big, rough, tongue gently soothed away the pain.

I'm sorry. I wasn't thinking.

S'okay. Oh . . . that feels so good.

Good enough that I'm forgiven?

Mei sighed. *I don't know. I'll tell you when it's okay to stop.* Then she giggled and whispered, "Like, uh . . . never?"

Oliver's purr rumbled in his chest. He licked slowly, careful of the sandpaper texture of his tongue against her tender parts. Just as carefully he cleaned away all traces of their loving while Mei sprawled bonelessly in the grass.

She closed her eyes and practically wallowed in the warmth of his tongue, the rough caress that soothed away the pain of sex with a big cat. It was hard to say which she preferred. She could choose sex as a wolf, as a woman, or as a leopard. Each had its own unique sensations.

Each left her replete, yet never satiated. Would this Chanku libido ever be satisfied?

Oliver's thoughts popped into her head. *Good Lord . . . I hope not!*

Grinning broadly, Mei opened her eyes just as Oliver shifted. She stared at her mate and smiled. There was something about him . . .

"He's still there, isn't he?"

Oliver nodded. "I can sense your spirit guide in me. Do you still . . . ?"

Mei grinned. "He's in me, too. How the . . . ?"

"I don't know. It's weird. Not in a bad way, but it just feels as if there's another someone in my head."

This time Mei laughed. "That's because there is, silly. Now you know how I've felt."

Oliver frowned and studied Mei for a moment. "What's really neat is that I feel an even stronger connection to you, through him. Can you sense it?"

Mei knew her eyes must look like saucers. The connection was so powerful, so visceral, it felt as if she and Oliver were one and the same. But if the same entity shared both their bodies at the same time, in a way, they were the same.

Weren't they? Totally confused, she decided merely to accept for now and ask questions later. "Yes. I do sense it. It's utterly amazing. I . . ."

Oliver leaned close to kiss her, then suddenly jerked back and leapt to his feet. Mei stood up and grabbed his arm. "What is it?"

Oliver frowned, and she knew he heard something . . . or someone. After a long moment, he relaxed and flashed a broad grin at Mei.

"Stefan heard two vehicles at the main road. It's the San Francisco pack. They decided not to fly, so they drove up in a couple of SUVs. Luc and Tia, Mik, AJ, and Tala in one, Tinker, Lisa, Eve, and Adam in the second. C'mon. Let's go back to the house. Stefan said Anton's called us in for dinner."

"But what if . . . ?"

"If anyone shows up, now we've got reinforcements.

Besides, I need to talk with Anton. I think we've gone from one spirit guide to two. Or one who's just cloned himself. Your guy's still with me."

Mei nodded. "With me, too. Do you have any idea what happened?"

Laughing, Oliver hugged her tight. "Not a clue, but it's not what I expected. I thought it would feel weird to have another soul inside, like a second intelligence. I've been wondering how you really felt. I definitely feel more connected to you because of him, if that makes sense."

Mei suddenly grabbed Oliver's hand and held it up. As dark skinned as her mate was, the small rosette on the back of his left hand was darker.

And it was a perfect match to the one that had appeared on her own hand after Igmutaka had settled in as her spirit companion, even more proof the spirit guide had now found a place in both of them.

Mei was still trying to figure that one out when Oliver shifted and stared at her with his wolven grin. Instead of worrying anymore, she joined him. Nipping at his flank as she passed him, Mei took off at a full run with Oliver right behind her.

She heard Igmutaka grumbling in the back of her mind and wondered if he was just as grumpy with Oliver.

Yes, he is. He really doesn't like it when we're wolves, does he?

He'll just have to get used to it. Mei nipped Oliver's flank and raced on ahead.

Chapter 7

Mei sat with Eve and Tia on the back deck. She adjusted the baby monitors for both babies and settled more comfortably into the deck chair. The men had gone for a run after dinner but Mei'd offered to stay and watch the babies. Keisha and Xandi wanted to join their mates—they needed a chance to work off some of their nervous energy, and Tala and Lisa decided to join them.

Tia and Eve had remained at the house with Mei.

She was definitely glad for the company. They all felt unsettled and out of sync and she really didn't want to be alone, especially after what had happened the last time she'd volunteered to stay with Alex and Lily.

She had to quit thinking like that! Mei took a sip of her wine. She heard a wolf howl in the distance and recognized Stefan's voice. He was quickly joined by a full chorus, and Mei laughed. "I think that's the biggest pack of wolves I've ever seen take off on a run at one time. An even dozen."

Eve nodded. Her slightly Southern drawl seemed more pronounced tonight for some reason. Stress? Hard to tell. "I know," she said, stretching out the *w*. "It almost made me sorry I'd decided to stay, but then I thought of how hard they're going to run. All that testosterone in one place is a bit overwhelming." She waved her fingers in front of her face as if cooling off.

"You should have been here the first time any of us got together." Tia stirred the ice cubes in her fruit juice with the tip of one finger. "When Dad was kidnapped, Anton offered to help us get him back. Luc, Tinker, and I came up here, total strangers to Anton, Stefan, and Xandi. They'd met Dad very briefly. Keisha's my cousin, so . . ."

Mei blinked. She'd not known that, though there was definitely a resemblance. "I didn't know," she said.

"Yeah. Our mothers were sisters, but we hadn't seen each other in ages so Keisha immediately dragged me off to catch up on stuff. That left Tinker and Luc standing here staring at Anton, Stefan, and Xandi. Luc said you could have cut the tension, and the testosterone, with a knife! Later, after they'd shifted into wolves, they spent a big chunk of time walking around stiff-legged, growling and peeing on everything in sight before they settled down and got past all their alpha male shit."

Eve and Mei both laughed.

"I didn't notice any of that tonight, did you?" Eve pulled her sweater around her shoulders. It was completely dark now, and the air was growing cooler.

Tia shook her head. "Things are better, now. We've all learned to work together." She laughed and blushed at the same time. "We've all had sex together, too, at one time or another. It's hard to pull that stuff with someone when you've been totally intimate with them. And, of course, there's Anton. All these guys are alphas, which isn't the way it would be in a regular wild wolf pack, but they still defer to Anton Cheval. Of course, Anton always defers to Keisha, which is the way it should be."

Mei laughed along with the rest of them, but Tia was right. Keisha did have full control of her mate, and in many ways the other females deferred to her just as the men respected Anton.

When the laughter died down, Tia took a sip of her juice. Then she got serious again. "As far as Anton's leadership, I don't think it's a question of size or fear. He just knows so much more than any of us, and he's always willing to share that knowledge. He's a natural leader and no one disputes it. I don't think anything scares the man."

Mei shook her head. "Not true. While he's definitely a leader, I think sometimes he's more afraid than any of us."

"I don't understand." Tia frowned. "How can you say that? He never shows it."

Mei smiled, remembering. If only they knew the real Anton Cheval. The night she'd spent in his bed had shown her an entirely new side of the man, and talking with him later had confirmed it. "He showed his vulnerability the night the spirit guide took over my body. Anton totally lost control. He actually wept because he thought he'd failed, and he was so afraid he'd lost Tala. I felt so badly for him. Think about it . . . we all depend on him for so much. We assume he knows everything, can fix everything. That's a tremendous amount of pressure to put on any one man."

Eve nodded. "Adam said the same thing about him a while back. Still, I'm glad Anton's the one who's called us all together. He tends to think of solutions when the rest of us can't. We have to do something to stop the attacks. I've never been as afraid as I was when those men came after us in Golden Gate Park."

"I heard about it." Mei sighed. "You're so lucky the guys were able to run them off without any deaths. It was bad here, too. They were so brazen! I've never killed before. I never want to again." She shuddered with the memory. "There's something so personal about death when you shift. A gun . . . that's not personal, but as a leopard . . ."

Sighing, Mei stared at the wooden deck beneath her feet. Eve and Tia sat perfectly silent. "Igmutaka was with me or I don't know if I could have done it. I jumped without thinking and grabbed the back of his head in my teeth. I think I broke his neck. He died instantly, but I held on until I was sure. I felt the spirit guide in my head, telling me what to do. What's scary is that the guy got inside the house without my seeing or hearing him. I was right here on the deck."

Mei realized her entire body had tensed with the memories. She consciously forced herself to relax. "We have to be on our guard all the time. We never know when one of them might be close."

"Is that why Anton told everyone to shift while they were still inside the house?" Eve sipped her wine and stared off into the dark forest. Her voice trembled.

"Yeah. He doesn't want us shifting in the open. We don't know for sure if anyone's watching the house." Mei shivered, as much from unease as the chill in the air. "Stefan and Oliver patrolled all day, but they didn't see anything. I imagine the run everyone's on tonight is more about checking the property for intruders than enjoying the chance to hunt game."

"You'd think, with all his money, Anton would have some sort of security," Eve said. "Even fences would help."

Mei shook her head. "Some of it's fenced, but do you have any idea how many thousands of acres Anton owns? Oliver said they've discussed it, but it's totally impractical. Besides, they've never really felt a need for that much protection until now. Not here."

"It's the not knowing that makes me crazy. Wondering if someone is watching us." Tia held both palms against her flat stomach. Mei caught the terror in her eyes.

"C'mon," she said, rising. "Let's get inside where it's warm. I'll feel better being close to the babies, too." She grabbed the monitors. "These are really great, but I'll still feel better if we're closer."

"Close to the babies and out of full view," Tia muttered. The relief in her voice was obvious.

Mei checked and locked all the doors in the huge house after they moved inside to the study. She looked in on the babies. Both of them slept soundly. Still, she shivered, but it wasn't because of the cold.

It was nerves, pure and simple. She'd never felt uncomfortable sitting on that deck before. Tonight she'd honestly been afraid. Igmutaka was restless within her. She wished Oliver would come home.

Both of them missed their other half.

Anton needed this time as the wolf. The freedom, the sense of the wild that took him out of his typically responsible, overly concerned self. He paced along the northernmost perimeter of his property with Keisha beside him and Oliver guarding their flank.

The night was rich with scents and sounds and it was good to run, good to be out with his mate and with Oliver, his oldest friend, running beside him.

If only they were running for the pure joy of the moment. This was business, in spite of the beauty of the forest, the inherent peace of the night.

He'd sent his packmates in every direction with instructions to search for anything wrong, any scent that didn't belong, any sign of trespass. They'd hunted near the house for cameras or sensors, something that might be passing information electronically, but they'd found nothing.

They'd searched the two vehicles that had brought the intruders onto Anton's land, but they'd been clean. Both SUVs now rested at the bottom of canyons many miles away. So far, there'd been no clue of any kind that would lead Anton to those who meant his extended family harm.

Now they spread out to the four corners of his extensive holdings. Stefan, Xandi, and Adam had gone south, while Tala, Mik, and AJ headed east, higher into the mountains. Tinker, Lisa, and Luc would check the western boundaries and all of them would report in before dawn.

The night was theirs and it was good.

At least it should have been good. He growled, aware of the changes, the lack of freedom he normally felt. The sense of communion with the forest usually consumed him. Not tonight. This night, he couldn't get the reason behind their run out of his mind. Couldn't find the peace he expected.

It was wrong. All of it wrong. The reason they had gathered. The need to check the perimeters to ensure their safety.

Never had he been put in such an all-consuming defensive mode before. Not since Keisha had been attacked by hunters shortly after she moved to his home had Anton felt truly threatened on his own land. Now, everything had changed.

Now Anton Cheval knew what it was like to be hunted.

He didn't like it. Not one bit. He had a responsibility to his mate, to his daughter, to his kind.

To all of them who looked his way for advice.

He'd not asked for this role. Not consciously taken it. Leadership had been thrust not so gently upon him, evolving over the past couple of years until he'd slipped the mantle of responsibility over his shoulders and done his best to wear it well.

Now, trotting along an imaginary fence line, Anton forced the threads of fear from his mind. He would never be a perfect leader. Far from it.

But he would lead as best he could. Protect with everything he had. Do whatever it took to keep his people safe.

Thoughts of the hijacking that had almost taken his life and the lives of Xandi, Stefan, Keisha, and their unborn babies made his veins run cold as ice. He shuddered.

His mate trotted close beside him. He knew that Keisha humored him tonight. Leaving Lily was not easy for her, but she'd agreed to trust Mei, Tia, and Eve to protect their daughter. Now that the spirit guide resided in both Mei and Oliver, the two appeared able to contact one another over long distances, so they had that link, should they need it.

Anton snarled at the night. He'd been completely involved in their ongoing attacks and hadn't had a chance to question either Oliver or Mei for details about Igmutaka. Something momentous had occurred between them and the spirit guide. Anton wanted to know more. He had to understand the motives behind the entity that now resided half in Oliver, half in Mei.

Did it mean them harm? Anton hoped not. He had no idea how to get the damned spirit to leave, now that he'd become such a powerful part of the two Chanku.

One more threat, or possibly an ally? He didn't know. Oliver and Mei didn't seem the least bit concerned. That alone worried Anton.

Keisha slowed and then drew to a halt behind him. Anton stopped and cocked an ear toward the beautiful dark wolf. Oliver paused beside both of them.

I feel your tension tonight. You radiate anger as if you were broadcasting to the trees. You've been telling me to be calm. Take your own advice, my love, before you have a stroke.

Anton hung his head. Keisha was right. His heart pounded. His blood raced through his veins. He was running through the night, oblivious to the beauty of the forest, the closeness of his mate and the support of one of his dearest friends.

Oliver rested his muzzle on Anton's shoulder. *Once everyone arrives, we'll have answers. Until then, we can only guard and protect. You can't solve everything, my friend.*

Anton raised his head and looked into Oliver's eyes. The same sense of a dual personality was there, a powerful presence residing within Oliver. *I sense Igmutaka in you, even though you're a wolf tonight. What is that like?*

He's a link to Mei. I'm never totally away from her, now that we share the spirit guide. And yes, even when I run as a wolf, I sense him. He's not happy, but he's with me, waiting until I'm a snow leopard again.

Amazing. In some ways I envy you. In others, I worry.

Oliver sat back on his haunches. *There's no need to worry.*

Good. Anton turned away and resumed his steady pace. Keisha ran beside him. Oliver guarded his flank. So did Igmutaka. The sense of the spirit guide was even stronger, now that Anton had acknowledged his presence.

He couldn't look at Igmutaka as a threat. No, he had to think of him as an ally.

If only he knew how to use the power Mei and Oliver shared.

Mik and AJ trotted at a steady pace along the eastern flank of Anton's property. Tala ran between them, protected by the two males yet well aware they deferred to her in almost everything they did.

It was a heady experience for a woman as petite as she was in her human form to have two such glorious male hunks at her beck and call, two beautiful men who swore undying love, who looked to her for leadership.

Not bad for an ex-whore.

Especially one who stood barely five feet tall.

The route they'd been given flanked the western slope of the Rocky Mountains. Rugged and isolated, the land had a magical beauty about it, a sense of power.

Tala inhaled the scents of the forest, then turned her attention back to the males running at either side. Their scent was even sweeter, their lure stronger than the innate beauty of this wild land.

Mik jumped across a rushing creek and waited on the far side. AJ made the leap, followed by Tala. Instead of continuing on, she paused in the lush grass where she'd landed, took her bearings and listened to the night sounds.

All was as it should be and her men were with her, protecting her. After the brief hesitation, she shifted and straightened up between her two male wolves. Mik's broad wolven shoulder reached higher than her waist. AJ was only a fraction shorter.

She rested her hands on their strong backs and once again breathed in the night air. After such a long drive from San Francisco and so much time confined to their vehicle, the freshness of the forest and the clean air felt like a benediction. Even so, her thoughts drifted once more to Mik and AJ.

The musky scent of the two males made her blood pound in her veins. A low ache settled in her belly. Need was an ever-present thing when she was with them, but it was always more powerful when they ran as wolves.

Eyes closed, Tala slipped into sensation, filling her lungs and her soul with the peace and life of the forest, with the love of both her mates, until everything she experienced deepened and intensified.

The coarse fur on AJ and Mik's wolven backs tickled her palms, the damp grass felt cool and luxuriant beneath her bare feet. The cool wisp of night air caressed her skin, raising gooseflesh along her arms, beading her nipples into tight points. She smelled her own arousal as it blended with pine and cedar and the damp mushroom aroma of forest humus.

Caught up in the smells and soft sounds of the forest, the nearness of the two wolves standing patiently beside her, Tala felt her arousal blossom and grow. Her breasts grew heavy and she yearned for the broad hands of one or even both of her lovers to support them. Her sex swelled and ripened and a single tear ran down her inner thigh.

Mik raised his nose and inhaled. AJ did the same.

Tala heard the soft, questioning sniffs and did her best to ignore them. She needed this moment, this break in time to feel the world around her.

To feel herself.

San Francisco was exciting and the city itself ever-changing, but this was where her heart lay. Here in the deep forest with her mates beside her. Here where the wild things lived was the one place she felt truly free.

Whoever dared trespass on this perfect ground had no right, no right at all. The thought had barely entered her mind when she heard a branch snap. The sharp sound echoed in the darkness. Tala's eyes flashed open and AJ growled. Mik nudged her forward, into the darker shadows beneath the trees and away from the sound. Tala walked quietly, her fingers wrapped in the thick fur of her wolves.

She wanted to shift, but not if there was any risk at all of being seen. *What is it?*

I'm not sure. Nothing, I hope. Mik's long tongue swept over her wrist.

The damp sweep made her shiver.

AJ sniffed the air and his hackles rose. *Not human. Grizzly, I think. Upstream from us and moving this way.*

Tala breathed a sigh of relief. Damn, they were all so jumpy, but bears belonged here. Whoever was after the Chanku didn't. She stood in the thick moss between the two wolves and shifted.

A moment later, a large bear wandered through the small meadow where they'd been standing only moments before. He raised his head, sniffed the air and looked their way, alert to their presence. Then he crashed through the undergrowth and continued his lumbering way on down the hill.

Tala stood there between her two men and listened to the crunching, swishing sounds of the bear moving through the thick growth along the stream. The sound of his passing slipped into absolute silence. Not a cricket chirped, no night bird called. Not even a whisper of wind in the pines disturbed the perfect quiet of a late summer's night.

Mei's voice intruded in her mind. Tala jerked to attention. Was something wrong?

Tala? I heard from Anton. He's calling it a night and wants everyone back for at least a few hours' sleep. You guys are staying with Oliver and me, so just come straight to our cottage.

Gotcha. Tala glanced at Mik on one side, AJ on the other and shuddered with the sharp thrust of arousal. *We'll be there as fast as we can, okay?*

Oliver's dry comment slipped in behind Mei's. *Make it even faster. We're growing real anxious.*

Tala led the other two back to the house, leaping over fallen logs and ignoring a fat doe that jumped out of their way. It took only a few minutes to race down the steep hillside to the front door of Oliver's small cottage across the driveway from the main house.

Mei and Oliver waited on the front porch. Mei's dark hair was wet from the shower. Both she and Oliver wore plain white caftans.

Oliver reminded Tala of a desert sheik in his, with his dark, dark skin and finely chiseled cheekbones. She paused, one paw lifted, and studied the two people in front of her—Mei so perfect with long, black hair that flowed to her hips, caramel-colored skin and the sexy Asian tilt to her green eyes. Oliver, just as perfect, with skin the color of dark chocolate and neatly trimmed black hair.

Tala treasured her amazing link with Mei, the fact Tala had been the original receptacle for Igmutaka when Mik called on the spirit guide to help them. In fact, the spirit guide had briefly controlled her mind when she'd traded her wolven body for Mei's leopard, in a convoluted plan of Anton's that allowed Oliver and Mei to bond.

The plan had worked better than even Anton expected. Not only was Oliver able to bond with Mei while she borrowed Tala's wolven body, he'd learned the mechanism for shifting into a leopard.

Oliver made an absolutely magnificent snow leopard.

Tala had hoped for the same knowledge, since she'd spent time inhabiting Mei's beautiful snow leopard body. So far, though, her shifting was limited to the body of a wolf. Even the perfect rosette that first appeared on the back of her hand when Igmutaka entered her consciousness had disappeared once he'd moved out of Tala and into Mei's body. Tala's memories of that brief time in such a sinuous, yet powerful, form still attracted her.

At least she'd managed to control Igmutaka long enough to get her own body back. She still felt a sense of pride that she'd had the mental strength to vanquish an ancient and powerful spirit guide.

Thank the Goddess she had! Tala doubted either Mik or AJ would have been happy with a leopard as a bonded mate.

Now, the crusty Sioux spirit lived in both Oliver and Mei. Tala wondered if he'd acknowledge her presence. Wondered what the night ahead would bring. There was only one way to find out. With a flirtatious tilt to her head, she shifted and became Tala the woman.

She stood there, smiling, a tiny little ex-whore with two absolutely gorgeous men standing beside her. She'd thought it didn't get any better than this, but after looking at the couple on the porch, Tala expected it was going to be absolutely mind-blowing, very, very soon.

Chapter 8

Millie locked the door to her cabin and followed Ulrich out to the Land Rover. The engine was already running, a subtle hint from her mate that it was time to get moving. Still, Millie paused beside the vehicle and took a final look at the seemingly endless list of things she'd had to deal with before they could leave.

"C'mon, Millie, m'love. We've a long ride ahead of us."

Ulrich climbed out of the driver's seat and walked around to her side. His thinly disguised impatience was beginning to get on her nerves, but she understood how anxious he was to be on the road and moving. It was going to be a long drive to northern Montana.

With a loud sigh, Millie tucked the list into the hip pocket of her jeans. Ulrich held the car door open for her. Millie stretched up on her toes and kissed him hard on the mouth, then climbed into the front passenger seat before he could respond.

"What was that for?" Ulrich leaned over and made eye contact with her inside the Rover. He had the look of a man who wanted another kiss.

Millie knew they'd never stop at just one if she gave in. They never could. "It was an apology," she said, meaning it. "Ric, I'm sorry it took so long to get things squared away. Now you know why I don't go anywhere."

Ulrich merely grunted, walked around the front of the vehicle and climbed in beside her. Then he threw the gears into reverse and backed out of Millie's driveway. She gazed longingly at the perfect little cabin nestled in the tall pines and wondered once again if she'd covered everything at the wolf sanctuary.

Ulrich turned to her and smiled. "Quit worrying. You've got a good crew. Let them show you how well they can do on their own."

Millie sat back in the comfortable seat. "You're right. It's just hard to relax when I leave this place. I never go anywhere. I never left even when I wasn't the director. Now it's really hard."

They passed the sanctuary and continued on. Millie watched until the curve in the road took them out of sight of the front gate. Then she turned forward in her seat and checked her watch. It was already after three, which meant even if they were to drive straight through, they wouldn't get to Anton Cheval's until sometime in the middle of the day tomorrow.

She glanced at Ulrich. He had a look of grim determination on his face. Millie sighed. No doubt he was going to try and make the trip with as few stops as possible. She'd packed sandwiches and soft drinks so they wouldn't starve, but she wasn't looking forward to the long drive. Still, it beat trying to fly and make connections.

The inconvenience of living in her beautiful but isolated mountains was only obvious when she needed to be somewhere far away in a big hurry—a very good reason for avoiding travel whenever she could.

Thank goodness Ric was doing the driving. There was no way in hell she could drive for so many hours. Trusting him to get her to Anton's in one piece, Millie leaned back in the seat and closed her eyes.

* * *

Ulrich yawned and stretched. They'd been on the road for what seemed like forever. Millie had been asleep for the past couple hours, but now she was awake and he knew she'd eventually see the signs pointing to Salt Lake City. They should be headed north, not west.

"Where are you going?" Millie turned and stared at him with the sexiest little frown between her beautiful amber eyes.

Ulrich flashed her his best grin and shrugged. "I wondered when you'd notice."

"I noticed about half an hour ago but figured I'd let you discover you were headed the wrong way before I said anything." She turned around in her seat and faced forward, but Ulrich could still see the curve of her lips as she fought back a smile. "Unfortunately, you obviously haven't done anything about it yet and we're well past the turn we should have taken. In a bit we're going to go flying by our second option. I figured it was time to speak up."

"I appreciate your restraint." Ulrich laughed, and then he drove by the exit Millie was talking about.

"What are you doing?"

Ulrich gave her what he hoped was an innocent look. "I'm following a hunch." He tapped his fingers on the steering wheel, and searched for the best way to say what he had to tell her.

No matter what he said, the memories he'd be dredging up were going to hurt. "I talked to Anton this morning, while you were getting things done at the sanctuary, but I haven't said anything because I was waiting for a bit more information. He called back a little while ago and gave me what I needed. Between Jake and Anton, they've got quite a collection of identification papers, including information from a cell phone belonging to one of the men who was involved in the attacks in Maine. So far, everything points to the San Francisco Bay Area. The area down around San Jose and Palo Alto known as Silicon Valley, to be exact. Lots of high-tech firms there. Lots of laboratories."

He paused and concentrated on the road for a bit, better to organize his thoughts. This was not going to be easy on Millie. He wanted to spare her, but there was no way.

"Many of the companies went under during the dot-com bust a few years back, but there's been a resurgence in the industry and some of those businesses are coming back to life, including one in particular."

He turned then, and looked directly at Millie. She watched him, her eyes bright and clear and unsuspecting. *Damn.* "Sweetheart, it's the one where Manda was held the longest. Anton's got enough evidence to believe some of those employees have hung on to records and information about your daughter."

Millie's fingers brushed her lips, but they didn't silence the gasp of pain. Ulrich jerked around in his seat and stared at the road ahead. He couldn't bring himself to look at his mate. It made him feel like a damned coward.

He opened his thoughts, though, and found her pain, a raw, open wound that still hadn't healed. Millie would forever mourn the time she'd lost with her babies, fraternal twins taken from her at birth. Adam had turned into an amazing young man after a fairly normal childhood, but Manda's life had evolved into a twenty-five-year nightmare.

Seeing the lab where her daughter had been abused and raped, held prisoner for so many terrible years, wouldn't be easy for Millie. Ulrich wondered if his mate would ever forgive herself for something over which she'd had no control.

As painful as it would be, he hoped a journey to the place where Manda had been imprisoned the longest would help Millie find closure. Especially if they were able

to find and stop the man Luc and Anton suspected was behind this latest series of attacks.

If they didn't, none of them would be safe. Ever.

Ulrich glanced in Millie's direction. "You couldn't protect her then, my love. We might be able to now, but only
if we're willing to take some serious risks. If we don't stop
these people, none of us will ever find peace. Our children
are in danger, Millie. I want to break into the lab and take a
look at their records. Anton's given me everything he has
and Jake recovered some pretty specific info from the cell
phone they took off of one of the guys who attacked them.
Luc's managed to get more info after hacking into their
computer system. Are you willing?"

Millie turned to him with damp streaks of tears glistening on her cheeks. She looked so much like her daughter,
just as stubborn and proud and determined. "I will do
anything to protect Manda. Anything to keep her from
more pain. Just tell me what we've got, my love, and what
we need to do."

Ulrich reached out and touched Millie's hand with his.
Goddess, how he loved this woman! "I knew I could count
on you. It may be risky, but sometimes a wolf can go
places a man or a woman wouldn't dare travel."

He smiled and realized what he really wanted to do was
pull off onto a deserted spot beside the road and make
love to her now, while his heart pounded and his chest
burned with the powerful love he felt for his very special
woman.

Instead, Ulrich patted her hand and turned his attention
back to the road. It would take close to twenty hours of
driving to get to San Francisco. He hadn't stayed in his
own home for ages, though for all intents and purposes, it
was now Tia and Luc's.

And, in less than a year, it would be home to Tia's babies. He chuckled. She insisted there was only one in there,

but Ulrich had it straight from his late wife's mouth. Two little girls with Camille's sass.

Of course, there was the off chance Tia could end up having them one at a time with a few years in between, if he'd misinterpreted Camille's comments. That wouldn't be at all bad, either.

For them, for those beautiful babies yet unborn, he was willing to risk anything.

Everything. He would give his life to keep them safe. To keep his own baby safe. Damn, he was so proud of Tianna, of the beautiful young woman she'd become. A perfectly wonderful daughter, a strong mate worthy of the powerful man who loved her, yet she was at risk.

All of them would be, until this series of deadly assaults ended.

Focusing on the road ahead, Ulrich and Millie headed west.

Tala sat in Mik's lap with her feet stretched over AJ's thighs. Mik's heavy forearm rested across her belly and AJ absentmindedly rubbed her feet. She sipped her glass of wine and hoped like hell his fingers wouldn't get tired, because it felt like heaven.

They'd all showered and dressed in loose, comfortable clothes after returning from their run across the eastern border of Anton's property. Tala's body practically hummed with sexual tension after all the tricks AJ and Mik had pulled on her in the shower without letting her come. She'd been stroked and rubbed, her hair washed, her pits and legs shaved, her crotch thoroughly washed, all without doing a bit of it for herself.

Of course, she'd helped bathe both AJ and Mik, making certain their genitals were thoroughly scrubbed and rinsed. By the time she'd finished, both men were hard as posts. As far as she could tell, they'd only continued to get harder.

The need for sexual release after a run was something none of them was very good at containing. Knowing what Oliver and Mei probably had on their minds didn't help a bit toward finding any kind of calm before the storm. The extra activity in the shower had added an even more powerful level of arousal.

The silky caftan she'd slipped over her damp body raised her desire even higher. The fabric whispered over her skin like a cool caress and left her sensitized to every touch. The fact Anton had called it a night and said he felt they were safe for the next few days hadn't been lost on them, either.

The relief from worry was almost as exhilarating as foreplay.

Tala hoped like hell Anton knew what he was talking about. She glanced toward the dark forest, but there was no sense of danger. An owl hooted, another answered.

All was well, and she needed to be outside. All of them did. It was like eating and breathing, the only way to feed their feral Chanku nature.

Oliver and Mei sat across from the three of them, gently rocking the small porch swing back and forth. They were every bit as aroused as Tala and her guys. The air practically dripped with the musk of three horny men and two very aroused women.

Oliver had carried a tray outside over an hour ago, loaded with cheeses and sliced meats and all kinds of fruits. They'd all tried to act relaxed and calm, but Tala felt as if every bite she'd taken, every morsel AJ or Mik shared with her, carried an extra message, reminding her what was to come.

Acting civilized was fast becoming an unpopular option.

Now the tray rested on the table between them, covered with nothing more than a few scraps. Empty beer bottles filled a paper bag for recycling and the ice chest was still half-full of more bottles and cans. Mei opened a second bottle of wine.

Tala held her glass out for Mei to fill. "Thanks. This is really good. I'm stuffed, though. The munchies were wonderful."

Oliver laughed. "You can thank Mei. I was going to barbecue, but she didn't want us eating anything too heavy."

AJ's fingers stopped rubbing. "You planning to run again tonight?"

Tala wiggled her toes so he'd get back to work. Luckily he took the hint.

Oliver grinned. "Run? I don't think so. I've done all the running I could possibly want to today." His hand slipped across the top of Mei's leg until his fingers rested at the juncture between her thighs.

She moaned and parted her legs, but he didn't move any closer. One finger tapped her, as if he was deep in thought. Tala was positive he tapped directly on Mei's clit.

She realized she was squirming in Mik's lap. His cock felt like a steel bar along her side. It was hot and she'd felt it twitch and jerk when she moved her body against him. Hot, lively steel, exactly the way she liked it.

She'd caught AJ's erection between her legs almost an hour ago and held him there. He didn't seem to mind being trapped at all, especially now, when she flexed her calf muscles across his solid length.

She felt his moan sort of crawling through her head and squeezed again.

"I was hoping for more indoor activities," Oliver said, dragging Tala back to the conversation. She tried to pay attention, but Mik's cock was even hotter and harder than it had been a moment ago. There was a damp spot in AJ's cotton pants where his broad glans stretched the material.

Oliver added softly, "Something we could all play."

Tala rubbed her side against Mik and slanted Oliver a glance. "Would this activity require everyone's participation?" She wondered if he noticed the breathless quality to her voice.

Oliver nodded, but his eyes were directed at the point where Tala's calves held AJ's cock at attention. Every vein, every wrinkle was visible through AJ's soft, cotton pants. So was the dark, wet spot where the broad tip stretched the fabric, and it was spreading outward, expanding.

Tala shifted her eyes from AJ's erection and found herself staring at Mei. Her beautiful green eyes sparkled. She licked her lips and grinned at Tala.

"Igmutaka bids you hello. He remembers you."

Tala swallowed. She'd wondered about the spirit guide. Their association hadn't been all that pleasant, as far as she recalled. Having a borrowed body taken over by a foreign presence was enough to leave anyone with concerns.

"What does he have to say about me?" Did she really want to know? She held up her hand. "His mark is gone. It disappeared when he left me for you." Tala felt Mik straighten up a bit and knew he was more than a little interested. Of course, Igmutaka had originally been his grandfather's spirit guide, until the old man's death.

What a convoluted journey the presence had taken, from whatever place it was where spirit guides hung out when their hosts died, through Mik and into Tala's wolven body with Adam Wolf's help. Then when Tala had switched bodies with Mei, the spirit guide had followed her into Mei's snow leopard.

Since his avatar was the panther, the snow leopard had held a lot more appeal to Igmutaka than Tala's wolf. It had taken a bit of sleight of hand on Anton's part to get Mei back into her snow leopard form and Tala in her wolf, but Igmutaka had made his own choice.

He'd stayed with Mei.

"Igmutaka remembers you as a powerful foe. You were able to control him when he wanted the snow leopard for himself. He's willing to share with me and he accepts the fact I am stronger than he is, but I have the feeling he's a bit afraid of you."

"What's that going to mean when we're all naked and fucking?" Mik's question hung there for a moment.

Mei shrugged. "I don't know. I've grown to trust him, though, especially since he's sort of split up between Oliver and me. There's a bit of him in both of us. He's fairly quiet when we're in human form but quite talkative when we're both feline. No matter. I have no intention of allowing him to keep me from doing what I want tonight."

"And what, exactly, is that?" AJ's fingers trailed along Tala's leg, but his eyes pinned Mei.

"I'd like to know as well." Mik's soft words hung in the night air as if held there by the strength of his will.

Another woman might have been intimidated. Tala was actually surprised when Mei laughed. Then she leaned forward, crawling across the low table that separated them. Her breasts swung freely, fully visible beneath the loose neckline of her cotton caftan.

She shoved the empty tray of what once had been a wide selection of hors d'oeuvres aside, and stretched like a cat in heat. Her black hair draped forward over her shoulders, covering one eye, adding to the sensual image she made, poised there on the tabletop.

"Whatever feels good, Miguel."

Tala felt the catch in Mik's breath against her throat. His heart pounded in his chest and she heard the sound as if it were her own heart beating. His arousal was a living, breathing thing, surrounding Tala, reaching for Mei.

Tala leaned close and wrapped her fingers around his cock. Like AJ, he wore loose cotton flannel pants and the contours and heft of his erection filled her palm. At the same time she clenched her legs tightly around AJ, compressing the base of his penis between her calves.

Oliver stood up, ran his palm over Mei's rounded buttocks and then went to stand behind Tala. His hands skimmed over her shoulders, down her arms, across her chest to cup her breasts beneath the silky fabric.

Mei blinked. A lazy smile parted her lips. Her tongue traced her upper lip and then the lower one. Mik swallowed. The sound was audible above the beating of hearts, the subtle shift of bodies barely moving.

Mei stretched and then crawled the rest of the way across the low table, her movements sinuous and slow like a panther on the hunt. Instead of heading for Mik, though, she paused beside Tala.

"We've got a huge bed in there. It has room to spare for all of us. Our room is right next to yours. Come with Oliver and me, or you can go to your own. The choice is entirely yours."

Tala cupped Mei's cheek in her palm. "I know. That's what I love about being Chanku. The choice is always mine. It wasn't, not when I had a pimp who called the shots." She leaned close and pressed her lips against Mei's, testing the seam of her mouth, using the tip of her tongue to gain entrance. They kissed, touching only where their mouths met, but Tala sensed the guys' growing excitement, knew their arousal grew even more intense, watching two women explore one another's mouths.

Mei was the one who ended the kiss. Sighing, she slipped off the table and stood up. Her nipples beaded visibly against the soft cotton of her caftan. Her breasts were high and firm and the shape of her nipples was clearly defined through the almost sheer white fabric. She looked at all three men, and then held out both hands. Oliver took one, Tala the other.

Tala unwound herself from Mik and AJ's laps and allowed Mei to lead her into the cottage. With bemused expressions on their faces, Mik and AJ followed the three of them inside and down the hall to Mei and Oliver's bedroom.

"You weren't kidding!" Tala looked at the huge bed. It was at least the size of two kings together and even longer, sort of like the ultimate playground for grown-ups.

"We just got it," Mei said, running her fingers over the crisp linen bedding. "One night a few weeks ago, before Keisha and Xandi were all that interested in sex because they were both tired from the babies, we had Adam and Eve and Stefan and Anton here, and our regular bed was too crowded for all of us. Anton ordered this one specially made for Oliver and me. Sort of a mating gift, I guess, but it's become the playground of choice."

Mik flopped down on the bed, stretched his full six-foot-five-inch length out and laughed. "I feel like a little kid on this thing. How does Oliver find you in here, Mei?"

Oliver laughed. "Notice the headboard and footboard? Set up for bondage. It has built in padded restraints so she can keep me locked in place."

AJ gave him a look that was filled with questions. "And you're okay with that? With the bondage thing?"

Oliver grasped Mei's slim fingers. "Oh, yeah." He looked at Mei with what could only be pure adoration. "She knows how to make it work."

Silence followed his heartfelt statement. Mik nudged AJ. "Some day I'd like to try that. Let Tala tie us up and . . ."

AJ shook his head. "I don't know. I'm still not real comfortable with restraints." He shrugged and lowered his eyes before softly adding, "Prison definitely did a job on me with that sort of thing."

Tala leaned against his back and ran her fingers down the inside of his pants. She found the cleft between his buttocks and followed it all the way to his ball sac, where she gently squeezed him. "Are you sure about that? Really certain you don't want me to have my way with you?"

AJ groaned. "Okay. I'll think about it." He leaned down and slipped his pants off. Mik did the same as Oliver tugged his caftan over his head. Mei stepped up to AJ and ran her fingers along his chest. She followed the thick mat of dark hair from his navel to his groin and tangled her fingers in the soft bush just above his cock.

"Would you trust me if I tied you up, right between Oliver and Mik? Her whisper had to tickle his chest. She breathed the words over his left nipple. AJ tilted his head back. His tangled dark hair cascaded over his shoulders. His nostrils flared and his eyes closed, but his lips parted as he sucked in a deep breath of air.

Both Mik and Oliver watched AJ, apparently mesmerized by the sensual nature of each move he made. Tala'd always thought of him as the most beautiful man she'd ever seen. Now, with his obvious arousal—such a powerful force—locked by his indecision, he was unbelievable.

Mik slowly stroked his cock, as if totally unaware he touched himself. Oliver had his arms folded tightly across his chest, but his lips were parted, his nostrils flared with arousal. Both men seemed to hang on AJ's answer.

"I would give you a safe word," Mei whispered, seducing him with her body and her voice. She pressed both palms against his chest, directly over his flat copper nipples. Rubbed them with her fingertips until they drew up into tight little knots beneath her touch. "Actually, you won't even need one. I'll promise to release you immediately if you ask. . . . I have such wonderful plans for the three of you tonight." As if to emphasize her words, Mei squeezed both AJ's nipples between thumb and forefinger.

His torso jerked, but he groaned and his big body flowed toward her, not away.

Tala leaned closer to AJ and ran her fingers along his spine. She trailed one finger down between his muscular cheeks and stopped at his anus. Slowly she pressed her fingertip against the taut, puckered ring of muscle.

She felt the tight clenching of his buttocks when AJ instinctively flexed at her touch. She withdrew, then pressed again and felt the muscle begin to relax. "We're guests in Oliver and Mei's home, sweetheart. I hate to think we might mess up their carefully organized plans."

"Now, Tala, don't pressure the boy." Oliver leaned

close to AJ and ran his fingers along AJ's right side, then over his flat belly to the point where his cock rooted to his groin. With slow, steady, strokes, he encircled AJ's cock and began jerking him off, almost as if it was an afterthought.

AJ moaned again, and his hips thrust forward into Oliver's tight grasp. Oliver accommodated him for a few slow strokes, then turned him loose. AJ's cock immediately rose up and brushed his belly.

Then he laughed. "You're all pretty convincing. I'm just not . . ."

Mik quickly knelt in front of AJ and took his cock in his mouth.

"Oh, shit. You've called in the big guns, now." AJ's strained laugh sent shivers along Tala's spine. He tangled his fingers in Mik's black hair and tried to ease him away from his cock, but Mik held on, sucking and licking until AJ looked like he might break down and cry from the pleasure.

This was, after all, the man he loved above all other men. His mate. Only Tala knew as much as Mik, exactly what turned him on more than anyone else.

And Tala was otherwise occupied, doing exactly that.

She kept up her pressure against his butt. Mei pinched and pulled AJ's nipples. His big body shuddered. A low, desperate moan slipped from between his parted lips.

As if they'd planned it, everyone backed off. Tala slapped his butt just as Mik released his cock with a loud, wet *pop*. Oliver patted AJ's shoulder and stepped away. Mei pinched both his nipples, then gazed up at him with an innocent expression on her face. "But if you're really not interested . . ."

"Oh, shit." Gasping for breath and laughing, AJ held out his hands. "I give. Go for it."

Within minutes Mei and Tala had all three men, hands tightly secured, lined up in a row with Oliver on the left and Mik on the right. AJ lay in the middle. His cock stood high and forlorn, bobbing against his belly when he moved.

Tala tied blindfolds on the three of them while Mei secured their feet. Then the two women sat back to admire their creation.

What now?

Mei grinned. *Right now I just want to admire our handiwork.*

It was truly admirable. Mik, even when restrained, radiated a frightening level of power. Huge and dark with the slashed cheekbones and black hair of his mixed Hispanic and Sioux heritage, he looked even more dangerous when restrained, as if he was merely accommodating the women's silly wishes. Knowing he could probably bend the metal headboard and free himself without any trouble increased the inherent threat in the man.

The muscles in his chest rippled and flexed as he tested the restraints holding his arms overhead. The headboard creaked when he flexed first one arm, then the other. His thighs were each as big around as either Mei or Tala at their widest point, and his cock stood upright, brick red, lined with dark veins and curving only slightly toward his flat belly.

His skin was a deep bronze, his hair so black it seemed to suck the light from the candles Mei had placed around the room. He gave the shackles one last tug and then turned in Tala and Mei's direction. "Do you want me to test them, see if they'll actually hold me?" he asked. "Just say the word." He grinned and his perfect white teeth made for a gloriously evil-looking slash across his face.

"Do not speak without permission. Also, none of you are to communicate with one another or with us in any form, unless it's to ask us to stop." Mei's voice carried a hidden threat of punishment should they not obey. The corner of Mik's lip twitched. Tala knew he'd winked beneath the blindfold.

As if he merely toyed with them for now.

Tala shivered in spite of herself. She knew Mik. Loved

him to pieces and knew he felt the same about her. Why then, she wondered, did he actually frighten her when he was the one restrained and she was free?

She turned away from Mik and studied Oliver. He seemed made of shadow with his closely cropped black hair and skin the color of strongly brewed coffee. Slightly built, he had an almost graceful beauty about him in comparison to AJ and Mik, but his chest was broad and muscled and his legs perfectly formed. His cock begged to be touched, the way it curved over his flat belly. His glans flared like a broad cap, and the single drop of white precum glistening at the tip emphasized his dark elegance.

Mei slipped out of her flowing caftan and leaned toward him, seemingly drawn by an invisible thread. Tala licked her lips as Mei touched her mouth to the tip of Oliver's cock, wrapped her lips around the small bead of white at its tip, and gently sucked.

Oliver moaned and his hips arched upward. Mei backed away, smiling. She glanced toward Tala and licked her lips.

Tala imagined she felt Mei's tongue between her legs and shivered again, only this time it was pure arousal, not fear. She looked away, and her gaze rested on AJ, lying in the middle.

His calves rested atop both Oliver and Mik's, held in place by the soft restraints that tied him to the footboard of the bed. It made for a fascinating design across the dark green bedspread. Tala stripped her caftan off and threw it on the floor. Then she crawled up on the bed to study him more intimately than she usually felt comfortable doing.

Andrew Jackson Temple wasn't the largest of the three, but there was something about him that drew women like flies to sugar. He was a truly beautiful man, with dark lashes and deep amber eyes, hidden now beneath the blindfold. His lips were full, his mouth wide and sensual, especially now when most of his face was hidden. His hair curled over his ears and touched his shoulders so that he always looked in need of a barber.

His chest was mostly bare and he rippled with the kind of lean muscles swimmers and runners tended to develop. Mik loved to tease AJ about his perfectly aligned happy trail, the dark line of hair that ran from his navel to his groin. Thick, black hair surrounded the broad base of his cock and dusted his thighs and legs, and the tops of his long, narrow feet.

Tala licked her finger and traced the line of hair from his navel to his cock. At the first contact, AJ's body jerked and he tugged at the restraints.

She watched him bite his upper lip, sliding his teeth over the full curve as he obviously struggled to control his nervous reaction. That small sign of vulnerability made him appear even more beautiful.

Mik might be the more powerful of the two men, but there was something so special about AJ, something Tala was still trying to understand.

She'd never expected love like the love she'd found with her men. Mated to one another as the only gay couple in the San Francisco pack, they'd welcomed her into their bed and their hearts, protected her, and given her a reason for living when they'd brought her into their family as their Chanku mate.

Neither of them had ever expected or wanted a woman in his life. Tala's addition had surprised everyone, but she knew AJ had been the most shocked. He'd always preferred men and he loved Mik beyond all others.

The same way she knew he now loved her.

Mei reached for Tala's hand. "I feel your love, just as I feel theirs. It's a powerful force. You and your men are very lucky."

Tala nodded, afraid if she tried to speak she'd break down and cry. *What now?* she asked, shaking herself free of her introspective thoughts. The guys were waiting for something, but it was obvious that the waiting itself was making all three of them even more turned on.

Haven't got a clue, Mei said. Her mental voice rippled with laughter. *But I've got some new toys we can try on them.*

Tala held out her hand. Mei reached into a drawer of the bedside table and pulled out three large phallus-shaped vibrators, all obviously new and still in their wrappers.

"I guess we treat this as an assembly line, right?"

The men writhed slowly at Tala's flip comment. Their shared anticipation beat against her senses and made her sex clench with need. Images speared her mind, a kaleidoscope of sexual positions and acts from each of the men that fed her growing desire. Chuckling like a mad scientist, Tala ripped off the wrapper, checked for batteries and flipped on the first of the toys. The vibrations shook her hand with a low, steady hum.

Mei handed her a jar of some kind of clear gel and Tala slopped a bit on the curved head of the first plastic phallus. Running her palm over the slick, vibrating tip, she imagined it filling her, pictured the image of the bright plastic riding against her clit or sinking deep inside her ass.

It was so easy to adjust the image to one of the guys.

Choosing Oliver first, she knelt between his spread legs and ran the vibrating toy the length of his cock. Oliver bit his lips, cutting off his startled cry. He jerked his hips, raising higher to increase the contact. Tala took advantage of the arch in his back and pressed the phallus against his anus.

With the gel coating the tip, she was able to slip it inside Oliver before he realized what she was up to. He cried out as Tala placed it deep inside him. His hips rolled and bucked in place until Tala put her hand on his clenched abdomen.

"No more. You are not to move."

Oliver groaned and held still, though his body quivered.

Leaving him there with his cock standing at attention and the vibrator going like crazy, Tala patted him again on his taut belly and moved over AJ's bound legs to Mik.

Like a nurse handing a scalpel to a surgeon, Mei slapped another vibrator into her hand. This one was already unwrapped and vibrating. Laughing, Mei took it from her and ran it over Mik's flat nipples. Both of them jerked to attention.

"Ah, you do like that, don't you?"

His lips parted, but he remained silent. When she leaned over and licked his tautly beaded nipples, he groaned. His thoughts were totally blocked to her, but Tala knew what Mik liked best. Leaning down, she took his erect cock between her lips and sucked hard. He lifted his hips to force his cock down her throat. Mei shoved a pillow under his buttocks.

Grinning broadly around her mouthful of hard, male flesh, Tala handed the vibrator back to Mei, who ran it over and under Mik's balls. She touched it to Tala's lips and then slowly dragged it the length of his cock.

Oliver moaned beside them. He obviously couldn't hold still any longer. He rolled his hips as much as he could, as if trying to dislodge the vibrator or drive it deeper. Tala wasn't sure which, but watching the way his huge cock swung to and fro as he thrust his hips had her growing wetter by the second.

She worked her teeth around the tip of Mik's cock as Mei rubbed the vibrator against his sphincter, then traced the ring of muscle with her lube-covered fingertips. She slipped one long finger inside. Mik's mouth twisted and his body writhed against the restraints. Tala sucked him hard and deep as Mei slipped a second finger inside, followed by a third. Mik was moaning now, a soft sound of need rolling out from deep in his throat. He thrashed his body in time with Mei's thrusting fingers until it was all Tala could do to keep his cock in her mouth.

When Mei slipped the vibrator deep inside, Mik groaned louder and his body tensed. His cock seemed to double in size. Tala sucked harder. She ran her tongue over the tip and the vibrations welled up through his penis and tickled her mouth. Her pussy clenched, but she didn't want to come. Not yet.

She released him with one long, hot lick.

The big man whimpered. His massive erection, shiny and damp from Tala's mouth, bobbed against his flat belly.

AJ lay perfectly still. Tala sat back on her heels and studied him a moment. *I think he's hoping we'll forget he's here.*

Mei giggled. *I've been checking, and they're not communicating with each other. He's got to be wondering what's happening to Mik and Oliver.*

Either that or he's worrying what we're going to do next. Tala winked at Mei. *He likes to get sucked off.*

Ah . . . I've got an idea. Mei straddled Mik and slowly eased his thick cock between her legs. Tala did the same with Oliver, placing the broad glans of his erection between her legs and sliding slowly down his full length.

Vibrations radiated through his body into hers. She bit back a low moan of undiluted pleasure and clenched her inner muscles tightly around his cock. Eyes half-closed, she angled her hips and pressed her clit against his vibrating shaft.

Her muscles immediately spasmed and she twitched away.

"Oh, crap." Giggling, Tala slapped her hand over her mouth. It was so much more fun when the guys didn't know for sure who was doing what to them. She rose up and then settled just as slowly back against Oliver's groin.

Twisting her torso, Tala leaned over and took AJ's cock

in her mouth. He jerked at her first touch. Then he sighed as she sucked him deep. Mei twisted at the waist, leaned over from her position straddling Mik and suckled AJ's balls. He cried out and arched his hips as much as the restraints would allow.

It took a few minutes to get it right, but Mei and Tala found a rhythm with their guys, rising up and flowing back down as they rode them in tandem. Bending supple bodies, they used lips and tongues on AJ, trading back and forth between his balls and cock.

Tala's body undulated with the rhythm they'd all finally found. Oliver's cock vibrated deep inside and AJ's weeping penis stretched her lips with its powerful length. Sound filled the room, all wet and breathy—the rhythmic rush of air in and out of straining lungs, the rustle of bedding, the occasional throaty whimper as each man fought for control.

Tala released AJ's cock and blew cool air over his wet length. He cried out. Then he clamped his lips shut. She opened her mind and found only Mei. The men were all blocked, locked away in their own fantasies, but Mei's busy mind was more than enough. She reveled in the beautiful man beneath her. His thick cock hit her cervix on every downward thrust of her hips and she loved the bunch and play of his muscles as he tugged against his restraints.

She continued to lick and suck AJ's wrinkled sack, mouthing his testicles and sucking each ball into her mouth, one at a time. When she pulled away to concentrate on Mik, Tala took over, once again sucking his huge cock all the way to the back of her throat. It wasn't easy from this angle, but she managed to swallow him and take his entire erection deep. Breathing through her nose, she slowly raised and lowered her head, milking AJ with her lips and tongue on each stroke.

His taste filled her mouth, so familiar yet somehow more

exciting. There was something almost magical knowing his eyes were covered, his arms and legs restrained.

Oliver bucked beneath her. She felt the tension beneath her thighs, the steady vibration spreading from his ass to his cock. Releasing AJ, Tala concentrated on Oliver. Glancing to her left, she saw that Mei was doing the same with Mik. Rising and falling to take him deep inside on every thrust, she rode him as if he were a stallion.

Tala reached behind herself and found the third vibrator. It was already slick with gel. She slipped it between AJ's legs and held it against his testicles for a moment. When he cried out and raised his hips in response, she carefully pressed it against his anus, slipped through the tight muscle and buried it to the hilt.

AJ groaned, Oliver shouted, Mik cursed, and suddenly Tala was overwhelmed with the arousal of all three men as each one neared his climax, opened his thoughts, and accepted the total experience of warm and willing woman, well-placed vibrator, and sensual need.

Arousal . . . extreme arousal as thoughts flew from one man to the other, overlapping and circling back once again, flooding the consciousness of the two women who controlled them.

Tala read their thoughts as if they were spoken aloud, and the explicit details seemed to suck away all conscious thought. She shuddered, immersed in sensation that turned her into nothing more than a desperately aroused body, a shivering creature of nerves and needs, of pounding heart and swollen, receptive tissues.

She sensed how Mik reveled in the restraints of the ties that held him. How he needed the blindfold, the one step that truly carried him into the captive experience and beyond, into his own world of sensual fantasy.

She saw how Oliver was caught in the shared aspects of the experience, the pressure of AJ's long leg resting over his, the knowledge that Mik, so big and powerful, lay on the other side of AJ, secured as tightly as Oliver was to the bed. Even more, Oliver relished the smells and sounds of sex he couldn't see or feel. His mind spun wild fantasies of the things the women might be doing to the men who lay beside him.

But AJ's impressions affected her most. Powerful and extremely explicit, so stunning and clear that Tala might have been AJ Temple, captive. He shared all he felt until she virtually lived through his senses, absorbed each touch and scent, each sensual impression, while the frantic hum of the vibrator underscored his freely broadcast thoughts.

Restrained, blindfolded, at the mercy of both Tala and Mei, two women he trusted implicitly, AJ soaked up every nuance, every new sensation. From his own barely controlled fear of bondage and his aversion to any level of vulnerability, to the unbelievable freedom of being held as a captive, open to his captors' every desire, a slave to their imaginations—he absorbed it all, and shared his feelings freely with Tala and with Mei.

Shared and relished, even though bondage was most obviously something he'd never choose on his own. He concentrated on the clasp of the padded cuffs around his wrists, the tight pressure of the blindfold across the bridge of his nose, the way his lashes felt when he blinked them against the slick fabric.

He shared the sensation of cool air currents floating past his damp cock after Tala released him, and the stricture of his balls, the way they felt, sucked up so close between his legs when Mei's long fingers and then her mouth caressed them. He couldn't allow himself to think about the vibrator and the way it felt deep inside his ass, or he'd come in a heartbeat.

Tala was suddenly dragged free of AJ's impressions when she sensed Oliver's climax, at the precise moment that Mei felt Mik's body tense. As if they'd choreographed the motion, both woman backed away from the men and held as still as their own highly aroused bodies would allow.

Trapped as they were, senses raised to a feverish pitch, Mik, AJ, and Oliver trembled with unspent energy, their bodies rigid with arousal.

Mik was the first to move. He tugged hard at the restraints holding him.

"No." Tala used her most authoritative voice. Mik stilled. "We're going to untie you now. None of you has permission to come until Mei and I have reached climax. If you do, you will regret it."

She glanced at Mei and had to bite back a giggle. This was so not her!

Mei grinned and then she went to Oliver first and untied him. "Lie still, and don't you dare touch yourself," she said, leaving his blindfold in place and moving on to AJ while Tala released Mik. When Mik's hand moved toward his swollen cock, Tala stopped him. Then she undid the leg restraints for AJ and Mik.

Mei slowly removed the vibrator from Oliver. Tala did the same for Mik and AJ. As the women flipped each one off, the absence of sound took on a mesmerizing quality, broken only by the pounding heartbeats and heavy breathing of each of the men.

The candles had burned low and the room lay in darkness. Only the flickering glow of the tiny flames remained, casting dark shadows against the walls. Sweat glistened on Mik's chest and his jaw was clenched. AJ lay perfectly still with his fists clasped at his sides, and Oliver looked as if he was ready to explode.

Mei removed their blindfolds and sat back on her heels. She glanced at Tala and winked. "I think it's our turn, don't you?"

Tala noticed a strange light in Mei's eyes. They seemed

to glow with green fire in the candlelight, giving Mei an ethereal look, as if she existed on another plane.

Mik reached for Tala, and all thoughts of Mei fled. She flowed into his arms and he lifted her over him and beyond, until her sex was over his mouth and she was suspended, her knees barely resting on the pillow beside his head, her fingers wrapped tightly around the metal bars in the headboard.

Mik's fingers grasped her thighs and held her as if she weighed nothing at all. His long tongue found her clit and the puffy lips of her vulva. He suckled and licked, nibbled as if he'd not tasted anything as wonderful in his life. Tala glanced to her left.

AJ held Mei over his mouth. He buried his face between her legs and the sounds of a starving man feasting raised Tala's arousal to a fever pitch. Mei glanced her way. The green light in her eyes was even brighter now in the fading light.

Mei arched her back and groaned just as Tala felt long fingers caressing her bottom, sliding along the crease between her cheeks and pressing against her anus. She glanced over her shoulder and saw Oliver behind her. He straddled one of Mik's legs and one of AJ's and had a hand on both her and Mei.

Opening her mind to her friend's thoughts, she sensed the moment when Oliver penetrated Mei. She felt his finger sliding deep inside her own bottom just seconds later, at exactly the same time Mik wrapped his lips around her clit and suckled hard on the bundle of nerves. His big hands slipped along her sides, cupped both her breasts and squeezed her nipples.

Tala exploded.

Mei screamed, AJ cursed, and even Oliver let out a strangled cry. Mik grabbed Tala and flipped her over while her body was still convulsing in climax and his huge cock slipped into her wet and ready sex, filling her completely and bringing on another climax.

Tala lay there beneath Mik, loving the weight of his big body, the feel of his heart pounding against her chest, the musky, earthy scent of sex that permeated the room.

The bed still shook from someone doing something, and she slowly rolled her head to one side, just in time to see Oliver throw back his head and shout as he drove deep into AJ, who still covered Mei with his cock buried between her legs.

Mei cried out at the same time. She arched her back, meeting AJ thrust for thrust until he drove into her hard and held the position, his mouth twisting in a rictus of what had to be either pain or profound pleasure.

Tala opened her mouth to make an off-color quip when Mei started shaking. Oliver shuddered as well, practically convulsing as he wrapped his arms around AJ and held on.

"What the hell?" Frantic, AJ turned toward Tala and Mik. Mei flopped and jerked in his grasp. Oliver rolled away and his body arched and shook in the midst of a grand mal seizure.

Mik and Tala scrambled apart. Tala helped AJ hold Mei. Mik grabbed Oliver. The shaking continued. Even the room seemed to vibrate.

"Mik, what's happening?" AJ held tightly to Mei's thrashing shoulders.

"I don't know." He held Oliver's shoulders against the mattress, then threw one leg over his body to hold him in place with his weight. "Oliver? Oliver, can you hear me? C'mon, buddy. If you can, use mindtalking. Tell me what to do!"

Oliver arched his back and screamed. Mei fought AJ and Tala's grasp, but when Oliver screamed, she thrashed even harder. Suddenly her body arched and her scream was the cry of a panther, harsh and bloodcurdling.

Light from somewhere beyond the candles flickered and

burst into a brilliant glow, nearly blinding Tala. Mik jerked his head to his left and covered his eyes against his arm. AJ held a hand over his as the light grew brighter, hotter.

Suddenly it began to shrink in upon itself, and then with an audible *pop*, the light winked out.

Silence filled the room. Oliver and Mei lay perfectly still. Both of them were breathing, but appeared to be unconscious.

Something moved in one dark corner of the room. A low growl shivered across Tala's skin. She turned in the direction of the sound and saw green eyes staring back at her.

Mik? What the fuck is that?

Mik slowly turned in the direction Tala pointed.

Just as a large, tawny panther stepped out of the shadows and jumped lightly up on the bed.

Chapter 9

South Bay, near San Francisco, CA

Millie trotted along behind Ulrich, keeping to the shadows and avoiding the overhead security cameras. She knew damned well she'd not relax until they were back in the Land Rover and at least a hundred miles north of this place.

In a pouch hung around Ulrich's neck was a thumb drive carrying the disgusting records that had been kept on her daughter. Millie had tried to read a few of the files as they downloaded and she erased them off the main computer, but the content had sickened her.

Ric had followed after her, uploading a special code Luc had e-mailed to him, one that should totally wipe all traces of Manda's information from the system and any other that might try to access this one.

Hidden within the operating files, it should remain active yet totally undetectable while it ensured that any records on Manda Smith, under all her code names, would soon be nothing more than inaccessible bits of unconnected binary code.

She and Ulrich had done all they could.

Now Millie just wanted to go home. Or to Montana.

Wherever. It didn't really matter, so long as it was far away from here.

One man lay dead in the main office, but he'd deserved to die and she felt a small sense of justice that she had helped avenge her daughter's horrible life. Another man, a security guard, had escaped, but from what Ulrich could sense of his mind, he didn't have a clue about the Chanku or shapeshifters. He merely thought they'd been attacked by vicious dogs.

So be it. All in all, it had been a very productive visit.

Granted, there might still be files on laptops that weren't at the laboratory, but with Luc's Trojan, the moment those computers accessed the main file, the information would be compromised. For now, it looked as if they had everything from the main files that proved Manda's existence. The photos Millie discovered in a locked cabinet in one of the offices had burned quite nicely.

Others had gone through the shredder.

The images she'd seen would stay with her for a long time. Poor Manda! To think her beautiful daughter, once such a pathetic freak of nature, had been treated so obscenely. It was wrong.

Dead wrong.

Which was probably why the death of the one scientist they'd encountered didn't bother Millie one bit. He'd known who they were, what they were.

He'd known Manda.

Even though he'd realized there was a sensitive, intelligent young woman beneath the horribly disfigured body, he'd still treated her like a lab rat.

Worse, in fact. Even rats had more rights.

Millie had recognized him in some of the photos and realized he'd been the one in charge of the lab when Manda was there. He'd orchestrated so much of her horrible life and had followed Milton Bosworth's despicable directions without question. He'd even tried a few disgusting things on his own, "in the name of science," according to his records.

She was only sorry Ulrich had been the one to kill him. Millie had never killed before, but it would have been easy to make an exception for that particular beast.

No, calling him a beast was an insult to wolves everywhere, but at least his death should give Manda some small sense of closure.

Millie wasn't at all certain exactly what it gave her.

They reached the dark street where the Land Rover was parked. Ric shifted and unlocked the door so quickly Millie hardly saw him move. He opened the passenger door from inside. She leapt in, still in wolf form, but shifted the moment the door was closed.

The eastern sky had begun to lighten with the first signs of the coming dawn and the industrial area they'd parked in would soon come to life.

Ulrich dressed quickly and backed out of the dark lot where he'd parked behind a warehouse. Millie was still tying her boots when they hit the freeway and headed north.

Neither of them had spoken.

Finally, Ulrich broke the silence. "I doubt we got all the information, but we cleaned out everything in that particular lab that proves we exist. I don't know what else we can do."

"We can go to Montana and see what the others have found out." Millie touched his arm and fought the urge to weep. So many years of her daughter's life, wasted.

If only she'd known.

"We'll need sleep, first." Ulrich grabbed his cell phone and handed it to Millie. "Call Anton. Let him know we'll be there sometime tomorrow. Tell him what we've done."

Millie dialed Anton's number while Ulrich headed into the city. She had to admit, a few hours' sleep in Ulrich's old Marina District home sounded better by the minute.

* * *

The big cougar sat on the end of the bed and growled. Oliver moved his head to one side and blinked. Mei lay beside him, breathing steadily but still unconscious. Mik, Tala, and AJ sat still as statues, watching the animal.

Someone pounded on the front door, and from the sound of the noise, they were coming through. The cat flinched but it didn't run away when the house shook with a loud crash. The door must have hit the wall when it was forced open. Oliver heard more than one person racing down the hallway.

Anton and Stefan burst into the room. Stefan flipped the light switch. The cat blinked when the overhead light came on, stared at the newcomers and growled low in its throat.

"What the hell? Oliver? Mei? Is Mei all right?"

Oliver shook his head to silence Anton and sat up with Mik's help.

Mei rolled over slowly, blinking against the bright light. She ignored everyone in the room except the cougar.

The cat stretched forward and sniffed her face. Mei lifted up on her hands and knees. She reached out with her right hand and stroked the animal's broad forehead and then scratched behind its ear.

A deep purr rumbled in the cougar's chest. Mei turned to Anton as she grabbed for Oliver's hand. "Don't you recognize him?"

"You can't possibly mean . . ." Oliver shut his mouth. That was exactly what she meant. "Igmutaka?"

The panther turned and gazed at Oliver. "But how could he . . . ?"

Anton stepped forward with Stefan right behind him. "Do either of you sense the spirit guide within you?"

Mei shook her head. "No, and it may sound weird, but I sort of miss him."

"I know." Oliver agreed. "Me, too." He scooted across

the bed and stroked the animal's broad shoulder. The cat leaned into his touch. "He certainly feels solid. There's nothing ephemeral about this creature at all."

"I wonder if he can take on human form?" Anton frowned. "Mei, can you still communicate with him?"

Mei shook her head. "Not like this. Maybe if I shift . . ."

"Not now." Anton held his hand out to stop her. "The snow leopard and American cougar aren't normally close associates. The last thing we need is a catfight in the bedroom."

Oliver bit back a laugh. He honestly didn't think Anton intended his comment as a joke. AJ and Tala weren't as successful. Anton's eyebrows raised when both of them turned laughter into quiet coughs.

"Let me try." Mik scooted closer and stared into the cat's eyes.

He'd been able to mindtalk with Mei when no one else could. Oliver grabbed Mei's hand. Her fingers were ice cold and trembling. He turned his head and caught her wide-eyed gaze. *Are you okay?*

Yes, but still a little shaky. Do you remember anything? What did it feel like for you, when Igmutaka left?

Like someone ripped out part of my guts. You?

Same thing. The pain was intense, as if he'd somehow melded with my cells. I never really thought of how we were connected. I didn't realize he had an actual presence beyond the spirit.

Me, either. Scary, now that I think of it, but it explains why he'd get so pissed off when we ran as wolves.

Mik sat back on his heels with a bemused expression on his face. "I'll be damned. It was the bondage, something about the fact the men were restrained and the women free, but I don't fully understand the reason. That and the energy from all of us having sex, the frustration that built up. It gave him the strength he needed to make a break for it when we all climaxed together. All that energy releasing at once released Igmutaka as well." Mik shook his head and turned to Mei.

"Mei, when you suggested bondage, it wasn't your idea at all. It was Igmutaka *pushing* you. His desire was controlling you. Did you realize he had that kind of power?"

Speechless, Mei shook her head. Oliver squeezed her hand and glanced at the big cat. He thought it had a decidedly smug expression on its face. Suddenly Oliver didn't miss the sense of Igmutaka's presence inside himself at all.

Had the spirit guide controlled him as well? The mere thought of it made him nauseous. "I never had the feeling he was exerting any influence on me at all. Now I'm beginning to wonder at decisions I've made since he moved in." Oliver shook his head and added, "Bastard."

"So, what now? Does he want something? Is he a shapeshifter? Can he become human?" Anton frowned and stared at the cougar. It was obvious Anton was trying to communicate with the big cat, and just as obvious it wasn't working.

Either that, or Igmutaka was ignoring him.

Mik caught the animal's attention once again. The cougar stared steadily into his eyes. After a moment Mik sat back on his heels and chuckled. "He's never been human and can't understand why we think he'd want to be one now. He wants only to return to the wild. He was a cougar long before he was tapped by the Great Spirit to become a guide. Already his interest in the world of men appears to be fading."

Stefan sat on the edge of the big bed and stared at the panther, frowning. "What about this ability to communicate? Will he keep that?"

Mik shook his head. "I don't think so. It's already getting harder for me to understand him, as if the human words are slipping away from his memory."

As if in agreement, the cougar narrowed its eyes, glared at Mik and snarled. There was a greater sense of wildness about him now than there'd been just minutes earlier.

Oliver reached for Mei's left hand and held it up. The dark rosette that appeared when the spirit guide first entered her consciousness was gone. Mei gasped and grabbed Oliver's hand and turned it over.

His mark was gone, too. They both turned and looked at the huge panther.

He stood up and stared back at them. His silent speech now, for some reason, was clear and easy to understand. Oliver couldn't help but wonder what power remained within the beast.

You gave me a home within you, and for that I am grateful. Now you have given me an even greater gift—my freedom and a chance, once more, at the life I left so long ago. I can never repay you, but know that I will always watch over you.

With great dignity, he jumped lightly off the bed. Then without a backward glance, the cougar walked with majestic grace out of the bedroom and down the hallway.

"We left the front door open. Should I try and stop him?" Stefan was heading for the door as he spoke.

"No." Oliver shook his head before Anton could answer. "Let him go. If what he said to Mei and me is true, we've just gained ourselves a trustworthy watchdog."

Mei jabbed her elbow in his side. "*Watchcat*, Oliver. Don't insult him."

Before he could come up with a properly pithy response, Oliver heard the sound of an engine. Someone was coming down the driveway and it sounded like they were in a really big hurry.

Ulrich decided he truly loved the way Millie clung to his hand as they entered his old home in San Francisco's Marina District. She'd not been here before and he wished they'd made the trip for a different reason, but at this point the big bed in the master bedroom sounded like heaven.

He'd shared this home with his late wife so many years ago, raised his daughter here until she'd gone away to school, but now the subtle changes Tia and Luc had made had erased any of Camille or Ulrich's lingering touches. Fresh paint, rearranged furniture and a big-screen TV in the once formal living room reminded Ulrich of both his daughter and son-in-law's youth—and his own advanced years.

But Millie, bless her, made him young again. He set their bags down on the floor, pulled her into his arms and kissed her. Her lips were warm and pliant and her body molded to his as he licked and sucked at her mouth. When Millie finally came up for air, there was a dazed and distracted look on her face.

"What was that for, Ric?" She touched his cheek with her fingertips.

"A reminder of how much I love you." He rubbed his scratchy face against her palm. It had been ages since he'd shaved and he imagined there was more than a little gray showing in his stubble.

"Why don't we continue this discussion in the bedroom?" Millie yawned. "I'm practically asleep on my feet."

He chuckled, grabbed their bags and led Millie down the hallway to the very back of the house. The master bedroom looked out on a miniscule backyard filled with flowers and small trees. Morning sunlight filtered through the blinds and left shadowy bars across the pale yellow bedspread.

Millie groaned as she stared at the bed. "I'm exhausted, but I know I'll regret it if I don't shower, first. As tired as I am, I'm still wound tight from everything."

Ulrich was already stripping out of his clothes. "The shower's big enough for two." He kicked off his shoes and stepped out of his pants. "Besides, I have a wonderful idea of how to help you relax."

He grabbed her hand as she walked past him and pulled her close. Millie draped her arms over his shoulders and buried her face against his chest. His cock rose to greet her and he chuckled as his sensitive nostrils picked up the musky scent of her arousal.

It was enough that they'd shifted and not had a chance for sexual relief afterward, but the events of the past few hours had kept both of them on an adrenaline high. Of course, even if they'd spent the day sitting on Millie's front deck, he would want her. The desire he felt for his woman was both profound and unrelenting.

He rubbed his palm along her spine, tracing each vertebra with his callused fingertips. She groaned when he found her tailbone and spread his fingers to cover her perfectly shaped bottom.

Was there anything about Millie that wasn't perfect?

She giggled and ran her tongue along the very center of his chest. "A lot, my love. I will never be perfect, and I love it when you broadcast without realizing it."

"Witch." He lifted her easily in his arms and carried her into the large bathroom with Millie grinning like the cat who got the cream. He set her on the counter.

"Ric!" Laughing, she slapped her hands down on the counter and raised her bottom up off the tile. "Do you have any idea how cold that is?"

"Of course," he said, trying to look innocent. Then he turned on the shower and waited a moment while the water heated.

Millie slipped off the counter and stepped under the spray. Ulrich got in behind her and grabbed a washcloth, but before he could add soap, Millie turned to him. Her chin wobbled and she blinked.

Were those tears on her cheeks, or the water from the

shower? He couldn't tell, but when he opened his arms, she slipped into his embrace with a shivering sob. Standing there beneath the stinging spray, Ulrich held her while she cried as if the tears would never end.

He opened his thoughts and found Millie's twisted in a convoluted morass of emotions. Regret over Manda's foul treatment, fear of more attacks, love and thankfulness for Ulrich . . . he paused in that part of her mind, wallowing for a moment in that sense of pure love he felt for his mate.

Then he felt a dark shadow and knew she thought of the hours just past, of the body of the man they'd left on the floor of the main lab, his neck broken, his sightless eyes staring at the ceiling.

The autopsy would show animal hair and possibly saliva, but Ulrich had managed the kill without breaking the man's skin, so it had, at least, been a bloodless death. A well-deserved death.

He'd seen into the man's mind and knew he killed their greatest foe. He'd seen the threats against the Chanku, the ongoing search the scientist had orchestrated against all of them. He'd also sensed Millie's anger, her satisfaction when she'd walked up and sniffed at the body. So why the shadows? Why the tears now?

Ulrich grabbed the washcloth and soap and began to gently bathe her. Millie's shoulders shook and she trembled, but he sensed her gaining control over her emotions with each soothing caress of the soft terry cloth.

"Why?" he asked, tilting her chin up and kissing her lightly.

She blinked with tear-spiked lashes. Took a deep breath so that her chest rose and fell. "I saw you kill a man a few hours ago. I wasn't horrified by his death. I wasn't even frightened by the unemotional calculation I saw in you when you killed him. I was glad he was dead. I know he's the one behind so much of what's been happening and I was glad he was no longer a threat. Then I thought about him all the way here."

Ulrich brushed her wet hair back from her face and used the handheld shower to rinse the soap off her body. "What were you thinking?"

He could have gone into her mind and searched for the thoughts, but he sensed her need to explain this to herself as well as to him. He remembered his own feelings after his first kill, so many years ago. His sense of detachment that a man had died because of him, and the effort it had taken to come to terms with his lack of emotion over the kill.

"I was thinking that he deserved to die. That I was sorry it had been so quick and clean because what he did to Manda had been neither quick nor clean. Then I realized how easily I'd rationalized the need to kill someone I didn't know." She looked up at him, blinking rapidly through tear-filled eyes. "That's not me, Ric! I save lives with every wolf I protect. I've never been violent, never once wished for the death of another, human or animal. What's happened to me?"

Ulrich quickly rinsed the soap off of both of them, turned off the shower and handed a fresh towel to Millie while he dried off with another. Steam filled the small bathroom and it made him think of how clouded some of the decisions they made had become. He wondered how he should phrase his words. How could he explain what was, in essence, an entirely new reality that came with life as a wolf, as Chanku?

He followed Millie to the bed and pulled the blankets back for her. She crawled under the covers naked. He curled in behind her and wrapped her damp body close to his.

She fit so perfectly against him, as if they were created,

one for the other and it made him think of Camille. Of all the nights they'd slept together in this bed.

Camille had never felt remorse over anything she'd done. She'd been the ultimate free spirit, whether it was in her sex life with her other lovers, or the few times she'd taken a life.

Millie was almost the opposite. She agonized over so many things and cared deeply about making the right decision. Even now, the part of her that would always remain human tried to rationalize her behavior as a wolf.

"You're not going to answer me, are you?" She didn't turn to look at him, but he felt her disappointment, that he'd not offered at least consolation if he couldn't help her find forgiveness.

"I was trying to come up with a simple answer to a very complex question." He nuzzled the soft skin behind her ear and inhaled the mixed scents of bath soap, shampoo, and woman. "What has happened to you is terribly complex. You have made a much larger change than merely that of a woman into a shapeshifter. You've taken on more than just the appearance of the wolf, my love."

Millie turned in his embrace until she faced him. "Explain, please?" She kissed him and wrapped her arms around his neck. "I want to see you talk your way out of this one."

"I knew you had an ulterior motive." He kissed her, and then rolled to his back with Millie on top of him. Her wet hair hung in damp strands to his chest. "You've taken on the credo of the wolf as well, the behavior patterns of the animal. You're a carnivore, my love. A killer capable of truly vicious behavior when it is necessary."

"Then why do I feel . . . ?"

It hit him, then. Why she was upset, and why this past night's activities bothered her so much. "No remorse? That's it, isn't it?" With both hands he brushed her hair back behind her ears and tucked it in place. Then he cupped her chin in his palms.

"You're thinking you should feel badly over the death of that man, yet you don't. You feel guilty over your lack of remorse, the fact you could be a partner to a killing and not somehow feel at fault."

She nodded as if mesmerized by the movement of his lips, so he raised his head and kissed her. His cock rose with her taste and they both adjusted their bodies until his shaft rested between her thighs. "The wolf kills when it's necessary. To feed. To protect its young. To protect territory. That's what happened this morning. We killed to protect our young. No more, no less."

Millie swallowed and chewed on her lower lip for a moment. Then she nodded. "What about the police? What if . . . ?"

Ulrich shook his head. "Remember, I disconnected their security system before we went in and severed power to the cameras. We wore rubber gloves that we disposed of and we destroyed all evidence of the very existence of your daughter. I saw nothing that mentioned Chanku as a species, only a lot of notes and questions. Once Luc and Jake have time to go through the files, we'll know for sure if there are more men stalking our kind from this particular lab. And, if it comes down to questioning, ever, we have ways to stop even the most curious of detectives."

Anton had been teaching some of his powerful mental skills to both Ulrich and Luc. Bending and reshaping the thoughts of a human weren't easy skills to learn, but Luc, especially, was quickly picking up on much of what Anton knew. Adam Wolf was also proving adept at many of the things Anton had learned over the years.

As a group, they were becoming stronger and more proficient. Individually, Ulrich knew each of them had developed a more powerful sense of self as Chanku. They identified totally as shapeshifters and the issues and politics of humans had become less important.

Maybe they had erred in their avoidance of the world of man, especially since it appeared that world was determined to intrude upon theirs. Ulrich hoped not. There was integrity and honor among the Chanku, a need to do good for human and animal alike, unless they were threatened—then all bets were off.

He did not want to lose what they had worked so hard to gain.

Millie raised her head and stared into his eyes. She still looked troubled. He ran his fingers across her brow, trailed along the line of her jaw. She turned her head and kissed his fingertips.

"As we were leaving tonight," she said in a whisper-soft voice, "I kept thinking about the man you killed, thinking he deserved death for what he'd done to Manda. I was sorry he died so quickly, that it had been so neatly and cleanly accomplished." She dipped her chin and rested her forehead against his chest. "I wanted him to suffer. The way he'd made Manda suffer. I wanted him to know who killed him, and why. A wolf wouldn't think that way."

Ulrich chuckled and lifted her face with both palms. "That wasn't the wolf thinking. That was a mother. Human, wolf, wildcat . . . it doesn't matter what species. First and foremost, my love, you are a mother."

Tears filled her eyes. "Not a very good one. Not when it mattered."

"I thought we'd gone through that. Your children don't hold you at fault. They loved you immediately. If anything, they feel only sorrow that you were separated for all those years, but they don't blame you. Never you." He kissed her.

She kissed him back. He felt her surrender in the sudden rush of heat, the pounding of her heart, the strength of her lips against his. Her tongue swirling around his, the soft moan as he rolled her over and broke the kiss to find her breasts with his mouth.

She arched into him as he sucked at first one nipple, and then the other, moving back and forth between the two, drawing them into his mouth, shaping them with the flat of his tongue. His palms supported the silky curve of her breasts and he kneaded them as a kitten would its mother.

Leaving her nipples wet and swollen, he slipped lower, kissing the sensitive skin beside her belly button and running his tongue along the slash of her hip bone. She reached for him and threaded her fingers through his hair when he finally knelt between her legs. Resting her thighs over his forearms and holding her buttocks in both hands he raised her hips off the bed and held her there, a veritable feast for his senses.

He studied her for a long moment while her pulse fluttered in her swollen clit and her thoughts rolled through his mind with all the subtlety of a growing thunderstorm.

She wanted, needed, *demanded* he touch her. Now.

He exhaled. His warm breath swept over her damp nether lips and he saw the flutter of muscles at the mouth of her sex. She was wet and glistening and he couldn't tease her any longer.

Leaning close, he touched the very tip of his tongue to her clit, licking her so softly he knew she would barely feel him. The muscles in her thighs clenched and her heels locked against his back.

He licked her again, sweeping through the dark gash between her labia and plunging as deep as he could. She raised her hips and pressed against his mouth. He thought of shifting, of using his wolven tongue to lap up her flavors, but this was more fun, more frustrating for Millie, more fulfilling for Ulrich.

He sucked first one swollen lip and then the other into his mouth, then circled her clit with the tip of his tongue before finally suckling the entire little organ between his lips.

She screamed and climaxed, but it was much too soon. Her fingers tore at his scalp as he continued sucking and licking through her orgasm. Then he lowered her bottom to the bed, drew himself along her warm body and plunged into her with the full length of his cock.

Her inner muscles were still pulsing and flexing with her climax. They grabbed at the head of his cock and tightened around the shaft, holding him, drawing him deeper. She wrapped her legs around his hips and fucked him hard and fast, forcing her rhythm on him, taking him deep inside with every lift of her hips.

Laughing, Ric rolled to his back. Millie went with him, only now she straddled him with both hands on his chest. As she raised and lowered herself along his full length, Ulrich caught the full force of her thoughts, the power of her love, the eternal, unwavering strength of the alpha bitch.

She had her head thrown back and her hands gripped his sides as she rolled her hips over him. The sensual sway of her pelvis atop his, the swing of her amazing breasts, the look on her face of a woman totally involved in the sensuality of the moment, stirred him as no other sight possibly could.

He could stay with her like this for hours, so caught up in sensation and pure, overwhelming lust. He wrapped his fingers over her hips and closed his eyes, losing himself in sensation right along with Millie.

Which was why he didn't see her hand move behind her and down between his legs to grasp both his testicles in her long fingers. He felt her, though, when she squeezed them in a gentle hold.

Her unexpected touch sent a jolt of pure electric current racing from his nuts to his brain and back to his cock. With a roar, Ulrich bent his knees, planted his feet on the bed and slammed upward. His cock filled her, lifted and held her completely immobile while he filled her with his seed.

By the time his cock finally quit pulsing and his breath returned to normal, Millie was almost asleep. Still planted firmly within her slick passage, he rolled her gently to her side and kissed her forehead. She snuggled against him with her head resting on his arm, her hands clasped between her breasts and her lips against his chest.

Within seconds her breathing had slowed and evened out and he knew she slept. Though his erection had subsided, his penis remained within the embrace of her tight folds. As tired as he was, Ulrich lay there holding her, his body totally relaxed but his mind a flurry of activity.

Goddess, how he loved her! She was everything to him, a wonderful gift he'd never expected so late in life. She was an amazing woman who fulfilled the roles of lover and wife, alpha bitch and mate, even as mother to two grown children she'd not known until recently. Millie West had slipped seamlessly into his life as if she'd been made for him, adjusted to his ways and challenged him to learn hers. She amazed him.

And all of this after so many years alone. How had she managed? His woman was full of fire and light, a sensual creature who never seemed to laugh enough, or to have enough of sex. He wondered how she would be around the other Chanku males. She'd not ever been with the others, and in fact only knew a few of them.

Would she want to make love to the younger men? To the women? Other than her own children, Manda and Adam and obviously, their mates, or Ulrich's daughter and her mate, Luc, Millie could go freely to any of the others. He wondered if she would, if she even realized she could?

He tried to remember, but they'd never really discussed it. Holding her now, soft and warm and totally pliant in his arms, he thought of her with another man. Could he handle it if she went to Anton or Stefan, if she chose Jake or even Tinker?

He'd not been with any of them, either, not the women or the men. Holding on to the role as leader of the San Francisco pack, he'd maintained a certain aloofness as part of his control.

Luc was the leader now, by virtue of the fact he was doing a hell of a good job while Ulrich stayed in Colorado with Millie. Maybe it was time to make the leadership role official. Deed this house over to Luc and Tia, take his things and make the move to Colorado permanent.

Millie snuggled against his chest and the decision was essentially made. She would never leave her beloved wolves. He would never ask her to. Once they settled the current situation, it was time to ask Millie if she truly wanted him as a permanent houseguest, maybe even as her husband.

He lay back against his pillow with a stupid grin on his face. She was his bonded mate. Of course she did.

Chapter 10

Oliver crawled out of bed around ten. Mei, Tala, AJ, and Mik still slept, so he left them in bed, dressed quietly and headed for the main house. Anton was up, sipping coffee and checking the stock market reports on his laptop. The house was still and quiet.

Oliver poured a cup of coffee and sat across the kitchen table from Anton. "Anything new? Did you get the Maine group settled in okay?"

Anton nodded. "They were exhausted. Drove straight through from Maine, trading driving. Jake turned over all the info he had and then they crashed. I don't expect to see them for a couple hours."

Oliver chuckled. "I take it they left the motorcycles at home."

Anton nodded again. "They know how much is riding on this visit. After Manda's attack, there's no way Baylor would ask her to come on the bike." He stared at his clasped hands for a moment, and then raised his head. "You know about the tunnel, don't you? The doorway we've been working on?"

Oliver met Anton's steady gaze. "Yeah. I saw it in Mei's thoughts a while back. I was surprised because you hadn't said anything, but . . ."

"I planned to, and then all this started to happen. I didn't mean to keep it as any deep, dark secret. I found the opening to the tunnel years ago, when you were still living with Stefan. At first it was nothing more than a tiny fissure in the rock wall. I worked off and on at enlarging the opening, but when you, Stefan, and Xandi moved in, things got busy. I'd pretty much forgotten about it. When the attacks started, I got to thinking how great it would be to have a way to escape, should we need to."

"How did you find it?" Oliver wrapped his hands around his coffee cup and stared into the dark surface. He'd never once thought any of them would need to worry about finding an escape from this place. It had always seemed like an impenetrable fortress to him, surrounded, as it was, by forest and private lands.

Anton chuckled. "I went down for a bottle of wine one night and noticed a draft. I could smell sulfur, sort of like the hot springs in Yellowstone. I figured it was either my invitation straight to hell, or possibly something at the back of the wine cellar. When I followed my nose, I found a crack in the wall. I was here all alone and there wasn't anything going on, so I found a pick and started digging."

"And?"

"And I eventually broke through the concrete, but that's as far as I got. There was a solid wall of rock with just a tiny little fissure in it behind the cellar wall. The house is actually built over solid rock beside a natural tunnel, but the wine cellar appears to be the closest connection. There was enough of a draft of air to keep me interested. I put Stefan to work on it a couple days ago and he managed to break through into a tunnel that leads to an amazing limestone cave not far from here."

"How far is it?" Oliver's eyes twinkled. "Does it link to any of the other caves on the property?"

"Possibly. I've only done a cursory exploration, but there's a whole system of narrow tunnels shooting off in all directions. It would be really easy to get lost down there. One tunnel looks like it goes for miles, deep into the mountain. Another leads to a huge cavern with a hot spring. The water has a faint sulfurous odor, but it's palatable. There's also another smaller tunnel that opens into the high meadow near the northern border of the property."

"An escape route?" Oliver grinned. "Sounds like a place where you could hide out for a long time if you had to."

Anton nodded. "Exactly. I've decided it's also the perfect place for all of us to gather where we know we won't be observed, but I'd rather keep the location private, for now." He laughed. "I need to keep a few of my mysteries intact."

"I won't say anything, and you know you can trust Mei."

"I sure hope so. Did she tell you she's been in my head for the past couple weeks? All the time?" Anton raised one dark eyebrow.

Oliver laughed. "Yes, she did. She's been very disturbed about it. Not everyone wants to know every move you make."

"Thank goodness for that."

"Any news from Ulrich?" Oliver sipped his coffee and politely changed the subject. At least Mei thought Anton appeared to be blocking better since she'd talked to him.

Anton nodded. "Yes. He called. He and Millie are getting a few hours' sleep and will head north as soon as they're able."

He stared at his cup for a moment, then raised his head. "They raided the lab where Manda was held for so many years. Collected or destroyed all the records. Dumped one of Luc's targeted Trojan viruses into the computer system. Burned and shredded a lot of incriminating photos. Ulrich killed one scientist. He might be the one directing a lot of the attacks. We'll know more once Luc and Jake go through the files they got out of his computer. A security guard escaped, but all he saw were some really pissed off wolves."

Oliver looked at Anton. "That's good news, right? How come you look so glum?"

Anton shook his head slowly and stared at his coffee. "I had the dream again last night. The one where someone is stealing Keisha and Lily out from under my nose, and I can't do anything about it. I still don't know if it's merely an extraordinarily detailed nightmare or a premonition. It's scaring the crap out of Keisha." He raised his head and stared at Oliver. "It's scaring me just as badly. I tell you, I had no idea how vulnerable loving a woman or having a baby would make me."

Oliver reached across the table and wrapped his fingers around Anton's hand. "Are you saying you would change things? That you wished you didn't have Keisha or Lily?"

Anton rolled his hand beneath Oliver's and squeezed his fingers. "Never. I can't imagine life without them. Without any of this." He locked Oliver's gaze with his. "Did you ever imagine, all those years ago when it was just the two of us, that our lives would ever be this full?"

Oliver shook his head. "Never. Not in my wildest dreams. I was a eunuch, for crying out loud." He grinned. "Do you honestly think I ever dreamed of having my balls restored, of having sex with a beautiful woman, much less a mate who loved me?" He raised his head and looked directly into Anton's eyes.

The eyes of a wolf stared back at him. The eyes of the man he loved above all others. "If I were to lose everything today, have to give up all that I've experienced in the past few weeks, it would be worth it to have known love."

Anton nodded. "I feel the same way, which is why we will do whatever it takes to protect our loved ones."

"So, you don't think Ulrich's raid has taken care of the problem?"

Anton shook his head. "I wish I could say it had, but I'm afraid to relax too much at this point. We don't know how many people knew of Manda, how many are in on whatever scheme was hatched, what the goal was. Even if the one he killed was calling the shots, we can't relax. Not yet."

Stefan wandered into the kitchen dressed in nothing but worn black sweatpants. He scratched his chest and yawned. "Relax? Obviously you don't have a two-and-a-half-month-old. I forget what relax means."

Oliver stood up and gave his seat to Stefan. "Let me get you some coffee, old man. Before you fall over."

Stefan sent him a dirty look and took the seat. Oliver handed him a steaming cup of coffee and then opened the refrigerator door. There would be a very hungry crowd looking for food before too long. The least he could do was start cooking.

The phone rang. Anton picked it up, spoke for a moment and then set it carefully back in the cradle. "That was Ulrich. He and Millie have decided to fly. He's got a buddy who can bring them straight through to Kalispell, but it will be around four this afternoon before they can get in. Anyone want to . . . ?"

"I'll pick them up." Oliver went back to the refrigerator. He liked Ulrich. The man had always treated him with respect, even when Oliver had little self-respect of his own and had been nothing more, by choice, than Anton's personal assistant. That position had broadened considerably, yet Ulrich had never once questioned Oliver's role in the pack hierarchy.

By the time the rest of the visitors from the various packs wandered into the dining room, Oliver had warming trays filled with fried potatoes and sausage on the sideboard, along with toast, bacon, biscuits and gravy, and scrambled eggs enough to feed an army.

Or a houseful of hungry wolves.

Luc, Tia, Tinker, and Lisa were the first to arrive. A few minutes later, Adam and Eve showed up. Jake, Shannon, Baylor, and Manda finally made an appearance. They all still looked half-asleep, but then they'd gotten in late last night, shortly after Igmutaka's dramatic exit. Now everyone except Keisha and Xandi and Oliver's housemates sat at the breakfast table with filled plates and way too many ideas on how to deal with the attempted kidnappings.

Finally, Anton raised his hand and the babble immediately came to a halt. "This conversation may all be a moot point. Ulrich and Millie had a very successful raid on the Silicon Valley lab last night. They've confiscated files, destroyed photos taken of Manda and managed it all with very little collateral damage. Ulrich said he was forced to kill one scientist who may have been behind the current attacks on us. We know he was heavily involved in the experimentation carried out on our packmate."

"Oh!" Manda's sharp exclamation caught everyone's attention.

Frowning, Anton turned to Manda, who looked shell-shocked by what he'd said. "I'm sorry. I didn't mean to be so unfeeling. I didn't think. I had hoped you would be pleased with the news."

"I am. It's just . . ." She turned to Baylor and touched his arm, as if anchoring herself. "It was a horrible time in my life, but it was the only life I knew. Many of the scientists, while they treated me as nothing more than a lab experiment, were still the only friends I had. Not all of them were mean to me. Most of them were just doing their jobs, and some were actually very kind. Do you have any idea who died last night?"

Anton shook his head. "No. But Ulrich and your mother are flying in this afternoon. We'll get details once they arrive."

Manda nodded, but Oliver noticed she sat closer to Bay and clung to his arm.

Keisha wandered in with Lily in her arms. She greeted everyone, kissed Anton's cheek and put Lily in the small portable crib Anton had placed near the table. Then she found a seat beside Anton. He got up and began filling a plate for her at the buffet. Stefan joined him.

"Xandi will be out in a minute." He glanced at Oliver. "Where's everyone from your cottage?" Then he laughed. "Are they still sleeping off all the excitement from last night?"

Just then, Mei wandered into the dining room with Mik, Tala, and AJ trailing behind her. "What excitement? You mean Igmutaka taking corporeal form and becoming a cougar? You think that was exciting? Or are you talking about our buddies from the East Coast flying down the drive and scaring the crap out of all of us? Now that was exciting." She laughed and reached for a plate as the questions started flying.

And they weren't about the pack from Maine.

Once the flurry of questions and explanations about Igmutaka's escape from Mei and Oliver slowed down, Manda rested her chin on her palms and asked, "So, where is he now?"

Mei flipped one hand in the air as she chewed and swallowed. "Out there somewhere. Last any of us saw him, he was trotting down the hall to our front door like he owned the place."

Tala grabbed another piece of bacon. "He did offer his protection. I wouldn't take that lightly. I imagine it means he'll stay in the area, don't you think?"

"I hope so." Mei looked sort of wistful, as if she actually missed the spirit guide who had shared her body for just a few short weeks.

Oliver touched her hand and she wrapped her fingers around his. "Me, too," he said, only half-teasing. "I was just getting used to the guy."

Mei laughed and pulled her fingers free. "So was I. He

made leopard sex a lot more tolerable. Now I've got to deal with that barbed cock of yours all on my own!"

"Tolerable? You're saying I'm merely tolerable?" Oliver leaned over and smacked Mei's butt as she walked back to the buffet for seconds.

He wondered if he was the only one to notice when Manda quietly left the room.

Manda found a spot on the front deck where the sounds of laughter coming from the dining room were muted, and birdsong filled the air.

She heard a loud honking and looked up in time to see a flock of geese flying overhead. They were going south, moving ahead of the coming cold weather. There'd already been ice on the ground when they left their home in Maine.

She wished she were back there, now.

She wished she felt safe.

Of course, it had been great to see Adam again, and her mother would be arriving this afternoon, but there'd been so much death lately. So much to fear.

She wondered who had died last night in that laboratory. She hoped it wasn't someone who had been kind to her, but even if it had been one of the others, his death was still on her head. All of them were. Every person who had died over the past few days had died because of her. She was the link that held them all together, the one common denominator, the freak who had given away the Chanku secret.

How many more would die? How many Chanku? So far they'd been lucky, but one of these days, their luck was bound to run out.

If anything happened to Shannon, or Jake, or Bay . . . or the babies. She'd held Keisha's little girl this morning and suddenly the attacks had seemed even more frightening than they already were.

And there was nothing she could do.

"You okay, sweetie?" Shannon plopped down next to her on the steps and wrapped an arm around Manda's shoulders. "You look like you're carrying the weight of the world on your shoulders."

Manda brushed her long hair out of her eyes and tried to smile, but it was a halfhearted effort, to say the least. "Actually, not the whole world," she said, struggling to keep it light. "Maybe the polar ice cap and a continent or two."

Shannon chuckled. "Want to go for a run? Sometimes that helps to clear your thoughts. The guys are doing dishes. I'll go and tell Bay and Jake we might take off for a while. Bay's worried about you."

"He shouldn't be. I'll be fine. But yeah, a run sounds good."

Shannon leaned over and kissed her cheek, then got up and went back into the house. Manda stood and stretched. Brush crackled nearby. She turned her head toward the noise just in time to see a flash of metal against the dark trees of the nearby forest, followed by a muffled *pop*.

She felt the dart pierce her skin and reached to pull it from her shoulder. Her fingers slipped on the cylinder. They were numb and she couldn't hold on. The dart fell free and she watched it fall, spinning slowly on its long way to the ground.

She swayed, standing there on the top step, trying to make sense of the fuzzy world around her, the strange man racing across the driveway.

Help me, Bay! I've been shot. Help me! Manda's world turned fuzzy and dark and the ground spun up to meet her.

Bay!

Manda! Baylor threw the dish towel on the floor and raced through the house to the front door. He met Shannon halfway, but he didn't slow down. "They've got Manda!"

"What? I just left her!" Shannon turned and raced after Baylor. The others followed in quick pursuit.

Bay stood on the front deck, disbelieving. She was gone. He called out, mentally trying to reach her. Nothing.

Anton grabbed his arm. "What happened?"

Numb, Bay shook his head. "I don't know. I heard Manda's voice. Said she'd been shot. Then nothing."

Shannon raced down the steps. She leaned over and picked something up out of the grass. "They darted her. Look." She held up a feathered syringe.

Anton grabbed Tinker McClintock's arm. "You and Lisa check around back. Mik, AJ, and Tala—can you guys watch the house? Make sure the babies are safe?"

"I need to go look for her." Bay ripped at his shirt, but Anton stopped him. "Shift out of sight. They could be watching. All of you," he raised his voice, then switched to mindtalking. *Inside to shift. We don't want anything on camera in case they're watching.*

Bay started undressing the minute he hit the front door and was a wolf by the time he reached the back deck. Keisha held the door open for him and he ran through without breaking stride. Leaping over the railing, he raced around to the front where Manda had fallen.

Frantic and furious, he sniffed the damp grass. The scent of a strange male filled his nostrils. Baylor growled. Four large wolves joined him as he took off on the trail, nose to the ground, following the scent into the forest. Jake and Shannon, Mei and Oliver raced directly off his flank, following Baylor's lead.

They didn't have to go far. The man holding Manda had her over his shoulder and his back to the door of an older model pickup truck sitting way off the ground on over-sized tires.

In front of him, snarling and pacing, stood a huge panther.

Igmutaka? Bay stayed back while Mei sniffed noses with the big cat. The animal's ears flattened to its skull, but as soon as it got a sniff of Mei, even though she was in her wolf form, it stopped snarling and slipped away into the bushes. The guy holding Manda watched the panther until it was out of sight.

"No one is going to believe this," he muttered. He reached for the handle on the passenger side of the truck. Bay snarled and moved closer.

The man dropped his hand, but continued holding on to Manda. It almost looked as if he were protecting her from the five wolves that now circled him.

Suddenly Anton strode into the ring of wolves. Wearing his usual attire of dark slacks and white shirt and looking every bit the wealthy landowner he was, he stopped beside the pack of restless, growling wolves.

"Give her to me. Now."

"Now, mister, I just . . ."

"Now. Or I turn my wolves loose on you before I call the sheriff."

Bay and Oliver growled louder. Mei took a step toward the man. Shannon and Jake looked ready to go for the guy's throat. He quickly stepped forward and handed Manda over to Anton, who carefully took Bay's woman in his arms and held her against his chest. He leaned close to listen for her heartbeat. A moment later, he raised his head.

"You're damned lucky she's still alive. If you want to remain breathing, you'll tell me why you're here and why you have tried to kidnap this woman."

Baylor snarled, baring his teeth and moving closer. The other wolves stayed perfectly still. There was a tangible sense of menace in the air. The panther screamed. It sounded close, as if it had merely faded into the forest, but stayed nearby in case it was needed.

The guy had twice Anton's bulk and was easily as tall, but he looked like he was ready to wet himself. He opened his mouth a couple of times before any sound emerged, and then it was spit out in a single breath.

"It was a wanted poster. I saw it on the Internet. Said this was a hangout for terrorists with some really strange powers. There's a five hundred thousand dollar reward for bringing in a man, but for some reason, it's double that for a woman." He looked at Manda as if he was trying to figure out how to get her back and get out alive. Then he sighed. "They gotta be alive for questioning. She's not hurt. That drug just knocks you out."

"How do I find this ad?" Anton looked as if he could tear the bastard apart with his bare hands. "I want to know who is offering the reward, where you are supposed to take the person you kidnap. Do you have any idea what you people are doing to my family? To my friends? We are not terrorists, damn it, and we have no special powers. But you . . . you are most decidedly an idiot."

The man swallowed and his eyes flipped from one wolf to the other and on around the half circle guarding him until he landed back on Anton. "I've got a copy in my pocket. If you'll just let me . . ."

"Try anything and you're a dead man. Do you understand?"

The guy swallowed again. The sound was audible in the deathly, unnatural quiet of the forest. He reached into his pocket, pulled out a crumpled piece of paper and handed it to Anton. Anton looked at it a moment, then held the paper out to Mei. *Take this to Luc. Have him check the address, see what the hell this is all about.* "You . . ." he pointed at the man, "Don't move."

Mei caught the edge of folded paper between her front teeth and raced back toward the house. Manda began to stir. Anton whispered something in her ear. Her eyes opened and she struggled for a moment. He loosed her legs so she could stand, but held his left arm around her waist for support.

Bay fought the need to shift, to go to her, to hold her. *Don't shift*, he said, staring at her. *Are you okay?*

Manda nodded. Then she pulled out of Anton's embrace but her legs still looked pretty shaky and she sat on the ground, next to Bay. He pressed his nose against her cheek and whined. She threw her arms around his neck, buried her face in his thick fur and hung on tight.

He whined again. The sad sound caught the attention of the man who'd tried to kidnap her. He straightened up a little and looked at the remaining wolves. "Okay, if you're not terrorists, what the hell are you?"

"I am a rather well-known magician. My name is Anton Cheval. I'm retired, now, but these animals were part of my act. The young lady is a guest. And you"—he took a deep breath—"you have no right to come on to my property, much less to harm anyone."

"The Web site says . . ."

"I don't give a fuck what the Web site says. You're lucky I didn't turn them loose on you." Anton didn't have to raise his voice to get anyone's attention, especially with wolves as backup.

Stefan walked into the clearing. "Luc found the Web site. He's tracing it now. What are we going to do with our visitor? Should I call the sheriff's department?"

"There are better ways to make him disappear." Anton seemed to be talking to himself. The huge man's face went deathly pale. He looked from Stefan to Anton and back to Stefan, as if weighing which man might help him.

Bay tensed his muscles. All he wanted was for Anton to say the word. One word and this guy was toast.

Say it, Anton. Say it—let me have him. I'll make sure he never hurts Manda or anyone else again.

Anton turned and looked down at Bay. "Bay, take Manda back to the house."

Bay jerked his head in Anton's direction and growled. Anton dismissed the sound as if Bay were nothing more than a well-trained pet. Bay growled once more, but Anton ignored him, which was probably a good thing.

Bay got himself under control when Manda stood up and tugged at the thick fur on his neck. He turned away, leaving Oliver, Jake, and Shannon on guard. He walked slowly back to the house with Manda's fingers still tangled in his fur. She moved carefully beside him on shaking legs. It took every bit of training Bay had not to turn around and rip the bastard's throat out.

He decided it was a good thing Anton had sent him away. A very good thing.

Anton breathed a silent sigh of relief as Bay slowly, reluctantly, escorted Manda back to the house. He'd wondered if the alpha wolf would obey his command—Bay was, of course, not a member of his pack and not really required to pay any attention at all to anyone from the Montana pack, up to and including the pack leader.

Times like this Anton decided he truly appreciated his position, true or imagined, as *uber alpha* to all the Chanku. He took a long, shuddering breath, eminently relieved the moment Bay and Manda were out of sight.

The last thing they needed was another body to deal with. There was no doubt in Anton's mind that Manda's mate was primed to kill.

Anton focused his attention and stared into the eyes of the kidnapper. Deeper, holding the man immobile with nothing more than the power of his mind, searching the interloper's thoughts and memories, looking for information. Anything to help them find out who else was behind the attacks. Anything to explain the Web site offering a million dollar reward for the capture of "the terrorists in Montana, California, and Maine."

A Web site that gave Anton Cheval's address. Lucien Stone's address. Jacob Trent's address.

Someone with a more powerful mind might easily have broken free of Anton's blatantly intrusive mental search. A stronger man might have subconsciously managed to hide his private thoughts, but this poor loser was nothing but a forty-three-year-old unemployed carpenter, trying to feed his family.

He was no match for Anton Cheval. Desperate, Freddy Martin had stumbled across the Web site and thrown caution and good sense to the wind. His wife and children waited for him at home. They thought he was out job hunting right now, not attempting to commit a felony.

At least he would not die today. Anton retreated from the man's mind and released him. Freddie stumbled backward, caught his balance and swayed in place for a moment. He blinked and stared wide-eyed at Anton. Before he could ask the questions that obviously hovered close to the surface, Anton silenced him with a raised hand.

"You will leave, Freddy. Go home to your wife. Take care of your kids. Don't ever bother me or my family again."

Freddy blinked again and shook his head. "How'd you know my name?"

"I'm a magician, Freddy. A very good magician. I know everything about you. I also know that if you don't leave now, my wolves will make sure you never leave. Ever. Go, while you can, and don't come back."

Anton whistled and turned away, following the narrow trail back to the house with Stefan walking silently behind him. He didn't wait to see if Freddy Martin would leave.

He didn't have to. He could practically taste the man's terror. Anton heard the engine start, the sound of gears grinding, brakes squealing and tires searching for purchase in the wet grass. The wolves slipped out of the brush and walked ahead of him; the panther had disappeared into the forest.

Within seconds, the truck was out of sight, following the fire road it had come in on. Anton paused at the edge of the forest and wrapped his hands around his waist in a vain effort to stop shaking.

Freddy Martin might have been a loser, but he'd come

very close to capturing Manda today. Too damned close to harming one of those Anton had vowed to protect.

Stefan put his hand on Anton's shoulder, offering support.

"We were lucky," Anton whispered, looking into his friend's amber eyes. "This time."

He knew, now, why they were being stalked. Why the threats had suddenly come from all directions. It was so simple. There was a million dollar bounty on their heads. Posted now, on the Internet for all the world to see. How the hell was he going to fight this battle? How would they ever protect their families?

Like a ghost in the night, his recurring nightmare flitted through his mind. He thought immediately of Lily and his heart nearly froze in his chest.

Stefan drew him close and cupped Anton's shoulders in his warm palms. Even with his dear friend's healing touch, Anton felt empty, powerless. Emasculated.

Oliver, Jake, and Shannon sat at his feet, their wolven eyes bright with human intelligence. He couldn't meet their steady gaze, couldn't acknowledge his failure or his abject fear and heartrending frustration

Stefan pressed his forehead against Anton's. He easily dismissed the blocks and barriers Anton had set to guard his distress and spoke directly to him, mindtalking in a silent voice filled with passion and strength.

Don't forget what you have told me in the past, dear Anton, that when we stand together, no one can hurt us. Nothing can touch us. Together, we are stronger, smarter, more powerful than any enemy. Remember that, my friend. Remember all of us. We stand behind you, beside you, wherever you need us.

Anton nodded. He raised his head, held Stefan's face in both his hands and kissed him. "Thank you. It's easy to forget when we're so intimately threatened, when one of us is actually harmed, but you're right. No man has truer friends than I. No man has a better army at his command."

He stepped back and took a deep breath, drawing the fresh forest air into his lungs, clearing his thoughts and taking strength from his friends. "Ulrich and Millie will be here soon," he said. "This is the first time so many of us will gather in one place. The first time we will truly experience the combined power of so many Chanku."

He let the sentence stand alone as the others watched him. Then Anton swept his gaze over the three wolves waiting patiently at his feet and realized he felt their strength even now. Felt their resolve. Even more, he felt their love.

Like an idiot, even as his eyes burned and his throat choked with tears, Anton stood there and grinned. With Stefan's heartfelt words, he felt as if a huge weight had been lifted from his shoulders.

Chapter 11

Anton called them all together shortly after Oliver picked up Millie and Ulrich at the Kalispell airport and delivered them safely to his home. They'd grabbed a quick meal, gotten hugs from Tia and Luc and a very subdued Manda and Bay. Now the kitchen was filled to capacity with twenty-one adult Chanku and two babies. Both babies slept soundly in their mothers' arms, but the noise level from the grown-ups had continued to build from the time they'd started filtering into the room.

Anton raised his hand for quiet. He felt the power in the room even as the numerous conversations immediately ceased. "As you know," he said, "we have an alarm system we rarely use because it makes it inconvenient to come and go as we please. For the sake of this evening's meeting, however, I've armed both the outside and indoor sensors so we can concentrate without worrying about intruders."

"I think that means he's holding all of us prisoner until we agree to do whatever he wants." Stefan's dry comment broke some of the gathering tension.

Anton flashed him a quasi-dirty look just as Mik raised his long arm for attention. As big as he was, he flattened his palm on the ceiling. "Anton, don't you think it's a little tight in here for a group this size to hold a meeting?"

AJ jabbed him in the side with his elbow. "It's the perfect size for an orgy."

"Watch it, boys. There are women and children present." Tala's voice seemed to come out of nowhere. As small as she was, Anton couldn't even see her behind her guys.

"That's why we're not meeting here." Anton laughed and shook his head. "Although women were never a reason not to have an orgy, were they?"

Keisha glared at him, then broke into giggles.

"Okay, for the sake of the babies . . ." He took a deep breath. It was time to get serious. Anton grabbed the handle of the door leading into the wine cellar and pulled it open. A cool blast of damp, musty air filled the kitchen.

"I want to ask you not to discuss where we are, or where we're going. I'll explain later. For now, please follow me." He turned and stepped through the door, vaguely aware of the curious whisperings from the group.

As they followed him down the narrow stairs and across the dimly lit cellar, Anton thought of all that had happened since he first suspected the existence of a natural tunnel running parallel to, and below the foundation of the house.

He'd been Stefan's mentor then, steadily growing jealous of the young magician's skill. Then Stefan had tried to shift without realizing what he was capable of. He'd ended up trapped in a body that was half man, half wolf. Blaming Anton, he'd gone away, frightened and angry. For five long years, with Oliver watching over him, Stefan had stayed in self-imposed exile.

All that time, Anton had chipped away at the wall.

It had become a penance of sorts. A place to work off his frustration, his anger, and the self-recriminations that appeared to be a huge part of his basic personality.

He'd chipped a sizable doorway through the concrete wall that ended in almost solid rock. Solid, except for the tiny fissure that had led him to search in the first place. It had taken much longer to cut through solid stone, and he'd worked at it, off and on for a couple of years, without breaking through.

Once Stefan, Xandi, and Oliver moved in, life immediately became more interesting and his digging had been set aside. Anton had almost forgotten the mysterious tunnel he'd discovered.

Until the dreams began. Until the attacks.

He'd put Stefan to work enlarging the opening. Over the past week, Stefan had finally broken through and explored the amazing world behind the wine cellar wall.

The actual tunnel paralleled his house, ran the length of the foundation, and well beyond. It far exceeded Anton's hope for an escape route from the house, should they need it.

He hadn't expected the magnitude of the cavern they'd found. Just a few hundred yards down a narrow tunnel was a huge limestone cave, heated by a broad pool of water that was probably warmed by some of the same molten rock that flowed beneath Yellowstone. The main cavern was the size of a small auditorium. The floor was smooth and flat, the walls wide and high.

Another cleft in the rock at the far end of the cavern was hidden behind a small waterfall that led to a series of long tunnels, twisting and turning through the mountain. One led to a narrow fissure in the rock, just wide enough for a grown man to slip through. Totally hidden in brush and twisted roots, it opened out on a hillside overlooking a quiet meadow on Anton's property, over a mile from the main residence.

Originally he'd hoped for an escape route, in case of wildfire. Now he saw it as an escape from something even worse than fire, but also as something more. He'd never dreamed of the huge cavern they'd find, never thought of using it for anything such as this.

A meeting of minds, literally. A gathering of powerful

shapeshifters, each with his or her own special talent. Down here in the bowels of the earth, completely hidden, safe from their enemies so far underground.

He felt the power of the men and women following him. Felt their sense of unity, their purpose. No matter what happened, he would have the knowledge they worked together by choice—because they loved. Because they shared the common bond of Chanku.

He looked over the gathering crowd as the last of them reached the wine cellar, and caught Keisha's steady gaze from across the cellar. She smiled at him and the light in her amber eyes reminded him why it was so important they not fail. He nodded, acknowledging more than words could ever express.

Without breaking eye contact, she slowly walked through the small crowd to stand beside her mate.

Adam Wolf kept a tight grip on Eve's elbow as they climbed down the narrow stairway into the wine cellar. He'd been down here a couple times to grab bottles for dinner and loved the still darkness of the room, the pungent scent of old wine and the sense of age. The cellar had been dug out deep under the house and the temperature remained naturally constant around fifty-five degrees.

Now that he thought of it, the cellar should be much cooler than it was. Didn't a cave maintain the mean temperature of the area around it? This part of Montana got damned cold in the winter, which should make the cellar stable at about forty degrees or so.

He also couldn't figure out why Anton would be leading all of them down here. The wine cellar was large, by cellar standards, but filled with racks of aging wines. There was very little empty space.

They'd be more cramped down here than in the large kitchen above. Stefan was the last person to come through the kitchen door. Anton glanced in his direction. "Stefan, would you please close the door and bar it for me?"

Stefan saluted and did as he was asked. He waited on the stairs because there really didn't appear to be any place for him to stand in the actual cellar.

Growing more curious by the moment, Adam watched as Anton walked across the concrete floor to a large cabinet against the back wall. He pushed it, and the massive piece of furniture rolled easily out of the way on hidden wheels.

There was a quiet gasp as each of them stared into the darkness beyond.

"You need to grab a flashlight." Anton pointed to a table near the wall, covered with a vast array of flashlights of all shapes and sizes. It was obvious he'd dug up every one he could find around the house.

Eve turned and stared at Adam, but she didn't say a word. Instead, she reached for one of the flashlights and handed it to him. Then she grabbed one for herself. Each person took one off the table, and they all followed Anton through the rough-hewn door, into the darkness beyond.

"I had no idea this was down here." Even though he spoke quietly, Adam heard the echo of his whispered words.

"It's absolutely amazing." Eve held tightly to his hand as they followed Anton.

The soft shuffle of many feet echoed against the stone walls and strange shadows ebbed and flowed across the ceiling. Voices remained muted. It was obvious everyone was awestruck by the unique beauty of the narrow passage they followed into the mountain.

"I sure hope no one's claustrophobic." Mik laughed when he said it, but the big man had to walk bent over along the narrow passageway. With his eyes glinting from the reflected flashlight beams and his long hair loose and flowing over his shoulders, he reminded Adam of an ancient shaman.

Adam tried to keep track of their direction, but after a short hike he didn't have a clue which way they headed. The path seemed to be leading them slightly downhill, but he wasn't even positive of that. His senses were confused by the whispered exclamations and shuffling feet, the eerie beams of so many flashlights and the uneven surface of the tunnel walls. It felt as if they'd entered an alien universe.

Anton paused and gathered them all together. "I don't mean to make this all so mysterious, but I couldn't explain myself up there without mindtalking, and it's hard to speak to such a large group that way. I'm convinced the house is somehow bugged with microphones. How else would anyone know when we were running as wolves or going into town? Down here, I think we can talk freely."

He sighed as if he carried the weight of the world on his shoulders. "Follow me," he said. Then he turned away, slipped through a narrow passage and disappeared.

Adam glanced at Oliver. "Follow me, he says. Well, okay, mighty leader." Taking a tight hold of Eve's hand, Adam stepped through the narrow fissure, rounded a tight bend and gasped.

Anton was lighting lanterns placed around the perimeter of a huge cavern. Light flickered against glistening walls and illuminated strange shapes and waxy-looking formations. Stalactites hung from the ceiling and curiously shaped stalagmites grew from the floor along the edges of the cavern.

A small stream of water cascaded from an upper level into a glistening pool. The air was much warmer here than in the wine cellar, heavy with the humidity from the waterfall and pool. Adam walked over to the pool, knelt down and touched the water. It was warm and so clear he could see the colored minerals at the bottom, glowing in the beam of his flashlight like multistriped taffy.

He stood up and looked back toward the doorway. He

wasn't the only one struck dumb by the impossible cavern Anton had led them into.

"I didn't think any of you would believe this place without seeing it." Anton leaned against one wall with his hands shoved in his pockets. He looked uncharacteristically humble. "It's private, big enough for all of us to fit comfortably, and the acoustics are great." He chuckled and pushed himself away from the wall. "We needed a place where we can put together everything we know and hopefully find a way to end the attacks. This seemed to fit the bill."

"That's an understatement." Ulrich Mason reached out and shook Anton's hand. "This is amazing. Have you always known it was here?"

"No." Anton shook his head and gazed upward toward the ceiling where tiny crystals sparkled in reflected light. "Years ago I suspected something was down here when I noticed a different air current flowing into the wine cellar. I dug at it off and on for ages, but we didn't actually break through until last week. You have Stefan to thank for doing the dirty work."

He turned and stared at Keisha with a bleak expression. "It was the dreams. I've been having vivid nightmares where I'm caught in darkness. Where someone is trying to steal Keisha and Lily away from me. The dreams made me think of a cave, and that reminded me of the one I suspected ran parallel to the house. I'll admit I never expected anything as grand as this."

Stefan laughed, breaking the tension. "He was hoping for an escape route. We got that and more. This place is amazing, and we haven't explored all of the connected tunnels and rooms yet. As extensive as it is, I doubt we ever will."

Mik Fuentes walked around the far side of the pool, using his flashlight to illuminate what appeared to be scratches in the walls. "Looks like cave art. Hey, guys, you should . . ."

"Please." Anton held up his hand. "Another time. You're free to come down here at any time you wish to explore, but right now we need to put our heads together and figure out what the hell is going on."

Mik shot him a bright grin. "Okay. For now, boss."

Anton found a high spot and sat next to Keisha. He stared at his daughter a moment with such powerful love etched on his stark features that Adam felt the ache in his own chest. Lily had awakened during the walk from the cellar to the cave, but now she once again slept soundly in her mother's arms.

After a moment, Anton blinked as if remembering where he was. He focused on Luc instead of his daughter. "Luc, I know you've checked some Web sites. What have you got?"

Lucien Stone, the acting head of Pack Dynamics, and Tia Mason's husband, walked to the front of the group. Even with his dark hair worn long and the faded blue jeans and comfortable flannel shirt, his military carriage was obvious enough to paint him as the ex-Marine he was.

"Every one of the men we've disposed of was associated with the same lab in Silicon Valley that Ulrich and Millie visited a couple nights ago, so we have to assume that at least some, if not all, of the attacks were directed by people from that facility. Whether or not that's the only one we need to be concerned with, we don't know for sure. Manda has said she was held in more than one laboratory, though I think this is the one where she stayed the longest. I haven't had time to go through all the records Ulrich and Millie retrieved."

"What about the guy who tried to snatch Manda?" Baylor had an arm wrapped tightly around his mate.

Luc shook his head. "He's an idiot and he's out of the picture. I'm certain Anton scared him off permanently. I found the so-called wanted poster that brought him here, on a couple of popular survivalist Web sites. The sites have been removed and the Bureau is checking to see who's behind them, but at this point, everything is leading back to that same lab and the scientist who ran it . . . who, by the way, is the one Ulrich removed from the picture."

He glanced at Millie and Ulrich. "As I told you earlier, it's being blamed on gang activity and pit bulls. The authorities are totally discounting the janitor's description of two large, vicious wolves."

AJ leapt to his feet. "You brought the FBI in on this? Is that safe?"

Baylor Quinn answered. "I sent Luc to some people I used to work with. They know nothing about us, but they remember me from my government work. I told them I had no idea what the posters were about, just that I and my friends were being targeted by someone I must have dealt with in the past. These guys are good people."

AJ sat back down on the cavern floor. Mik put a steadying hand on his shoulder.

Xandi shifted her baby to her shoulder and patted his back. "Anton, you said you think the house is bugged. What are we going to do about that? We can't live in a cave."

Laughing, Anton shook his head. "I think that's where Adam comes in."

Adam blinked when everyone turned to look at him. "Me?"

"I hope so. It actually came to me when we were walking down here, or I would have warned you." His eyes narrowed. "You fix things that are broken, right? Machinery and people. What about houses? If you know the privacy, the sanctity of our home has been broken, don't you think you should be able to fix it? As in, find out how these guys are tracking us?"

"Hell, I don't know." Adam stood up. "How do you think I should approach it?"

"How did you fix Tinker's gunshot wound?" Anton smiled, encouraging him.

Adam shrugged. "I pictured it healed."

"You're shittin' me. That's all?" Tinker laughed and rubbed the totally healed spot on his shoulder where the bullet had grazed him. "Wish I'd known how to do that a time or two."

When the laughter died down, Adam realized everyone in the room watched him. Eve reached up and squeezed his fingers. He felt her love flowing into him. Her confidence gave him strength. He closed his eyes and thought about the beautiful house nestled in the deep forest, thought of the love and laughter that was so much a part of the structure.

About the goodness, the purity of the wood and stone and the metals, all of them woven into a perfect blend for strength and warmth and beauty.

And he felt a sense of wrongness, of evil at this corner and that, at a point under the eaves and near the base of the porch swing. He let his body flow upward, out of the damp cavern until it became part of the house, until his cells blended into the walls and entered the wiring, the lamps and light fixtures, the stones of the hearth and the fabrics covering the floors.

Then he returned to the humid silence in the cave, to the sound of his packmates' breathing, the trickle of water falling into the pool. Blinking himself back to the here and now, he asked, "Does anyone have a pencil and some paper?"

Oliver handed him a notepad. Adam sat back down on the sandy ground and quickly sketched a rough design of the house. He marked the points where he'd sensed something not right, and handed the pad back to Oliver.

Without a word, Oliver reached for Mei's hand and together they left the cavern, climbing back toward the surface.

"I take it you were successful?" Anton rested his chin on his steepled fingers. There was a very slight smile on his face.

"I hope so. That was weird. It's hard to tell, this far underground, but I sensed places that were wrong. They just felt . . . wrong." He shrugged, suddenly embarrassed when he realized everyone was still looking at him. He turned and glanced over his shoulder and caught Millie's eye. She smiled at him with such unabashed pride it made him blush. His mother. She'd never really seen what he could do, but now she practically wept with pride.

Adam sat a little straighter. He felt a hand on his shoulder. Manda leaned close to him and kissed his cheek. Then, without a word, she sat back and leaned against Bay.

His sister seemed just as proud as their mother. Two women he'd only known for a few weeks, yet who meant the world to him. Eve squeezed his hand again and he felt his heart stutter in his chest. Such powerful emotion took a lot of adjustment for a man who'd spent so much of his life alone.

"There's one more thing I want to try, but this will take everyone's cooperation." As soon as Anton spoke, Stefan stood up and began handing out computer-generated maps. "The map shows the boundaries of this property," Anton said. "You'll notice there's very little that actually meets up with privately owned land. We're almost completely surrounded by federal wilderness that extends over the mountains, and that limits the number of people who might stumble onto this property. I want to see if we can generate some sort of energy that will tell us when the perimeter has been breached. If we can figure out how to do it here, you should be able to create your own boundaries at your own homes."

"Sort of an electric fence to zap intruders?" Jake held Shannon close with one powerful arm. "If we could harness the power in those vibrators of yours, sweetie, then . . . oof!"

Shannon folded her arms demurely across her chest after jabbing Jake in the ribs. "As you were saying, Anton?"

Laughing, Anton shook his head. "I'm thinking more along the lines of a force field, but you're not that far off with the vibrators. What's the most powerful energy we generate?" When everyone laughed, Anton answered his own question. "You're right. Sex. As Chanku, we produce an amazing amount of energy during sex."

"Shit, Anton." Mik raised his hand. "You're not going to make us stay celibate for a week, are you?"

"No! Not this time." He held up his hands in mock surrender. "I merely want you to get some rest and then run as usual tonight. Report back here just before dawn. We'll use the natural arousal you feel after shifting and see what happens."

Jake Trent laughed. "There's nothin' natural about it, Anton. It's way too good for natural." He glanced at Shannon, who actually blushed. She, in turn, shot a quick look at Manda, who got the giggles. Adam realized he was grinning, wondering what the four of them had been up to.

Obviously something to take Manda's mind off the kidnap attempts. Just as obviously, it must have worked.

There was a scrape of rock and the sound of breathing. Adam started to rise when Oliver and Mei popped out through the narrow fissure in the cliff wall. Oliver carried a plastic bag filled with small dime-sized disks. "We found one of these at every point you mentioned, Adam. Thing is, we can't figure out how they could have been planted. There's someone at the house almost all the time."

Keisha bowed her head. "I've been wondering the same thing, Oliver. I think it's my fault." She looked ready to cry. "The carpet cleaners I hired, Anton. Remember? They did a lousy job and I told you I found them in places around the house where they didn't need to be. I never once thought of them being anything other than what they were. I never dreamed they'd be planting bugs . . . never."

Anton nodded and held out his hand to his mate. She grasped his fingers and pulled him close enough that he could wrap his arms around both her and Lily. "I'd forgotten all about them," he said. "I never thought to scan their minds or suspect anything, but after the work they did, they would know where the bedrooms are, where the babies slept. Do you still have the name of the company? I'll have Luc check on them."

Keisha nodded, but it was obvious she was terribly upset. Anton pulled her closer and rubbed his hand up and down her back. "This is a reminder, people. We can't trust anyone we don't know. Check the minds of everyone on the outside who you interact with. Until this threat is ended, we all have to remain alert."

Anton leaned down and pulled Stefan to his feet and he in turn grabbed Xandi. The four adults stood together, a united front filled with confidence and strengthened by love. The babies were both awake now, eyes wide open and alert. Though they were perfectly formed human children, and in fact would never become Chanku without the proper nutrients in their diets, Adam realized he thought of the two of them as pups.

He wondered what the future held for Anton and Stefan's children. For any children he and Eve might have. He felt a shiver run along his spine and glanced in Eve's direction. She smiled at him. The love in that simple glance calmed his suddenly racing heart.

The rest of them stood and quietly headed back toward the passage to the wine cellar. Eve stood beside Adam. They waited until only Anton and Stefan and their mates remained.

"I never thought of doing anything like that," Adam said. "Searching for something wrong in an inanimate structure.

It was an amazing experience. Thank you for suggesting it." He held out his hand.

Anton took it in a firm grasp. "I have a feeling you are capable of much more we've not even dreamed of. Thanks for being so willing to try my crazy suggestions."

Adam took Eve's hand and turned to leave when it hit him. He spun around and faced Anton. "Maybe that's it. Maybe you only have to suggest something for me to do it. Who's to say what I, or any Chanku, can or cannot do? Could it merely be the fact we believe ourselves capable that gives us the ability?"

Anton blinked. His amber eyes appeared almost black in the dim light remaining in the cavern.

Stefan and the women, including Eve, quietly turned off most of the lanterns and slipped out through the tunnel. Only one lamp now remained. Its feeble glow barely lit the way to the opening in the wall that led back to the house.

Adam and Anton stood facing one another in the still quiet of the cavern. Only the soft ripple of falling water broke the silence.

Until Anton spoke. "If that were true," he whispered, "there's absolutely nothing beyond your abilities."

"Or yours," Adam said. He grabbed Anton's upper arm, clasping the muscle tightly, anchoring himself with the man's power. His voice sounded harsh in his own ears. Roughened with the powerful emotion suddenly coursing through his body.

"I've heard of the things you've done," he said. His breath came hard and fast now, as his sense of wonder and excitement grew. "You're practically a legend among your own people, but there's a damned good reason for that. You've succeeded at everything you've attempted, Anton. You brought Ulrich's late wife back from the dead for an entire night. You rescued Ulrich when he was clear on the other side of the country. Luc told me how you put your thoughts into a raven's mind two thousand miles away to help free his father-in-law from kidnappers. You helped Mei and Oliver when they needed to cross species in order to bond. Think of it, Anton. Whatever you attempt, so long as you believe, you can do. That's the secret. You have to believe. Think of the possibilities."

Anton slowly nodded. Adam released his grip on the wizard's arm, suddenly ashamed of the force he'd shown a man he truly respected. Anton shook his head and smiled, but he didn't speak. He turned on his flashlight and turned the wick down on the last lantern. Then he followed Adam out of the cavern, walking silently behind him.

At first Anton's silence perplexed Adam, but then he sensed his mentor's growing excitement. Sensed the power filling the narrow passage. When Anton thought about something, things happened. Adam knew he was thinking right now. He just wished he knew what in the hell the wizard was planning next.

Chapter 12

They ran in shifts, small groups of wolves leaping from the deck to race through the woods. Adam, Eve, Tia, and Luc were among the last to go, but Tia's rest time had turned into hours of uninterrupted sleep.

"I hate to wake her," Luc said to Adam as they waited for their women in the study. "She looks so pale sometimes and I know she's not feeling well. I'm beginning to wonder if Ulrich is right and she's really carrying twins."

Adam chuckled. "That could certainly change things. Eve wasn't feeling all that great tonight, either, but I think she wore herself out helping Keisha with the meals and cleaning." Adam stretched and glanced toward the door just as Eve wandered through, rubbing her eyes. "You okay, sweetie?"

She shook her head. "Can you and Luc go without us? Tia's just beat and I'm tired, too. I was going to crawl into bed with her and just sleep. I told Keisha we'd stay and watch the babies so she can add her energy to Anton's experiment." She laughed and rubbed her cheek against Adam's arm. "I don't think I'd have anything to share, but I bet you and Luc can come up with something."

She stretched up on her toes and kissed Adam. He ran his fingers along her cheek, loving her more with every breath. She knew he'd been watching Luc, knew Luc was interested in him. And, she did look tired.

"Go sleep." He kissed her. "Watch over Tia, okay?"

"Hmm. G'night, my love." Eve shoved her long blond hair out of her beautiful gray eyes. Adam thought he could drown in her eyes, but then she shot a sideways glance at Luc. "Keep an eye on my guy, will you, Lucien?"

Luc leaned close and kissed Eve on the cheek. "How close an eye?" His voice was a deep, sexy rumble.

Eve laughed. "As close as you can get without getting off. G'night, boys. Be careful."

She spun away with a wriggle of her slim hips and disappeared out the door. Adam slowly turned and grinned at Luc. "I think she's planned our evening."

"Great night to plan it. Anton wants us horny, remember?"

"Oh, shit." Laughing, Adam stripped out of his shirt and jeans and shifted. Luc was right behind him. Together they slipped through the open door, crossed the deck and leapt out into the moonlit meadow behind the house.

Stefan and Anton were just returning. Xandi and Keisha followed close behind.

Where are your mates? Stefan paused and planted his paws in front of Luc.

The girls are tired. They're staying in. They'll watch the babies for you guys later. Luc snorted. *Adam's my date tonight.*

Adam yipped. *C'mon, sweetheart. We're running late.* He took off at a full run with Luc right behind him. Anton and Stefan's silent laughter echoed in his mind, but the two were quickly forgotten as Adam and Luc entered the silent forest.

Though he wished Eve were beside him, Adam embraced the freedom he felt whenever the darkness of the thick woods closed around him. He filled his nostrils with the myriad scents, the rotting wood and humus, the different kinds of fungus and mold and the faint trails of wild creatures. Over it all was the complex mix of other wolves that had run this way tonight, but the most powerful, the most alluring, was the rich scent of the male wolf running beside him.

As a man, Luc was everything Adam admired. Strong and self-assured, his honor and integrity as much a part of him as his broad shoulders, dark hair, and amber eyes. Adam knew Luc's history, knew he'd been the rookie cop who killed Ulrich Mason's wife, Camille, so many years ago. He also knew Luc had more than atoned for that terrible incident.

He must have, to have gained the unwavering love of Camille's only daughter, Tia. His men at Pack Dynamics admired and trusted him, the women loved him.

And Adam, since the first moment he'd met the man, had lusted after him. It was almost embarrassing, this need he felt for Lucien Stone. He'd talked about it with Eve, but she couldn't understand the driving force behind it, either. They were Chanku. If they wanted sex with another member of the pack, they merely had to make themselves available.

There was no reason for Adam to hide his desire, but hide it he did. And tonight, he could desire all he wanted, but he couldn't do a damned thing about it. He would have laughed out loud if he'd been human.

The wolf merely yipped and raced on ahead.

Luc occasionally sent his thoughts home and checked on Tia, but she slept soundly beside Eve. She'd shown him images earlier while he ran, of Eve sprawled between her long legs, feasting greedily on her sex. Then Tia had turned in the big bed and explored Eve with her mouth and tongue, suckling her swollen labia and using her tongue on the taut little bud of her friend's clitoris.

They'd loved one another to climax because they wouldn't be part of Anton's experiment, and the ripples of ecstasy had left Luc so hard he could barely keep up with Adam.

He'd actually been relieved when Tia and Eve had finally drifted off to sleep. He wondered if Eve was sharing her experience with Adam, but the big wolf beside him ran on as if he hadn't a care in the world.

They scared up a jackrabbit and chased it into a twisted bramble patch, but neither one of them wanted to risk the sharp thorns for one skinny hare. The night was still and it appeared the bigger game had been frightened off by the earlier groups of hunters, which left Luc more than enough time to concentrate on the wolf running along beside him.

He was hungry, but he wanted a different kind of meat. Running beside Adam wasn't helping his desperate arousal. He wasn't certain what it was about the man that attracted him. As much as he loved Tinker, the need didn't overwhelm him like this, and while he and Jake had been lovers for years, he hardly missed him now that he was in Maine with Manda, Shannon, and Bay.

Adam was different. There was an aura of power about him, a strength the man wore like a second skin, yet he appeared to be absolutely oblivious to it.

Anton wasn't. Luc couldn't help but notice how the wizard watched Adam tonight, mainly because Luc was watching Adam just as closely himself. It was obvious Anton recognized something rare in Adam Wolf, something special.

Luc had stood there in that amazing cavern and wondered if Anton and Adam were lovers. Then he wanted to slap himself for such a stupid thought. It didn't matter. None of it mattered. The night, the forest and the soft, springy humus beneath his feet—that mattered.

His wife, the woman who was his mate, who carried his child—she mattered. But if it wasn't for Anton and his need for all that sexual energy, Luc knew he and Adam Wolf would be screwing each other like a couple of horny bunnies right now.

They slipped beneath a tangle of shrubs and entered a quiet meadow near a shallow creek. So late in the summer, there was barely enough water to maintain any current, but it was clear and cold and both wolves drank their fill.

Adam was the first to shift. Luc shifted and rose to two legs mere seconds later with a wary sense of anticipation. His cock was already hard, pulsing with need as it curved upward, stretching almost to his belly.

The faint glow of moonlight provided more than enough illumination with their Chanku night vision. Luc stood perfectly still and studied Adam Wolf.

Adam stared back at him for a long moment without speaking. Finally he cleared his throat and said, "Anton doesn't want us to spend, but that doesn't mean we can't play, does it?"

Luc grinned at him. "Spend? Sort of an archaic word for a good fuck, don't you think?"

Adam chuckled and shook his head. He wrapped his hand around his own cock and stroked himself, lifting the thick length up and away from his full sac. "A good fuck generally means you get to shoot your load. We're on the honor system not to do that. But like I said, it doesn't mean we can't play a bit, does it?"

Luc's mouth went dry and he felt something in his heart spring to life along with his cock. "How much time do we have?"

"An hour, maybe. No more." Adam grinned. "I can get into a lot of trouble in an hour . . . even more trouble with help." Now he cupped his balls in one palm and held his erection with the other.

Laughing, Luc touched Adam's shoulder, though he really wanted to stroke his cock. For now, Adam's shoulder would do. "If we're good enough," he said, "we might be able to power that energy field of Anton's all by ourselves."

Adam's laughter died away on a sigh and his hands fell away from his genitals. "I've wanted you since we met, but there never seemed to be a chance to be alone." He stared down at his feet. "I love Eve, but it's not the same with the girls there, having sex with a guy. I feel as if I need to maintain a certain male dignity."

Luc grinned at him. "That's sort of an oxymoron, isn't it? Male dignity?"

"With me it is." Adam wrapped his fingers around Luc's upper arm and drew him close. "We promised Anton and I promise you I will stop whatever I'm doing before you come."

"Me, too." Luc reached for Adam and pulled him close. Adam's cock pressed against his hard belly, hotter and bigger than Luc had imagined. He felt his own erection stretch and grow as he hugged Adam close.

Their hearts seemed to stutter and slow, then speed up to find a pounding rhythm in perfect sync. When Luc breathed in, Adam exhaled and their chests followed one another in a dance of muscle and sinew and unbelievably sensitive skin.

Adam tilted his hips until his sac rubbed along the base of Luc's cock. Luc groaned, planted his feet, tilted his hips forward and pressed his balls against Adam's. The pressure was amazing, the sensation of intimacy bordering on pain. Their cocks were hard and heavy, leaning off to either side between their taut bellies. Luc concentrated on the hot pressure of his ball sac sliding back and forth over the wrinkled surface of Adam's.

Every sensation seemed intensified. The blood rushing in his veins made an audible sound, echoing in his ears like the rhythmic pulse of the sea. He felt the precise shape and size of Adam's balls against his own and the hard base of his cock. The rough hair on Adam's thighs scraped against the silky hair on Luc's. He wondered if, once Adam spent more time as Chanku, his body hair would soften as Luc's had. Even the coarse pubic hair Luc had as a youth was now fine and silky.

Tia's long blond hair had been a mass of frizzy curls when she was a kid, but now they'd turned to silken waves, every bit as curly, but soft and sleek. It had to have something to do with the act of shifting, but Luc had never understood why. Maybe it was the fact wolves had straight hair. He didn't know.

"One of life's many mysteries, eh, Luc?" Adam chuckled softly and leaned his forehead against Luc's. "You're broadcasting, buddy, and damn but you're turning me on, thinking about the soft blond patch between your mate's thighs!"

Luc laughed. He gave Adam's left nipple a sharp pinch between his thumb and forefinger. "Can you take any more without coming?"

A broad grin spread across Adam's face. "I can take whatever you dish out, my friend."

Luc bit back a burst of laughter. He wondered if Adam realized the gauntlet he'd just tossed. "We'll see about that."

Adam laughed out loud and shook his head. "Maybe that wasn't quite the way I should have expressed my . . ."

"Too late. That's as powerful and binding as a triple *I dare ya* in the third grade." He pressed his palm against Adam's chest. "Here, I want you to turn around and face this tree."

"Yes, sir." Adam looked him straight in the eye for a brief moment, as if judging him. They were about the same height, though Luc was broader in the chest, his build more muscular. Adam had the lean, rangy build of a swimmer with broad, bony shoulders, a narrow waist, and trim hips.

He might have a leaner build, but Luc knew his equal in

physical strength when he saw it. There would be no dominant male, no submissive partner. Not this time.

After a brief pause, Adam turned as directed and faced the thick trunk of a tall fir tree. Admiring the view, Luc slipped around behind him.

"Raise your arms and press your palms against the trunk." Adam silently complied, but there was a definite quirk to his mouth and Luc knew he was trying not to laugh.

Adam seemed to have a pretty good opinion of himself, but Luc was just as much the alpha as any male member of the pack. This was going to be so much fun. "Now we'll see just how tough you are," he said. "Remember, no matter what I do, you can't come. You can, however, ask me to stop."

Adam's laugh turned into a strangled gasp when Luc wrapped his left arm around his waist and flattened his palm against the rippling muscle just above Adam's navel. He slipped his finger into the sensitive indentation and swirled it in a small circle as he held his own cock down and pressed his groin against Adam's rock-hard buttocks. The length of Luc's erection pointed down the dark valley that led between Adam's thighs.

Luc slipped his right arm around Adam and wrapped his hand around the hot, pulsing length of his cock. He folded his fingers around the thick base and squeezed a couple of times, as if testing his grip. Adam's cock twitched and his body tensed, but he remained silent. Luc stood perfectly still for a moment, just soaking up the heat and warmth, the pure masculinity of the man in his arms.

All was silent around them in the very early hours before dawn. Luc felt as if the entire forest held its collective breath, waiting to see what he would do next.

He knew Adam wondered. When he felt the tension in Adam's body building, Luc began to move his hips, slowly moving in and out, sliding his thick cock back and forth between Adam's thighs, far enough forward to catch the underside of his sensitive balls with his own broad crown.

Luc slipped his hand down from Adam's belly and grasped his tight sac. He rubbed his palm over the broad tip of Adam's cock and felt the slick pre-cum already dripping from the small slit at the tip of his glans. Using the slippery fluid to lubricate his palm, Luc slowly and firmly stroked the full length of Adam's cock.

Adam groaned.

"Do you want me to stop?"

"Are you kidding?" Adam's words burst out on a gasp of expelled breath. "Damn, but that feels good."

Luc lay across Adam's back and rolled his hips back and forth in a slow, smooth rhythm. His cock pressed firmly into Adam's ball sac on every forward thrust as Luc continued to stroke his cock and squeeze his balls.

Adam's body quivered with the struggle to hang on to control. Fluid ran in a steady stream from Adam's slit, which merely made it easier for Luc to stroke the thick length of his cock. The big vein in the underside pulsed and Adam trembled, but still he held on.

Thoroughly enjoying the torment he was putting the other man through, Luc slowed the thrust of his hips and paused long enough to smear the crown of his cock with a generous amount of Adam's pre-cum. Mixed with his own, he knew it would make entry easier, though Adam was so caught up in trying to control his ejaculation, Luc didn't think he had a clue what was coming next.

Slowly releasing Adam's balls, he continued the slow back and forth stroke along his cock, but he slipped his hand around and stroked Adam's dark cleft with his slick fingers. Adam groaned. He leaned forward a bit more and spread his legs wider.

Luc grinned and squeezed his cock just a little tighter, just enough to take Adam's mind off what was happening behind him. Luc ran his fingers over Adam's sensitive perineum, but instead of retracing the route to Adam's sac, he slipped one finger through the taught ring of muscle protecting his ass.

Adam jerked. He cursed, but he held on. The muscles in his back tensed and tightened and his body quivered, but he didn't let go. His cock seemed to swell within Luc's grasp as he continued stroking. Adam whispered something just under his breath.

Luc strained to hear. *Hold on. Don't come. Hold on. Don't come.* Over and over again, like a solemn mantra for control.

"Do you want me to stop?"

Adam took a deep breath and shook his head, two sharp jerks back and forth. *No.*

Luc pulled his finger out of Adam and pressed the slippery tip of his glans against Adam's tight sphincter muscle. He gave him no warning, no time to prepare. He pressed forward, hard, squeezing the base of Adam's cock at the same time, preventing him from shooting his load.

"I'm helping you keep your promise, bro." Luc could barely get the words out. There was no place for laughter, not if he was going to keep himself from coming as well.

He buried himself inside Adam's damp heat, all the way to his balls, and he kept the tight grasp on the base of Adam's cock so that he could fuck him hard and long, at least until he felt his own climax gaining strength.

It was so damned perfect, taking him bare like this. They almost always used rubbers for anal sex, more for the aesthetics than anything else, since disease wasn't a factor for Chanku. Now, though, the tight clasp of muscle clinging to his cock as he planted himself deep inside, the amazing heat and the slick channel that stretched just enough to take all of him gave Luc the sense his cock was encased in a velvet fist.

Now, if he could only hold on until Adam cried uncle!

* * *

Adam's entire body was hard as a rock. Veins stood out along his arms and his legs quivered with his struggle for control. Even with Luc's steady pressure on his cock, he felt as if he might shoot any second.

Not if I can help it, damn it! He would have laughed at the stupidity of such a contest if he weren't in such a desperate struggle for control. This had definitely become a contest of wills and restraint, a test of mind over sensation.

There was a familiar buzzing in his ears, a sense of power above and beyond his barely rational mind. Adam felt Luc's thoughts as they breached the mental barriers he had so carefully erected.

How the hell . . . ?

He didn't have time to wonder. Their joining became a perfect mesh of two minds until they thought as one, breathed as one. Until their hearts beat in perfect synchronization.

Adam recognized the strange sensation taking over his body, the same sense of *other* he'd experienced when he and AJ Temple had sex just a few weeks ago. The feeling that their minds and bodies, hearts, lungs, and thoughts were now a single, powerful, pulsing mass of energy.

Luc's rhythm never changed, but Adam's perspective did. He felt himself leave his body, sensed Luc beside him, and as one they looked down on two men fucking in the forest.

Adam sensed Luc's fear. *It's okay. I'll explain later.*

He felt Luc relax a bit, but still they hovered, watching themselves from an impossible perspective.

Control of his climax was easier, now, and Adam felt himself relax just enough for the fear to subside. Unlike the time with AJ, he didn't feel so totally separated from the reality of Adam Wolf. This was something else, something unique, yet whatever was happening, he knew it had something to do with the sexual energy between Luc and himself.

Together—their presence mere thought without sub-stance or form—Adam and Luc hovered as a single entity of pure energy. Adam could have stayed there forever, watching the beautiful play of muscles across Luc's back and the taut line of his buttocks as he fucked Adam, driving deep and hard with each thrust of his hips. It was amazing.

Luc's mental voice interrupted Adam's eminently satis-fying voyeuristic experience.

How do we get back?

Go back? Luc wanted to go back? Adam realized the sky was growing light in the east and wondered how long they'd been here, floating in the air, completely apart from their corporeal selves.

Good question. With AJ, we returned as soon as we both climaxed.

We can't do that. We promised.

You're right, Adam said. *Let's just go back.*

Why does that sound too damned simple?

Because it is. He opened his mind to Luc and *thought* himself into his own body.

At the same moment Adam felt the grass beneath his feet and the weight of Luc's back over his, Luc released his grasp on Adam's cock and pulled his still-erect penis from his ass.

Adam's body throbbed with unmet needs. His cock bobbed mournfully against his belly and if his balls were to draw up any tighter between his legs, they might as well crawl back inside.

Luc spun around and leaned against the tree next to Adam. He broadcast his feelings of amazement at what they'd just done. Every bit as strong was the raging sexual frustration. Like Adam, his chest bellowed in and out, his balls ached, and his cock was still hard as a post.

"I think, considering the circumstances, Anton would have forgiven us if we'd gone ahead and shot our loads."

Luc's dry comment was all it took. Adam started to

laugh. He leaned over, hands on his thighs and butt against the rough tree bark, and tried to catch his breath. He'd get it under control, take one look at Luc, and start all over again. Luc held on as long as he could, but he ended up on his bare butt in the cold, damp grass, laughing so hard he could barely breathe.

Adam slipped down beside Luc, slung his arm over his shoulder and forced himself to take long, deep breaths until he had it all under control. It took Luc just a moment longer before his body stopped shaking with poorly suppressed giggles.

"Not a very manly response." Adam's dry comment set both of them off all over again. Finally, gasping for air, Adam leaned his head back against the rough bark and turned his head. His gaze locked with Luc's, whose amber eyes were filled with amazement and wonder, as well as a healthy dose of fear. Like Adam, it was obvious Luc wondered what in the hell had happened.

This was a power unlike anything Adam had imagined. That first time his mind had slipped free of his body, an early morning when he'd had an amazing sexual encounter with AJ, had been terrifying and wonderful. It happened again with AJ, Mik, Tala, and Eve, but they'd planned it and hoped to repeat what Adam and AJ had experienced.

The five of them hadn't had a clue what they were about, but they'd managed to call forth the spirit of Igmutaka, Mik's grandfather's spirit guide. Of course, the original goal was to plant him firmly in Eve's consciousness. The fact he'd ended up with Tala had been scary, but exciting, too. There had been a definite sense of wonder.

This time, though, Adam felt he might have lost himself in the sense of power and energy he'd experienced. If Luc hadn't wondered about returning to their bodies, would Adam even have cared?

He hoped so. Hated to think of himself wandering about

as some nebulous cloud of energy, unable to find his physical self. Still, the sense of mastering an unknown power was addictive. Already he was thinking of doing it again, of figuring out how he could leave his body without the need of another person, without depending on the power generated during sex.

Or was it sexual frustration that powered his ability to separate, in a most literal sense, mind and matter?

Maybe it was something even simpler. Adam banged his head back against the rough bark, grounding himself against the tree. Could it be nothing more than what he'd mentioned to Anton?

What if he merely had to *believe* he could float free of his body? Was that all it took to give him such an amazing ability? He'd have to think about that one. The concept certainly opened up a whole slew of new possibilities.

There was so much he didn't know. So many things he wanted to learn. How could he turn this dubious power into something useful? There had to be a way to use it to help protect all of those he loved.

Adam stood up, reached for Luc's outstretched hand and pulled his buddy to his feet. Luc glanced at Adam's painfully swollen erection. Then he looked down at his own and shook his head in dismay. Chuckling, he shifted, trotted a few steps away and peed on a low bush.

Adam did the same. He managed to place his stream just a bit higher than Luc's. Some instincts were just too cool to fight.

Ears and tail high, Adam slipped through the thick undergrowth and followed Luc along the trail back to the house. It was time to talk to Anton. If anyone had answers, Adam knew it would be the wizard.

Chapter 13

They gathered in the early morning as planned, all of them standing together, casually but warmly dressed against the cool air in the cavern beneath the house. The level of arousal in the underground grotto created a palpable, throbbing pulse that filled the room and replicated itself in the hearts and lungs of everyone there.

Anton looked at the familiar, beloved faces and realized each of them looked to him for answers.

He had none.

Frustration gnawed at him, a sense of failure that he couldn't promise any of them, even his own mate, safety. Luc may have managed to get the reward postings removed from the Internet, but what would prevent them going back up? What would stop the next mercenary from attacking any of those Anton loved?

What would keep other scientists, familiar with Manda and questioning her odd heritage, from searching for answers?

They trusted few people in the human world with their secret, but the ability to read their minds meant Anton could be assured of their loyalty. What of those he didn't know?

He did know of at least five men, still alive and willing

to risk their lives to capture a female Chanku. The ones who had gone after the women in San Francisco were still out there, putting Tia, Lisa, and Tala at the most risk once they returned home.

Damn. He felt so helpless. Completely emasculated by circumstances out of his control. Shaking his head slowly, Anton looked into the faces of the people he knew most intimately, and spoke what was in his heart.

"I don't know what to say to you." Anton flinched when every head turned his way. "I asked for your energy, but after hours of testing I realized my idea won't work. I've spent the night searching for a protective spell, something that would warn us if a particular boundary is crossed, but I haven't had any luck with it. I tried setting a ward on the doorways to the house, but I couldn't hold even that much. Even with our combined energy, it's not a practical solution. I don't want to risk weakening any of us for something that obviously won't work."

Keisha placed her hand on his forearm and squeezed. He felt her silent strength and stood a bit taller. "Do any of you have any suggestions?"

If only his request didn't sound so plaintive.

The silence told him more than it should have. Finally Ulrich spoke up. He sounded just as dejected as Anton felt. "I haven't got any ideas at all, other than to remain vigilant and keep close watch on our loved ones. For now, though, Millie and I need to get back home, and that means a trip to San Francisco first for our car, and a long drive to Colorado. She's not comfortable being away from the sanctuary this long."

"We need to go, too." Mik glanced toward Tala and AJ. "We've turned down a couple of calls since we've been here."

"And he's felt guilty about every one," Tala said. She slipped an arm around Mik's waist and hugged him.

"Tia and I should get back as well." Luc stretched his

arms over his head and yawned. "She's had a substitute teacher covering for her, but she doesn't have a lot of personal time left. Besides, I have a few leads I need to follow and I've got better access to information in the Bay Area. Tink? Are you and Lisa going to come with us?"

Tinker smiled at his mate and nodded. "Looks like."

Keisha stepped forward. "How about an end of summer barbecue tonight, and you can all get an early start in the morning, after a good night's sleep? I know for a fact every one of you has been up most of the night. I don't want to worry about a bunch of sleepy drivers hitting the road . . . or anyone else."

"That sounds great, Keisha. Thank you. Let us know how we can help you, okay?" Luc took Tia's hand and led her toward the stairs.

Anton watched in silence as everyone else filtered quietly out of the cavern and left. He sensed their frustration, a feeling of desperation bordering on anger. He wondered if his personal sense of failure caused it.

Keisha leaned close and kissed him. "I'm going up now. I'll pull some steaks out of the freezer. We'll put Stefan in charge of the barbecue."

Lily slept on in the sling that stretched across Keisha's chest. Anton stared at his beautiful daughter and felt sick inside. "That's fine," he said, though if Keisha had asked him what she'd just told him, he wouldn't have been able to repeat a single word.

"Don't do this to yourself, my love." Keisha's soft voice had an edge to it.

"Do what?" Of course her mind was blocked. It usually was when he wanted some idea what she was thinking about.

"Don't blame yourself for the attacks. You are no more responsible than I am. We'll stop these people. Agonizing over things you can't control won't help a bit."

"I've failed them." He sighed and held Keisha close. "But the worst thing is, I've failed you and Lily. I'm your mate, her father . . . I can't protect you. I can't keep Lily safe. I don't know where to turn."

"I'm not helpless, and you, Anton Cheval, are not the only one responsible for keeping Lily, or me, or the rest of our kind, safe. You don't share responsibilities well at all. In fact, I imagine you got crappy marks in school. You know, the little box on the report card that says 'plays well with others'? You probably got zeroes every time. Now come upstairs. I want this to be a fun evening for everyone, which means you have to quit brooding. We need to remember who and what we are."

Anton kissed her, even though he still felt sick inside. "And who is that, Ms. Alpha Bitch Rialto?"

She smiled and slowly shook her head side to side. "We are Chanku, Anton. We're wolves. The top of the food chain."

He ran his hand over her thick, black hair and tangled his fingers through the soft curls cascading over her shoulders. He shook his head, surprised he was smiling. "Actually, my love, man is at the top of the food chain, and we are being hunted by men."

Laughing, Keisha punched his arm. "Killjoy." She turned and headed up the stairs, but the somber mood was broken.

Anton followed her, still smiling. Thank the Goddess for Keisha. She could always make him laugh.

Adam waited for them in the wine cellar. He heard Keisha's soft laughter and stepped forward as she walked through the opening carrying Lily, followed by her mate.

"Hi, Adam. I didn't realize you were still here."

"Hope I didn't startle you, Keisha." He shoved his hands into his pockets and felt about six years old. To admire a man as much as he did Anton, and to essentially hang out here, waiting to proposition him . . . he cleared his throat and looked beyond Keisha. "I'd like to talk to you, Anton, if you've got a minute."

Anton nodded. He shoved the cabinet across the opening and closed off access to the tunnel.

Keisha kissed his cheek. "I'll go on up and get the steaks out to thaw. Then Lily and I are taking a nap."

Adam waited until Keisha closed the door into the kitchen. He took a deep breath and turned his attention to Anton. The man looked like hell. His face seemed lined and weary this morning. He looked every one of his fifty-plus years, and then some.

It wasn't right, that he took the attacks so personally. Just because there were a bunch of nuts out there with crazy ideas . . . ideas about as crazy as Adam's.

What was it about the wizard that left him feeling tongue-tied? Adam took a deep breath and realized he'd never know if he didn't speak. "Anton, remember a couple weeks ago, when I did that thing with the out-of-body experience? At first I thought it was a fluke, until five of us did it again when we called Igmutaka. I haven't tried it since, at least until a few hours ago. Luc and I . . . yeah. Well, it got me to thinking, that somehow, maybe we could . . ." He shook his head. "Maybe I'm nuts, but that's the third time it's happened. I'm not sure how we could use an ability like that, but I wondered . . . ?" He shrugged and grinned. "It's such a cool thing and I wondered if it might have any use."

At least the wizard wasn't laughing at him. Instead, Anton looked interested and there was that familiar gleam in his eye. "Maybe. Can you teach me? If I can follow the process in your head, see how it works, I might be able to figure something out. Believe me, at this point I'm ready to try just about anything."

Adam laughed and the tension went out of him. "I can show you, but only if you're interested in some heavy-duty fucking. So far the only way I've been able to do it is during sex. Really intense sex."

Anton grinned and the years fell away. "Really intense sex, eh? I'm always up for that."

"That's a really bad joke."

"It's the best I've got." He laughed. "When? Where?"

Adam swallowed. What if it didn't work? "Are you okay for a run? I want to be out in the woods where we won't be disturbed. I'm still not exactly sure what's happening when it happens, if that makes sense."

"Actually, it does. I imagine it will make sense very shortly, once I have a chance to observe the phenomenon."

"You'll do more than observe," Adam said. "You'll participate, if all goes well."

"Even better." Anton spun around, and stepped briskly toward the stairs leading to the kitchen. There was no sign of weariness in him now. "I need to speak with Keisha before we go. You let Eve know we might be away for a couple of hours. I'll meet you on the back deck in ten minutes."

Biting back laughter, Adam followed Anton out of the wine cellar. It appeared the wizard was back in charge.

They ran much farther than Adam expected, but the meadow Anton took him to was high on the mountain and beautifully secluded. A small stream ran from east to west and emptied into a shallow, sun-warmed pond.

Anton shifted first, standing tall and already partially tumescent. Adam circled the meadow, sniffing for signs of other visitors. Beyond the typical scents of deer and rabbits, there was nothing to attract his attention and no sign that humans had been anywhere near at all. He recognized the smell of a panther. Igmutaka had recently passed through, but Adam had no argument with the big cat.

Satisfied they were truly alone, he shifted. His body still throbbed with anxious arousal, a holdover from this morning's incomplete, yet amazing, sex with Luc. Now he stood face-to-face with an even more imposing figure.

Anton was tall and lean, his shoulders wider than Adam's, the hair on his chest thicker and darker. Where Adam was blond, Anton was dark as night.

His cock was even more imposing, swelling and growing even as Adam watched. It curved upward from the dark nest of hair at his groin. Thick at the base and long with a broad glans and thick veins running the length, it caught Adam's attention and sparked an entirely new level of lust.

When he finally raised his head and looked into Anton's gleaming eyes, Adam shuddered. Arousal coursed through his veins and set his heart thundering into overdrive. He felt the catch in his lungs, the tension between his legs as his testicles drew up hard and tight against his body, as his cock filled with blood and stretched long and hard.

He fought the need to grasp his full length and stroke himself. Merely touching it might send him over the top, but the need to touch, to find release for the pressure building inside was overwhelming.

Anton glanced at him as if only marginally interested in what Adam had to offer. "What do you prefer, Adam Wolf? Do you choose the top or the bottom, or is it the heat in a man's mouth that takes your control away?" Anton's voice, deep and seductive, echoed in Adam's ears. The cadence of his words seemed to segue into the beat of his heart, the rush of blood through his veins, the rapid expansion of his lungs and the slow, steady pulse in his cock.

Adam swallowed, suddenly feeling outmaneuvered and definitely outclassed. This man was a master of everything he did. All alphas, no matter their age or status within their individual packs, bowed to him, yet he asked Adam what he preferred?

His buttocks clenched and he imagined the slick feel of Anton's cock riding the tight cleft between, forcing entry and taking him. Then Adam drifted further into fantasy. He thought of the opposite, of covering Anton's lean body with his own, stroking the man's long, thick cock and using his own fluids to lubricate the tight muscle guarding his ass.

He groaned, picturing the way his glans would flare when he held his swollen penis in his fist and forced his way through Anton's puckered ring. As hard as he was, his cock would hold rigid as the glans reformed in the precise moment of penetration, squeezing through Anton's tight hole. He felt the first clench of muscle, the flutter of release, the slick entry once he'd breached the taut muscle. Felt the amazing pressure as Anton instinctively fought entry while Adam slowly pressed forward. He imagined the heat, the wet and warm passage rippling around his cock, the muscles fighting entry even as they pulled him deep.

The images in Adam's head flashed through in quick succession, so vivid he almost climaxed right there in his not-so-private fantasy. From the increased rate of Anton's breath, he knew the man read him, knew Anton saw exactly what Adam thought.

Felt what Adam felt, and responded. Anton stepped closer and wrapped his arms around Adam's waist. He tilted his hips forward and trapped the wet crown of his hard cock against Adam's belly, alongside Adam's shaft.

Anton stood perfectly still, but he opened his mind, opened his thoughts so that Adam felt and saw everything Anton experienced.

Adam saw Anton kneeling, bending over in a totally submissive position. Tufts of green grass flattened beneath his elbows and knees and his lean buttocks and smooth back seemed unusually vulnerable for a man as powerful as the wizard.

Adam nodded, and dug deep inside his mind for control. If he was going to be the top, he needed to last long enough to give Anton satisfaction. Long enough to force that same out-of-body experience he'd had with Luc.

Without a word, Anton turned and took the same position Adam had seen in his mind. Adam knelt behind Anton. His knees left smooth depressions in the damp earth between Anton's legs. The late summer sun beat warmly against his back.

Anton's forehead rested on his folded arms. If not for the explicit images still spinning in Adam's head, it would be an almost anonymous fuck, but the visuals were as real as the man. As powerful as the wizard, and in some ways, more frightening than anything Adam had ever experienced.

Meeting Anton Cheval as an equal was one thing. Kneeling behind him, cock in fist, preparing to fuck the wizard's perfectly shaped ass was something else entirely. Adam reached around Anton's hip and grasped his thick shaft. As big as his hands were, Adam barely encircled Anton's girth. He stroked the silken skin slowly to the broad head and found the slick trail of liquid seeping from the slit at the end. Rubbing his fingers through it, coating them thoroughly, Adam used Anton's own early release to lubricate the tight little rosette of muscle between his ass cheeks.

Anton moaned and his hips pressed back against Adam's slick fingers. He brought his fingers to his lips, tasted Anton's pre-cum and added his saliva. Then he rubbed harder, pressing into the puckered muscle, parting it just enough for one finger to slip through.

He slipped his finger in and out, slowly, aware of Anton's muscles trembling every bit as hard as his own. He could have thrust harder, but dragging this out seemed to be an important part of the process. Adam increased the pressure and added a second finger, and finally a third. Stretching slowly, pressing deeply, he felt the tight ring begin to soften and relax.

When he finally forced his cock against the stretched and softened muscle, entry was faster and deeper than he'd expected. Anton groaned and pressed back against him. Adam clenched his teeth and fought an almost overpowering need to let go and climax. He drove in as deep as he could, then grabbed both of Anton's hips and held perfectly still.

There was a rhythmic throbbing around his cock. He wasn't sure if it was his own or Anton's pulse. Then it came to him, that they shared the same rhythm, shared the pounding of their hearts, the *whoosh* of blood through their veins.

Adam closed his eyes and experienced the pure sensation, the unimaginable pleasure of such an unexpected and intimate connection with a man he admired above all others. His sac pressed tightly against Anton's and his cock was buried so deep that the pressure of his groin separated the two muscular globes of Anton's ass.

As he shared that sensation with Anton, the wizard spread his knees apart even farther and Adam felt himself slide a fraction of an inch deeper.

There was no desire to move. Not yet. Adam realized he was finding control by categorizing each sensation separately. The subtle contractions of the muscles in Anton's rectum, closing and releasing around the length of his cock, the taut pressure of Anton's sphincter where it clung tightly to the base and pulsed strong and steady.

There was dark hair on the backs of Anton's thighs, mingled now with the lighter hair on the front of Adam's. He ran his hands over the hard planes of Anton's ass, stroked his lean sides and traced each vertebra along his spine.

Anton groaned. Adam felt the vibrations. He reached around Anton's slim waist with both hands and stroked his belly. He trailed his fingers through the thick hair at the wizard's groin, cupped his ball sac in his palm, wrapped his fingers once again around the thick girth of the man's hard cock.

The skin was silky and hot, the full length curved up tightly now against Anton's belly, the veins distended and hard. Thick fluid dripped from the narrow slit at the tip.

Adam rolled his palm over the top, collected the moisture and used it to dampen the length of Anton's cock. Then he traced each throbbing vein with his fingertip, finding the start near the base and following it all the way to the tip, around and over the top of his shaft.

The tension in Anton's body grew. Adam reached for his thoughts and found Anton caught in a cycle of anger and self-recrimination. His plea sounded as much like a mantra as a request.

Move, damn it. Fuck me deep. Take me hard. Pound into me now, Adam Wolf. Hurt me. I need to hurt, to feel the burn and tear. I deserve the pain. I need the pain.

Adam's fingers tightened involuntarily around Anton's shaft just as his other hand squeezed the twin globes in the sac grasped in his long fingers.

Immediately he released the tension. It wasn't in him to cause anyone pain.

Anton moaned and his hips pressed hard against Adam's belly. Unmoving, Adam leaned his head forward and rested his cheek against Anton's warm back.

I can't intentionally cause you pain, my friend. Don't ask me to do anything more than love you. You're the one who taught me to fix more than machines. You taught me to heal, not to hurt.

Anton sighed, and some of the tension went out of his body. His disappointment became a living, breathing entity between them.

Understanding blossomed in Adam's mind. This was what Anton needed, now, at this point in time. Not tenderness. Not a gentle loving. He needed the pain if he was ever going to heal. This was the key to the experience both of them were seeking. Adam raised his head and breathed in. He closed his eyes, asked the Goddess for forgiveness, and then he slammed his hips hard against Anton's buttocks.

That doesn't mean I can't take you hard and fast,

Anton Cheval. Doesn't mean I don't know how to fuck. Adam tightened his grasp on Anton's balls and cock as he pulled his hips back again and slipped his cock almost free of Anton's hot, wet passage.

Then he slammed forward, filling him completely. His hand squeezed Anton's shaft, his fingers clutched his balls and he caught a rhythm of thrust and release, harder and deeper. Anton grunted with each powerful drive until Adam felt as if he moved with a metronome setting the pace.

He had complete control of his own arousal. This was for Anton, this powerful wizard, a man admired and respected by all, suffering as any man might suffer, awash in his own feelings of inadequacy, no matter how misguided those feelings might be.

Adam felt the power in him grow until he wanted to lean back and howl like the wolf he was. He opened his thoughts and found Anton. He shared his friend's pain, the burning agony of each powerful penetration as his cock tore into sensitive tissues not designed for such brutal treatment.

Adam slammed deep and hard with every thrust. Anton's body, writhing now, twisted beneath him as his level of excitement reached for the ultimate peak, climbing closer to climax with every thrust of Adam's hips, every brutally painful penetration.

Adam grasped the base of Anton's shaft and wrapped his fingers tightly around him, preventing Anton's ejaculation. Thrusting harder, faster, plunging in and out until he lost himself in the rhythm, fell even deeper into Anton's experience, and released his mind.

Adam felt the connection first, the sense of melding totally into Anton Cheval's consciousness. There was physical pain coupled with extreme arousal, emotional pain too deep to comprehend.

The rush of blood in his ears, the audible pulse of two

hearts joining, finding their rhythm, beating as one. Anton's thoughts, his experience now every bit as intimate as Adam's, intermingled until Anton's pain was Adam's, and Adam's arousal filled Anton.

There was a strange buzzing in Adam's ears, a sense of disorientation, coupled with Anton's gasp of wonder. And once again, Adam experienced a miracle.

Anton's body shivered with the need to come, his climax held at bay by Adam's powerful grasp at the base of his cock. His balls ached, his ass burned and he hadn't been this aroused, this frustrated, in months.

He felt the power in Adam Wolf and knew he experienced something amazing. Each thrust took Anton closer to some nebulous experience he still couldn't understand, but the sense of oneness, of joining, seemed to grow with each breath he took.

Until he realized he was breathing in perfect sync with Adam, his body moving as if they danced, flowing into each thrust, anticipating every touch and thought.

Blood pounded in his ears and down the length of his cock, and his heart pounded just as hard in his chest. Perfectly meshed with Adam. As if he controlled every response, every cell in Anton's body with his own driving need.

There was a strange buzzing in his ears, a sense of disorientation that reminded him of the completion of the mating bond. This bond was different, this link taking the two of them to a totally different level.

Literally.

About ten feet above the bodies of two men fucking in the forest. Anton might have gasped if he'd had corporeal form, but he was as Adam said he would be—nothing more than a shimmering ball of energy hovering above two familiar bodies.

His body. Adam's. *Amazing. Even though you explained it, I had no idea . . .*

It is amazing, but how the hell can we use this to protect the others?

What can you do, separated from your body like this?

Adam took a minute to think about it. *I don't know. All I've done before is hover here and wonder at the miracle, the absolute impossibility of being out of my body, yet watching my body.*

Can you feel what we're doing?

Adam wondered if he could shake his head, but he had no control over the body beneath him. *Nope. There's no sensation beyond what I can see and your voice in my head. I can't hear the forest, don't feel your ass clutching at my cock.* He laughed. *Damn. I know that feels really good, and I'm missing it.*

Anton laughed. *Let's go back. I feel vulnerable, not knowing if there's anyone near.*

I think you just want to come.

There is that.

It was a simple matter, really, to reenter his body. It happened just as Adam tore deep inside his ass with another powerful thrust, releasing his grasp on Anton's cock at the same time.

Orgasm hit hard and fast. Anton arched his back, his mouth opening in a silent scream. Excruciating pain and unimaginable pleasure, the hot spill of Adam's seed filling his bowel, the throbbing pressure of that huge cock pressing deep inside.

They lay there in the warm grass, bodies still linked, minds caught in the downward spiral of fading orgasm. Anton felt somehow cleansed, as if the pounding he'd just received from Adam had swept away most of the worries and self-condemnation that had plagued him for days now.

He'd needed the pain as much as he'd needed the amazing sense of separation, the chance to peer down at his body and realize Keisha was right. He was just one man. A man who did the best he could to protect his family, but still just a man.

Not a god, not all-powerful.

And, as Keisha kept reminding him, he was not to blame. That didn't mean he wouldn't do whatever he could to end this reign of terror. Now, though, he could face it with a clearer mind. For that, he would have to thank Adam.

Unfortunately, though the out-of-body experience Adam had just demonstrated was an amazing feat, Anton could see absolutely no practical application. He knew how to achieve it on his own. Already his mind was grasping the *how* though not the *why* of it, but he saw nothing applicable, at least to this situation facing the Chanku.

No matter. He wouldn't have passed up this past half hour with Adam Wolf for anything. So much of the tension, the frustration haunting him for so long seemed to have disappeared, at least for now. Anton rolled to his side and felt Adam's soft penis slide easily out of his ass.

Adam lay beside him in the grass with a big smile on his face. His lungs still bellowed in and out and sweat streaked his face. He stroked Anton's shoulder with his fingers. "Thank you," he said. There was a gleam in his brilliant amber eyes.

"I think I should be the one to thank you." Anton rolled over to his back and spread his arms out over his head. "That was an amazing experience."

"Yeah." Adam rolled over and lay beside him. "That out-of-body thing is pretty cool."

"That's not what I meant." Anton lay there grinning. He felt energized. Ready to face whatever might come. He turned his head and kissed Adam full on the mouth. Life was good again. "You, my friend," he said, meaning every word, "you are the amazing experience."

Chapter 14

Anton stepped out of the shower and glanced toward the bedroom. Keisha sat in a sunbeam with Lily at her breast. The baby had grown so much over the past few weeks. She smiled now, and babbled away like she knew how to speak, and her eyes were already showing the amber glow of her parents'.

Nothing, though, would ever outshine the glow in Keisha's eyes. She was meant to be a mother. Meant to be Anton Cheval's mate.

Love ripped through him, so powerful, so deep he pressed a fist against his chest, as if he had to hold his heart inside with the pressure of his hand.

He stood there a moment, struggling to catch his breath. Then he turned away and dried off quickly, shaken by the stabbing emotions that filled him.

Keisha raised her head and smiled at him. "You're worrying again, aren't you? And here I thought Adam helped settle your nerves."

Anton laughed, leaned over and kissed her soft lips, tracing the seam between them with the tip of his tongue before regretfully pulling away. "Trust me, he settled more than my nerves. I want to have just him and Eve here with us one night, all night. Luc wants them to come to San Francisco. I don't want to lose either of them."

"That good, eh?" Keisha held Lily to her shoulder. "You might mention that to them. Right now, I need to get down to the kitchen. Tia's meeting me there in a few minutes to help get things together for dinner." She stood up and kissed him again, taking longer this time, sipping at his mouth, sucking his lower lip between her sharp teeth. "Maybe after everyone goes home?"

Before he could answer, she turned away in a colorful swirl of her long gauzy skirt and was gone. Anton stood there, perfectly aware of the stupid grin on his face and her taste on his lips. Every time. She had this power over him every time she kissed him.

Anton! I think Igmutaka's been shot!

Shaken out of his sensual fog, Anton jerked to attention. *Oliver? Where are you? What's happened?*

I'm on my way to the south meadow. Alert everyone! Igmutaka contacted me, said there were two men with guns, probably hunters. Then his voice cut off. I can't reach him.

I'm coming. He sent a quick message to Keisha that he'd be out in the woods for a while. No need to worry her with incomplete details at this point. Then he opened the door from their bedroom to the back deck, shifted and raced toward the large meadow at the south end of the property. There were always deer there, occasionally antelope and elk and even bears.

Hunting season didn't start for a couple weeks, but the kind of hunter who ignored the NO TRESPASSING signs marking his property wasn't the type to wait for a legal season.

He put out a call to Adam. If Igmutaka had been shot . . .

What's up? Adam's voice came through clear and strong.

Igmutaka may be injured. Meet me in the south meadow. On my way.

* * *

Keisha checked her list while Tia counted out napkins and table service for twenty-one. The big table in the formal dining room was opened out to seat all of them, and the buffet table was cleared and ready for the trays of food.

"I pulled forty steaks out of the freezer. Think that will be enough?" Tia leaned against the doorjamb and shook her head. "I'm sure glad you guys are hosting dinner and not Luc and me. How do you manage to feed this army?"

Keisha took a quick glance at Lily. The baby slept peacefully in her portable crib. Then she smiled at Tia. Her cousin absolutely glowed with the early pregnancy and Keisha was really going to miss her when the San Francisco pack headed home.

"We always keep a lot on hand because we never know who'll be here," she said. "It's really going to be a simple dinner. Stefan and Xandi took Alex and made a grocery run for a bunch of those pre-mixed salads and plenty of potatoes. Since everyone likes their meat really rare . . ."

Tia laughed. "You mean raw?"

"Well, yeah . . . almost raw. We have to let Stefan think he's cooking something, right? Anyway, it's merely a matter of warming a bunch of steaks, putting out big bowls of salad, baked potatoes and all the fixin's, and of course, lots of wine."

"Thank goodness for a well-stocked wine cellar."

Keisha looked through a scattering of notes on the counter. "Isn't that the truth? Anton left me a list of wines he wants for tonight. Once I find it, we'll go downstairs and grab whatever we need."

"I'll set the plates out on the buffet."

Nodding in agreement, Keisha finally found Anton's neatly written list in the stack of notes and old mail. She wondered vaguely why he was going to the south meadow in the middle of the day. It was a great place for wild game, but they had more than enough for dinner tonight.

"Tia? Found it. Let's go down and get the wine while Lily's asleep. It's so chilly in the cellar, I'd rather not take her if we can avoid it. It will just take a miinute if we both go."

Tia grabbed a sweater. "Okay. Plates are out, silverware is on the table, and the dust bunnies are under control."

With one last glance at her sleeping daughter, Keisha opened the door to the cellar and headed down the steps.

Oliver knelt in the tall grass, stroking the velvety coat of the big cougar. Igmutaka's chest rose and fell with each labored breath he took. Blood covered Oliver's palm where he applied pressure to the cat's shoulder and tears coursed down his dark cheeks.

Anton and Adam reached them at the same time. Adam wasted no time in covering the gaping wound with his palms. Anton wrapped an arm around Oliver's waist and touched Adam's forearm, sharing whatever strength he could.

"He's alive." Adam closed his eyes and held very still. "The bone isn't broken but the bullet is lodged in the joint. I don't think it's damaged any internal organs. I'm going to see if I can pull the bullet out."

Anton looked at Oliver and shook his head in amazement. Was there anything Adam couldn't do? As they watched, the wound seemed to swell. Igmutaka growled, but he didn't move. A mushroom-shaped piece of lead worked free of the bloody hole. Anton plucked it out of the way with his fingers and dropped it to the ground.

Sweat beaded Adam's forehead. His body swayed with his own internal rhythm, but the blood stopped running from the wound. Fresh tissue seemed to grow from the inside out as the minutes passed. Slowly the flesh knit together until it completely closed the ragged opening.

Adam sat back on his heels and let out a long, exhausted sigh. His hands were covered with blood and shaking from the effort, but Igmutaka's healing shoulder no longer bled and the cat's breathing appeared almost normal. The cat's eyelids fluttered but remained closed.

"Amazing." Anton gave Oliver's shoulder a squeeze. He turned and looked into Adam's eyes and was surprised to see them filled with tears. "Are you okay?"

Adam nodded. His mouth worked, but it took a moment for him to speak. "Whenever something like this happens, I wonder what my life would be like if I hadn't found you . . . if Oliver hadn't found me." He ran his fingers over Igmutaka's bloody shoulder. The scar was fresh and pink. Dried blood matted his fur. "What I am able to do doesn't come just from me. I feel the power of the Goddess, the power of both of you . . ."

Adam bowed his head a moment while he regained composure, then looked up once again. "He's going to be really sore. I put his shoulder back the best I could, but it was badly damaged. Who would do such a terrible thing?"

Oliver touched Igmutaka's forehead and gently rubbed between his ears. "He called to me. Said there were men with guns. Two of them."

Anton nodded. "We need to look for them. Damn, this probably isn't related to the other attacks, but I'm not willing to take that chance." He stood up and pulled Adam to his feet. "You look like hell. I think you need some rest."

Adam laughed. "I feel like hell." He glanced down at the cat just as Igmutaka opened his eyes. "Probably no worse than he does, though."

Slowly, the big cougar rose. He swayed unsteadily, snorted, and turned his head to stare at the bloodstained fur on his right shoulder. Then he lifted his right front leg in an almost human gesture and stretched it out, bent and tested it. He put his weight on his right paw and took a couple of steps.

Then he turned and stared at Oliver for a long moment.

Oliver nodded. The cougar turned away and walked slowly into the thick brush at the edge of the meadow. He disappeared into the shadows.

Oliver shook his head. "He's really hard to understand, as if he's even more feral than he was. He says he's still sore but the leg is strong. And he's going after the guys who shot him."

"I'm outta here." Adam shifted. The big wolf glanced toward Anton. *Let me know what happens. As much as I hate the idea of poachers on your land, I'd hate to see them get eaten by Igmutaka. That could create a whole new slew of problems.*

Hard to explain that one to the game warden. Anton waved him off and Adam trotted back toward the house.

Oliver shifted and waited for Anton.

"I guess we'd better see if we can find these idiots before Igmutaka has them for lunch." Anton took one last glance around them. The meadow was empty and nothing in the woods seemed out of the ordinary. He shifted and sniffed noses with Oliver. The two of them took off at a steady lope, following the trail of the cougar.

Keisha filled her arms with bottles of red wine and Tia grabbed the white. "We'll have to come back for the rest. You shouldn't be carrying too much weight."

Tia laughed. "I'm pregnant, not sick. Don't worry."

Keisha grinned. "You're right. I remember when I first found out I was pregnant. Anton worried about every little . . . oh, damn. I hear Lily. I was hoping she'd sleep longer." She glanced toward the closed door, set a couple of the bottles down and headed up the stairs with Tia right behind her.

She shoved the door open with her shoulder and stepped into the kitchen with Tia following on her heels.

"My baby!"

Three strange men waited. One held Lily in his arms.

The other two held guns. Very large handguns, pointed directly at Keisha.

Her blood went cold. She couldn't take her eyes off Lily, lying so comfortably in a strange man's arms. She sent out a silent scream to Anton.

Tia stepped in behind her and gasped.

Keisha very carefully set the wine bottles on the floor so that her hands were free. She sensed Tia's silent message to Luc. Tia set her bottles down beside Keisha's, and when she straightened up, there was more anger than fear in her eyes.

"I know you," Tia said. "You're the same ones who came after us in San Francisco. What the hell do you want?" She practically snarled when she asked, "Why won't you leave us alone?"

Anton paused in the shadows. His ears pricked forward and he strained to hear the sound again. Voices. Men's voices, low whispers on the far side of a deep and treacherous ravine. Too far to read their minds, the sound too distorted to pinpoint their location.

He and Oliver remained hidden beneath the low branches of a sprawling shrub, but he was positive he'd heard at least two men speaking softly to one another.

If only he could be certain of their location! The wind had picked up, though, and the rustling branches muffled sound as much as the wind confused the direction.

He and Oliver were well within the boundaries of his huge property. It might not all be fenced, but the entire perimeter was posted. Anyone who was not Chanku had no business here.

I'm going to see if I can get to the other side of the ravine. I think they're up in those rocks.

We know they're armed, Oliver said. *Be careful. You'll be exposed if you try to cross over.*

Not if I go down inside first. There are some fallen trees bridging that area near the slide.

Okay. I'll watch from here, let you know if I see anything.

Anton nodded. Belly low to the ground, he crept through the brush, moving uphill until he reached the edge of the ravine about a hundred yards north of where he'd been hiding with Oliver. He paused there at the rocky lip, ears cocked for any sound.

Keisha's cry slammed into his mind. He jerked around and stared in the direction of the house.

Help us, Anton. Men have Lily. We're in the kitchen. They're armed. Tia's with me.

Keisha! Panic powered his cry. *Oliver, Keisha and Tia are in trouble. We need to go back!*

Leaping to his feet, Anton sent a powerful cry for help to everyone within hearing.

He barely got his message out when something hard and hot slammed into his side and sent him tumbling.

No!

It was the nightmare, all over again. Darkness surrounded him, pain engulfed him. He opened his eyes but couldn't see, tried to scream but made no sound.

Keisha's plea for help filled his mind. Lily's cries.

Was it the dream, or did he truly hear them?

Keisha and Lily needed him, but he couldn't move. His body was leaden, his thoughts confused. He tried to run, but something held him. He struggled to breathe, but an iron band encased his lungs.

Oliver? He was certain he sensed Oliver nearby. But why? Oliver wasn't part of the dream. No, only Keisha and Lily and his own worthless, helpless self. He didn't remember the pain, but he'd never felt anything like this . . . his lungs struggled for air, his heart stuttered in his chest.

He tried to rise. Keisha needed him. Lily . . . he sensed his daughter, sensed her fear, but *he could not move!*

Keisha! I love you. I'm trying, my love. I'm trying so hard . . .

The darkness was absolute. The pain inside his chest, overwhelming. Even worse, the pain of knowing, once again, that he'd failed. Keisha and Lily were in danger and he was helpless.

Useless to his mate and his daughter. Unable to care for those he loved. Those who counted on him. Anton blinked and sensed, more than saw, a glimmer of light. A pale glow in the absolute darkness of his world. It seemed so far away, but he knew, if only he could reach it, the pain would stop.

He tried to stretch out his arm, but nothing happened. He tried to stand, but his legs refused to obey and the light seemed to fade.

No!

Then it came to him. His own light. His own action. Suddenly, Anton knew exactly what he had to do.

Oliver scrambled down the steep cliff, hiding behind boulders, finding cover wherever he could, scrambling with the agility of a wolf on the hunt. He'd heard the blast of the rifle, watched Anton's body jerk viciously and tumble over the cliff.

He called out to Adam. Sent out a cry to Mei and anyone else who could hear. Keisha and Tia were in trouble. Anton had been shot.

Anton!

Panting, scrabbling over loose shale and sliding through broken shards of rock, Oliver raced to the bottom of the cliff. He knew the men waited at the top, somewhere out of sight. Knew they followed his descent and could only pray they would let him live.

He had to find Anton. He had to! But the man whose mind was always a quiet presence in his own thoughts was silent.

And when he finally found Anton, his body tumbled and broken behind a massive boulder, Oliver understood why he'd not heard a sound from his mentor.

Blood pooled beneath the big wolf's head and body and there was a gaping wound above his ribs with white bone showing through the torn skin. His left rear leg was bent and twisted, his flanks covered in cuts, his thick fur tangled with twigs and stickers.

Without regard to anyone watching, Oliver shifted. He held his hand to Anton's chest, but he couldn't find a heartbeat. Sobbing, he held his face next to the bloody muzzle, but it was impossible to tell if Anton breathed.

Impossible to tell if he lived.

Frantic, grief-stricken, he called out again and again, praying someone would hear.

Praying for a miracle.

"There's a million dollar bounty on your heads, ladies, and we've struck gold." The closest man waved his pistol in Tia's direction. "I heard you say you're pregnant. That's even better."

"The reward's no good anymore. How long since you checked the Internet?" Tia shoved Keisha behind her and faced the two like a warrior goddess, standing in front of their guns without fear.

Keisha felt cold inside. She'd had a moment's connection with Anton, then nothing. The man holding Lily hadn't hurt the baby, but Keisha could tell she was winding up for a good, loud cry.

Emotionally, Keisha should have felt numb. She didn't.

No, she was angry. Purely furious, in fact, and she'd had it with these bastards coming after them, turning their lives upside down, threatening them.

I've killed before.

And she would do it again. Keisha sent her thoughts to

Tia. *I'm going to shift. My clothes are loose enough, they should fall off. What about yours?*

I'll be fine. Luc's on his way, but I don't think we have time to wait for him. On my word, you shift and get the one on the right. I'll take the one on the left. If you can shift back and get Lily, I'll try and take out the third one before he gets his gun. It's behind him, on the table.

"What do you mean, the bounty's no good?" The one holding Lily glared at the other two. "You said . . ."

"It's good. She's lying." The one on the right emphasized his words with the barrel of his pistol.

Tia stuck her hands on her hips. "The one who offered the bounty is dead." She grinned. "He was killed by wolves."

The one holding Lily turned a pasty shade. Keisha shifted and lunged at her target. He twisted out of her way but his handgun clattered to the floor.

Tia had her target down, but he was big and powerful and managed to hold her away from his throat. The one carrying Lily turned and stuck the baby back in the crib. He reached for his weapon.

Turning toward the struggling pairs, he fired a single shot into the floor between them. Tia snarled, but she didn't turn loose the one she held. Neither did Keisha. Her jaws were locked on the throat of the man she'd attacked, but he was twisting her head, pulling her off as she searched for purchase with her hind legs, scrabbling and slipping on the tile floor.

The moment he separated from his body, the pain went away. Anton looked down at the body of the ruined wolf lying in the rocks beneath him and wondered how much time he had before his life force disappeared entirely.

Oliver lay beside him, his shoulders shaking as he cried silent tears. Anton wished he could comfort his old friend, but there was no time. He sensed others coming. Adam was with them.

If he could have, Anton would have sighed. Adam would try to save him. He had such a huge heart, so much love and such amazing skills, but they would never make it in time.

His wolven body was too badly damaged.

Even Adam wouldn't be able to fix this one. It bothered him, to think of the way his death would affect the ones who loved him.

Which reminded him of his reason for being here, floating in the air above the battered wolf. He needed to go to Keisha, now. He had to save Lily. Once again, he had Adam to thank, or he never would have known how to leave his dying body.

If only he could find them. He'd not moved far from his body when he and Adam shared energy this morning. Was that only a few hours ago?

So much had changed.

Lives altered. His ended? Soon. He sensed his own ending. He had to hurry. He knew that, logically. He sensed his waning power. When the wolf died, the energy would dissipate, though he didn't know how long he could last. He needed the energy to help his mate, if only he could find her.

Keisha? He was afraid of that. Mindtalking in this form wouldn't work. Something, though, seemed to draw him to the north. He visualized the kitchen where Keisha said the intruders had entered.

Suddenly he was there, hovering above Lily's crib.

Tia had her jaws clamped around a man's wrist, but Keisha's jaws were locked on another's throat. A third man held a large handgun, but it appeared he was afraid to shoot, afraid of hitting his own people.

Anton knew the moment when it came to the man, that if he were to grab the baby, the women would stop. Quick as thought, Anton wrapped himself around his daughter, covering her in an invisible cloud of pure energy.

He sensed Lily's mind. He was surprised to find it so filled with conscious thoughts. She was an infant, after all.

Enthralled, he wrapped his energy closely around her and totally dismissed the fight in the kitchen. Keisha and Tia were a formidable team and he had no doubt they would be victorious.

Anton was vaguely aware of the third man trying to grab for Lily, but he merely had to focus and block the man's grasping hands. He sensed a subtle pulse in his energy field.

Screaming, the man flew across the room.

Then Anton sensed Luc coming through the door and shifting, and another wolf right behind him. More were racing across the front drive. Keisha would be fine. He hoped she realized how proud of her he was. How much he loved her.

He settled himself closer around his daughter. For these last few moments left to him, he would soak up everything he could about her, every bit of the infant she was, the girl she would be . . . the woman who would one day become a wolf.

Thank you, Daddy.

Lily? How did you know it was me?

Because I can feel your love.

Her voice sounded so mature, so very grown-up and he ached when he realized he'd not be there for her.

Daddy, will Mommy be okay?

I hope so. She's very brave, and very strong and she loves you as much as I do.

They're not fighting anymore, Daddy. More good people are coming. I'm safe, now. You need to go back. Your body is waiting for you.

I can't go back, Lily. There's nothing to go back to.

But . . . you can't stay forever.
I know, sweetheart. But I'll stay with you as long as I can.

Adam shifted and knelt beside Oliver and Anton. He let Oliver know that Mik, AJ, and Tala should be here shortly. Mei, Tinker, Lisa, and Eve took off after the two hunters. Igmutaka had spotted them on the cliff above and was keeping them in sight.

They saw you shift, Mei said to Adam as she raced away. *They're the ones who shot Anton.*

Kill them.

It didn't bother Adam at all to order their deaths. They had, after all, tried to kill Anton.

He hoped like hell they hadn't succeeded, but he sensed no life force at all. It was as if Anton wasn't here.

Not here? Hope blossomed in his heart. Kneeling next to the bleeding wolf, Adam went about repairing the broken body that hovered on the cusp of death. Could Anton have slipped free of the wolf? Was he nearby, nothing more than energy?

Adam placed his hands on the wolf. He had to search for the tiny, flickering spark of life that was all that remained to link Anton to this plane. Finally, he found it, but he was dismayed at how pale it was, how faded and diminished. Not like the man he knew and loved. Not like Anton at all.

But it was all he had to work with, and it would have to be enough. Slipping inside Anton, Adam searched the extent of the wolf's many injuries, performing his own sort of triage. Stopping the bleeding was paramount, but the wounds were horrible. This damage went far beyond anything Adam had ever attempted to heal and he was already tired.

So very tired from healing Igmutaka.

He sensed others arriving, felt the energy they shared

with him. He wondered where Keisha was, how long it would be before Stefan and Xandi were back from town.

Wondered if he could save his dear friend.

So long as you believe . . . That's what he'd told Anton. If you believed you could do something, then you could do it. He had to believe. It seemed so trite, so utterly clichéd, but Adam knew that, should he give up hope, all hope was lost. He had to look at each injury separately, see each as an integral part of the whole. He couldn't look at the entire mass of injuries at once.

That would be too much. Overwhelming, in fact. One step at a time.

And with that in mind, he set about healing the wolf that was the wizard, Anton Cheval.

Chapter 15

"I want to go to him. I *should* go to him, but I sense him here . . . and even if I didn't, I can't leave Lily." Keisha wept even harder as Stefan and Xandi wrapped their arms around her. Luc sat with Tia, holding her close.

Keisha glanced toward her daughter and wiped her streaming eyes. "I don't know what to do." Remarkably, Lily slept through everything, curled up in her little portable crib with a smile on her face. Such innocence. She had no idea of the drama going on about her. She didn't know that the man who had given her life might be gone forever.

"I'd know if he died, wouldn't I?" She couldn't imagine a man as powerful as Anton Cheval, quietly submitting to death. He'd fight it with everything he had.

And he wouldn't go without telling Keisha he loved her. She knew that. She had to believe it.

Stefan led her to a kitchen chair next to the baby's crib and helped her sit. He squatted down in front of her and pushed the tangled hair back from her eyes.

"Adam's with him now. He can fix what's broken, sweetie. I'm sure they'll bring him home the moment he can be moved."

"They shot him, Stef. Oliver said it looks bad. What if Adam can't . . . ?"

"They're coming." Xandi stepped back from the window. "Mik's carrying a wolf. He has Anton."

Keisha raced from the kitchen and practically flew down the steps. She met the somber group halfway across the drive. The bloodstained wolf lay limp in Mik's huge arms.

"Anton? Is he . . . ?"

"He's alive," Mik said. "Barely. Adam's coming. He's totally drained, but he said this is all he can do for now. He needs to rest. The bleeding is stopped and the shattered bones are mended, but . . ." Mik sighed and started walking again.

"But what?" Keisha ran alongside to keep up with his long strides.

"Adam will explain."

Keisha stopped. She stood in the driveway and watched Mik's broad back as he carried her mate into the house. Adam was coming, his steps slow and labored. AJ was on one side of him, holding on to his arm, Oliver on the other. Tala walked silently behind them, her face streaked with tears.

All of them were nude. They'd raced to save Anton as wolves. Why hadn't they shifted to return?

She knew the answer as they drew closer. Adam's face was gray and haggard, his skin lined as if he'd aged years in the course of the day.

"Adam?"

Oliver and AJ paused. Tala stopped beside AJ. Adam's head drooped and it was obvious he remained upright only because Oliver and AJ held him. Keisha touched his cheek. Slowly he raised his head, blinking as if he'd just awakened from a trance.

"Adam, what happened? Where's Eve?"

He shook his head. "Don't know." His voice was rough, barely a whisper. "Is he here . . . ?"

"Mik just brought him home. He's putting him in our bedroom."

Adam shook his head again, stronger this time. "Not his body. Him. Is Anton here?"

"I don't understand."

Adam took a deep breath. "Body dying. Life essence left. I taught him how this morning. He's not in the wolf. I can't find him."

Keisha realized she was staring at him like an idiot. "He's not in his body?"

"He can't communicate this way. Do you sense him anywhere? Feel him near?"

Of course, she did. She'd felt him near ever since the intruders attacked. "Lily! He's protecting Lily." Keisha spun around and raced back to the house. It had to be. There was no other explanation. Lily hadn't cried through all the commotion. Keisha'd caught a glimpse of one of the men going after her baby and the next thing she'd seen him unconscious, lying against the wall on the far side of the kitchen.

She raced up the front steps and ran through the open door. "Stefan! Xandi! Where are you?"

Stefan came at a full run from her bedroom. "What's wrong? I was helping Mik get Anton settled." He grabbed her arms but she pulled herself free and ran toward the kitchen.

Xandi sat at the table with her head in her hands. Alex was asleep in the carrier wrapped across her chest. Lily slept on in her portable crib. Keisha knelt on the floor beside the baby, sobbing so hard she could barely catch her breath. "Anton? I know you're here, my love. You've been with Lily all along, haven't you? When you're ready, come to our room. Mik just put the wolf to bed."

Xandi knelt beside her. "What in the name of the Goddess are you doing?"

Gasping for breath, Keisha rested her forehead on her clenched hand at the edge of Lily's crib. "This morning,

Adam taught Anton something new. He showed him how to become pure energy, how to separate himself from his body. Adam thinks Anton did it again, when he was so badly wounded. I cried out to him for help, but he was shot at precisely the same moment."

She glanced up at Stefan, standing solemnly behind his mate. Sobbing, she asked them, "What would you do, if your body were dying and you knew Xandi and Alex needed you?"

Stefan slowly nodded. "I would move heaven and earth to help them." He gazed at the crib and his eyes were troubled. "And if my body was dying, I imagine I'd find another way. But shouldn't we sense him? Feel something if he's with Lily?"

Oliver stepped into the kitchen. He'd thrown on a pair of old sweats. Mei stood beside him with tears streaming down her face. "His life force could be very weak. His wounds were awful and the wolf is near death from blood loss. Maybe Anton doesn't have the strength to return to his body."

Mei's lips trembled. "I can always hear his thoughts. There's nothing there now. Nothing." She turned against Oliver's chest and cried harder.

Mik walked into the room. His hands and chest were covered in Anton's blood. He'd slipped on a pair of worn blue jeans and tears streaked the sharp angles of his face. "Maybe he knows if he returns, the wolf will die."

"What?" Keisha stood up and faced him. She realized her hands were clenched into tight fists. Slowly, she forced her fingers to relax. "Why would he die?"

"The wolf stays alive because there is no spirit within the body to pass on to the next life. Think of a mindless zombie. Right now, the wolf is like one of the undead. His wounds were too serious for him to survive. I saw him there, before Adam began his healing. He managed to repair the broken bones and torn flesh, but he can't replace the lost blood or heal the weakened spirit. If Anton is even able to return, unless he's strong enough to keep the body alive, it will be as if he's given it permission to die."

"I won't let that happen." Keisha lifted her chin and gazed around her. While she'd been kneeling at Lily's crib, the room had filled. It looked as if everyone had returned. "We're all here except Adam, who's resting, and Ulrich. Millie, where is he?"

"With Anton. He didn't want to leave him alone."

"Good. We need to move Lily's crib into our bedroom." Keisha looked at her sleeping daughter and shook her head. "Then we need to make the wolf as strong and healthy as we can. If we're going to get our alpha back, all of us will need to share everything we can."

Talking as much to herself as anyone else, she muttered, "I wonder how long Adam needs to rest?"

Manda and Eve sat beside Adam's bed while he slept. Manda had never seen her brother looking like this, so haggard and worn, as if each breath might be his last. She knew he'd given everything he had to heal Anton, but it hadn't been enough.

Can we somehow give him our energy? Is there a way to share? She turned and smiled at Eve. Shrugged her shoulders and wondered. *It seems only fair.*

But how? Eve frowned. She trailed her fingers over Adam's shoulder. *I love him so much. I'll do anything for him. Did you know he saved my life?*

He saved mine, too. Over and over again. When I was a child growing up, just a horrible freak in the labs, there was a stranger who came into my mind and gave me hope. I didn't know him, but he kept me going. Kept me from killing myself on more than one occasion. It was Adam.

He's your brother and he loves you.

He didn't know me, then. He only knew I needed help. He's so generous, but he never thinks of himself.

He loves Anton. Eve stroked his arm. *It will kill him if Anton dies.*

He won't die. Not if she could help it. Not if she could help Adam. He was the key. Manda showed Eve exactly what she had in mind, staring into her gray eyes and explaining, in no uncertain terms, the risks they faced.

Eve nodded and accepted without hesitation. She moved to the far side of the bed, swept her long, blond hair back over her shoulders and took Adam's right hand. Manda held on to his left. Then she searched inside herself, digging deeply for the source of energy that made Manda Smith exactly who and what she was.

And when she found it, when she figured out a way to channel it, she sent all that she could into the twin who had saved her, over and over again for so many years.

Keisha sat on the bed beside the wolf and struggled to contain her tears. Without Anton's life force, this was nothing more than an animal, yet as long as it lived, there was a chance for her mate to survive.

"At least we know he's still alive." Luc's soft voice caught everyone's attention. "If we die in wolf form, we revert to human."

Mik frowned. "How do you know that?"

Tia leaned against her mate. "Because Luc killed my mother when she was a wolf and she turned back into my mother."

A soft gasp filled the room. Keisha thought everyone knew Luc and Tia's story by now, but it appeared not.

Luc nodded. "I was a rookie cop and got a call on a wolf roaming loose in Golden Gate Park. I saw it, thought it was going after some kids, and I shot it. When I got to the place where it had fallen, I found a beautiful, naked woman lying in the grass. She was dead with my bullet in her chest."

Ulrich stepped to Luc's other side and put an arm around his shoulders. "Camille's loss was devastating, but it led me to Luc and eventually to you, Mik, and to AJ, Jake, and Tinker. It's hard to believe, now, but my wife's death was the catalyst that started Pack Dynamics."

Stefan ran his fingers through the wolf's thick fur. "So as long as he's a wolf, he's alive?"

"Yep."

Hope blossomed in Keisha's breast. She swung around and saw the last person she expected, standing in the doorway. *Adam!*

"And as soon as he's strong enough and we get his life force back where it belongs, we should get Anton back in whatever form he chooses."

"Adam!" Keisha ran to him and threw her arms around his waist. "I thought you'd be asleep for hours."

"So did I, but Manda and Eve had a better idea, one I think we can use with Anton." He turned to Baylor and grinned. "Your mate and mine shared their energy with me. It didn't take much, but I feel rested and strong. It feels like a transfusion!"

Baylor frowned. "Is Manda okay? I thought she was resting."

Adam nodded. "She's resting now. She and Eve are in our room, but they're both fine, just tired." He rubbed his hands together. "I'm going to need everyone here to help me. Keisha, did you ever figure out where Anton is? I sense him here in this room, but I can tell he's not in the wolf."

"He's with Lily." She stood beside her daughter's crib and fought back tears. All she'd done this afternoon was cry. There was no time for tears now . . . and, with the Goddess's grace, no reason for them later.

"Why didn't I think of that?" Adam walked over to the crib and smiled down at the sleeping baby. "He protected her during the attack, didn't he?"

Keisha nodded as Adam knelt down and stroked Lily's cheek. Her lips curved up to meet his fingertip, but she didn't awaken. "He's here." Adam looked up and met Keisha's eyes. "I feel him, but he's very faint. It's almost as if Lily is keeping him alive."

"He would never harm her." Keisha reached for her daughter.

"Of course he wouldn't." Adam gently touched her forearm. "Can you lay her beside the wolf? Close enough that their bodies touch?"

Keisha nodded and gathered the sleeping baby in her arms. She nuzzled the dark cap of fuzz on Lily's head and closed her eyes to whisper a quick prayer to the Goddess. Then she stripped away Lily's sleep sack and carefully placed the diaper-clad baby against her father's back.

Lily's café au lait skin seemed unusually pale beside Anton's dark fur, but she wrapped her tiny fingers in his thick coat, sighed, snuggled close, and then settled back to sleep.

Adam sat on the edge of the bed beside Anton. "We need to share our strength. Open your minds, see what I do when I touch the wolf. Take turns. Stay as long as you feel you have something to give. Then make room for the next person. Touch only the wolf. Lily should be able to take what she needs."

Then he put his hands on the wolf and closed his eyes. Keisha felt Adam's strength pouring into her husband, saw the path it took, and sighed. If this didn't work . . .

But it would. She felt the energy in the room as each one came forward. Ulrich and Millie, Mik, AJ, and Tala. Lisa and Tinker. Jake, Shannon, and Baylor, each one of them sharing whatever they could, pouring their own life force into the grievously injured wolf lying so still on the bed.

Stefan and Oliver were with him now, their faces showing the intense amount of concentration this took.

Keisha looked away from the men and realized there was a glow around her baby—a shimmering cloud that seemed to grow and pulse with life. She shot a worried glance at Adam and saw him frown.

The wolf seemed to waver and suddenly Anton was lying on the bed with Lily close behind him. The shimmering cloud still hovered over her daughter.

There was no sense of life in the man. His chest was still, his powerful muscles slack. Horrified, Keisha raised her eyes and met Luc's grief-stricken expression.

A low moan seemed to fill the room as each of them recognized death for what it was—something unimaginable, unbelievable.

The wizard could not die.

Keisha cried out. She flung herself forward and covered his body with hers.

Adam, Stefan, and Oliver came together as one, each of them touching a part of Anton's still body. The others, recognizing this for what it was, Anton's final battle, joined forces. Crowding around the bed they placed their hands on his body, sharing whatever each of them had left to give.

You need to go, Daddy. Now!

I know. Don't be frightened. It's just . . . I have to choose, Lily, but which way? The light calls me. Do you see it? It's beautiful, so warm and gentle. The body calls me, too, but it's filled with pain.

It's filled with love, Daddy. Don't you recognize love anymore?

I recognize you. I love you.

Then choose life, Daddy. For all its pain, choose life.

* * *

What a strange dream. He felt as if he'd been run over by a Mack truck and it was damned hard to open his eyes. He sensed a lot of people around him. Sensed their thoughts, even their memories, in him.

All of them, Chanku.

He tried to move and groaned.

There was a collective gasp that was more than enough to force him to open his eyes.

Keisha leaned over him, crying as if her heart would break. He reached up and touched her tear-slicked cheek with his trembling fingertips. She pressed her hand over his and cried even harder.

He slowly turned his head to one side and saw Oliver, Stefan, and Adam. Oliver and Stefan cried openly, but Adam had a huge grin on his face.

He must have fixed something. Adam loved to fix things.

Anton recognized the bedroom, but all the faces sort of blurred together. He hurt like hell and his mind was confused, filled, as it was, with memories from more than one person.

He'd have to figure that one out.

Later.

He heard a squeal and felt little arms and legs against his side.

Lily!

He tried to reach for her, but Keisha lifted the baby and placed her, tummy side down, on his chest. She raised her head and gave him a drooly, gummy grin.

He tried to see into her thoughts, but found only the incoherent babble of a typical three-month-old.

Had all of it been a dream? He'd figure that out later, too. Now, though, he just wanted to sleep. He reached for Keisha and found her mind wide open to his.

Make them all go away, my love. I want to sleep. You and Lily may stay.

232 / *Kate Douglas*

She laughed. He frowned. What the hell was so funny? "He's back," she said, giggling. "Grumpy and arrogant as ever, but he's back."

Grumpy? He was never grumpy. . . . Arrogant? Well . . . Anton felt his eyelids flutter closed. Heard the soft shuffle of many feet as his room emptied. With Lily back against his side and Keisha holding them both in her arms, he drifted slowly in the direction of sleep.

There was a sense that something momentous had occurred, but he didn't have a clue what it might have been.

He'd figure that out later, too. Right now, everything that mattered was here with him. His beloved mate. His amazing daughter. Nothing else mattered. Nothing at all.

"I never thought we'd be celebrating anything tonight, not after what's happened over the past couple weeks, but what you accomplished is nothing short of a miracle." Stefan held his beer up to tap Adam's bottle. "Thank you. I would have lost my dearest friend if not for you."

Adam stared into his beer bottle and smiled. "I'm still a bit overwhelmed. The fact we were all able to share bits of ourselves . . . I wonder what he'll remember?"

"I'm sure he'll tell us."

Adam laughed at Stefan's dry comment. Then he socked him lightly on the shoulder, turned with Eve and followed her to the small group standing near the deck railing. Stefan watched them go. He took a long swallow of his cold beer and his gaze drifted over the amazing cadre of individuals sitting and standing around the deck, all of them laughing and talking as if they didn't have a care in the world.

Of course, now that Anton rested comfortably and Luc had discovered no more wanted posters for them littered about the Internet, it might mean they could actually relax. For a while, anyway.

Xandi slipped in behind him and wrapped her arms around his waist. "It's going to seem so quiet when everyone goes home."

"I know, but it's time. Anton will probably need a few weeks to completely recover. Adam said the long period out of his body might affect his short-term memory for a while."

"Thank goodness he's alive. I was so afraid. . . ."

Stefan nodded. "I know. I think all of us were."

Ulrich stood up and tapped a fork against his wineglass. All heads turned in his direction. "Millie and I will be leaving early in the morning, most likely before most of you bums are awake. With my daughter and son-in-law's permission, I have a couple of announcements I want to make before we go."

Millie slipped in beside him and he wrapped his arm around her waist. "First of all, I've decided to make my retirement official so that I can help Millie with the High Mountain Wolf Sanctuary."

Millie interrupted. "He hasn't worked in weeks. I guess he's been practicing." She flashed him a saucy grin and he kissed the end of her nose.

"As I was saying, before I was so rudely interrupted . . . I love Colorado, and I love Millie. I know she can use my help. With that in mind, I'm naming Lucien as the head of Pack Dynamics and granting ownership of the Marina District house to him and Tianna."

"Dad! The house?"

He grabbed Tia's hand and held it to his lips for a kiss. "My grandbabies need a nice place to live that's all theirs. That's a good house for raising babies. It's where I raised you."

Luc grabbed Ulrich's hand and was quickly pulled into a tight embrace. Everyone applauded. Stefan realized he had a death grip on Xandi's hand and a huge smile on his face.

234 / Kate Douglas

It was time for good news. He just wished Anton was out here where he could hear it.

Xandi agreed. She kissed his cheek and let him know he'd been broadcasting again.

"Think of the devil." Stefan tugged on Xandi's hand and nodded toward the front door. Anton stood in the open doorway with a big smile on his face. Keisha held Lily in one arm and supported her mate around the waist with the other. Stefan quickly moved to Anton's other side to help him walk.

Oliver gently shoved Keisha aside and slipped his arm around Anton's waist opposite Stefan. They walked him across the deck to one of the comfortable lounge chairs and helped him sit comfortably with his long legs stretched out in front.

Xandi quickly brought him a plate of steak and potatoes from the dining room. He ate quickly, efficiently, and it was obvious his body was crying out for food to replenish the calories he'd burned.

When he finished and raised his head, everyone sat watching him. He blinked, and his skin darkened to a ruddy shade.

Stefan laughed. "You're blushing, my friend. I didn't think you had it in you!"

Anton turned with his usual superior air. "So would you, if your head was filled with the carnal memories of over a dozen sex-starved shapeshifters."

"Sex starved? When is anyone here starved for sex?" Stefan touched Anton's shoulder. He needed the contact, the proof his friend was alive and well.

"Since they all shared so much of their life force with me today."

Obviously, Anton had meant it as a joke, but his voice cracked on the final word and he bowed his head. Stefan rubbed his shoulders and waited.

Finally, Anton raised his head. Tears sparkled in his amber eyes. "I died today. I remember the cold and the emptiness. I remember a pale light glowing in the distance, calling me and I had a choice between that light and the peace it offered, or a body filled with pain. A voice told me it wasn't pain. What I felt was love, and life, and I was instructed, in no uncertain terms, to choose life. I only had that option because of all of you. Because of your love."

Stefan frowned. "Who was the voice, Anton?"

The wizard shook his head. "It was Lily. She said in spite of all its pain, I should choose life." He reached up and grabbed Stefan's hand. Keisha took his empty plate and set it on the railing. She grabbed his free hand. Xandi moved around behind him and rubbed his shoulders.

Oliver and Mei stood to one side, all of them touched by Anton's words. No matter the risk, Stefan thought, they would always choose life.

He raised his beer in salute. "To my dearest friend, Anton Cheval. May you always choose life, Anton, and may we always be lucky enough to share it with you."

Laughing, Anton touched his wineglass to the side of Stefan's beer. "Oh, you have, Stefan. You have all shared it with me. There are no secrets anymore."

Mei clinked her wineglass against Anton's and slanted him a sly grin. "There never were, Anton. Remember that."

The wizard snorted. Not his usual witty comeback, but at least he was alive and laughing.

Stefan stepped back and leaned against the railing with Xandi close beside him. Alex lay comfortably in the ever-present sling stretched across his mother's chest. It was time to count their blessings, not worry about what the future might bring.

Xandi glanced up at him with eyes filled with love, and his heart overflowed with memories. So many years lost and alone, half man, half wolf, wondering if he would ever know love. Now he had more than he knew how to handle. More than he'd ever dreamed.

He glanced at Anton and found the wizard staring back at him. Once more his eyes were filled with tears, but there was a smile on his lips.

Stefan raised his beer in toast. Anton saluted.

Damn, no matter the risk, it was all good. And for all its pain, Stefan knew each of them would always choose life.

Epilogue

San Francisco, California

Montana was nice, but it really felt good to be back in the city. Tala picked up her pace as she headed down Stanyan to Haight where she planned to cut through the park to check on Keisha's memorial garden. She'd promised, after all.

Like she'd had a choice?

That thought alone was enough to make her smile.

Are the plants doing okay? Is the rock work still in place? Please, don't let there be graffiti . . . like that's all Keisha had to worry about. Still, Keisha had won a national prize and the chance to design the garden, and it was lovely. Planted with grasses native to the Himalayan steppe . . . amazing, the varieties she'd chosen.

The same mix of grasses the Chanku needed to shift.

Only Keisha hadn't yet known of her Chanku heritage. That alone made her choices special.

Tala reached the corner of Haight and Stanyan. The usual group of homeless youths whistled and made lewd comments. No big deal. She smiled and waved when she walked past the half dozen young men lounging around the street corner.

At another time, she might have been terrified by the suggestive leers and off-color comments, given her small stature and feminine gender. Since becoming Chanku, it took an awful lot to frighten her.

She held her head up and kept walking. The sun passed behind a small cloud. Tala shivered. Moments later, as she drew near Keisha's garden, she caught the sound of footsteps behind her. Memories of the recent attack here in the park were way too fresh to ignore. Luc had assured all of them that the wanted posters were off the Internet and no one seemed to be hunting Chanku, but . . .

Tala risked a look back. Two of the young men she'd passed had broken off from the group and now followed her toward the memorial garden. Dressed in black, lips, noses, and eyebrows pierced with metal studs, they both had the glittery-eyed look of chronic drug abusers.

Rather than risk a surprise attack, Tala turned and faced them.

The taller of the two kept coming until he was well within her personal space. He reached out to touch her hair, but Tala twisted away. She sent out a mental call for help and hoped like hell Mik or AJ heard.

"Bitch. Think you're too good?"

Tala heard movement behind her, but who? She'd only noticed these two and her senses rarely failed her. She heard a low growl, sensed Chanku power—a wolven presence.

An unfamiliar wolven presence. The kid groping her had his eyes glued to her breast. He grabbed her right arm with one hand, her left breast with the other.

His friend screamed and took off running.

A flash of gray knocked Tala to the ground. Her head hit the pavement hard. She saw flashes of light, a dark shape spinning. Nausea welled up with a rolling wave of vertigo when she tried to raise herself on one elbow.

She heard snarling, growling, a choked scream.

Another scream, behind her. A woman crying out, "Ohmygod, Nicky. Ohmygodohmygod . . ."

Tala blinked. She was too close to focus. Her nostrils twitched with the thick smell of blood. Lots of blood, and bits of gray spinning, a kaleidoscope of life and death and horrible sounds that seemed to go on forever.

And ended in a heartbeat.

Then there was silence.

All but for the harsh sobs of the woman who now knelt beside her. Who put her hand out and touched the naked shoulder of a slender young man lying on the path in front of Tala.

All around them were pools of blood, and the torn, lifeless body of the one who had grabbed her.

Tala shook her head and caught her breath. She waited for her vision to clear. "Who?"

The young woman kneeling beside her looked totally shell-shocked. She raised her head and stared at Tala. "He just changed," she said. "He said he knew how, but I didn't believe him. Nicky saw that guy grab you, and he changed." She shoved her knuckles into her mouth and closed off a sob.

Another young woman ran up and wrapped her arms around the first girl. Three young men appeared, all of them dressed in black, faces pierced, arms and hands tattooed, heads shaved in strange patterns. They knelt beside the unconscious youth lying in the trail.

They'd come from the direction of Keisha's garden.

The garden where the Tibetan grasses grew.

Suddenly Mik was there, and AJ beside him. The young people pulled back, obviously afraid, intimidated by the two large men.

All but the first young woman who knelt beside her comatose friend.

"Are you okay? What happened?" Mik touched Tala's shoulder, but his eyes were on the naked young man lying on the ground. He was still breathing, but barely.

"Do you have the car?" Tala glanced at AJ.

He nodded. "I do."

"We need to take them with us. All of them. Now." Tala grabbed the forearm of the young woman kneeling beside her on the path. "I want you and your friends to come with us. We can help you, but not if the police get here first."

The girl nodded. Her black hair swung like a silken curtain, her eyes still looked glazed.

Her amber eyes.

Mik carefully picked up the naked youth. The others watched him, each with an almost feral gleam in eyes the color of dark amber. All five of them shared the same look—the tall, lean bodies, the golden eyes with flecks of green. Tala took the hand of the young woman who'd cried out. She gestured to the other girl. "Come with us. We'll keep you safe. We'll take care of your friend."

"Why?"

It was one of the guys, a tall, lean kid with silver studs in his eyebrows and one side of his head completely shaved. "Why would you help us?"

"Because your friend helped me," Tala said, rising to her feet. "And because we,"—she gestured at AJ and Mik, and then herself—"we are just like you."

Read "Chanku Honor" in Sexy Beast VI

Turn the page for a sizzling preview of Vonna Harper's
NIGHT OF THE HAWK!

Coming soon from Aphrodisia!

Captured in flight, the hawk commanded most of the photograph. Its wings were spread as if it were embracing its world, talons stretched, haunting yellow eyes seemingly trained not on the world below but on whoever had taken the picture. The rest of the picture was a blur of greens and browns, undoubtedly the forest it lived in, but the hawk's image was so sharply defined Smokey could make out the individual tail feathers.

Stepping closer, she continued her study of the eleven-by-fourteen-inch picture that had been placed at eye level on the wall of the art gallery. Except for the faint drum and flute notes from the Native American instrumental playing in the background, the gallery was silent. She could hear her heart beating, feel the pull and release in her lungs as she breathed.

What came after *incredible, mesmerizing, captivating, eerie?*

Eerie?

Yes, she acknowledged, there was something otherworldly about both the hawk and the way the photographer had frozen the predator in time and space. It wasn't that large a bird, certainly not as imposing as an eagle or osprey, and yet there was no doubt of its confidence and power.

What would it be like to have such faith in one's physical ability, to be utterly at home in the wilderness?

"Pretty amazing, isn't it?"

Startled, Smokey turned around. Behind her stood the young woman who'd greeted her when she'd first come in the door. As they were the only two people in the building, she shouldn't be surprised that the woman whose name tag identified her as Halona had joined her, but the hawk had captured her attention.

"Amazing is the right word all right," Smokey acknowledged as she returned to her study of the photograph. Her fingers tingled, and she longed to be holding a paintbrush. "I wonder, do you know who took that shot? I'd love to paint the bird."

"That's one of Mato's creations. In fact, he's responsible for every wildlife and wilderness photograph in here."

"Mato?" The name seemed to settle on her tongue. "He's local?"

"As local as they get. I don't know how many generations his family goes back, certainly long before white men arrived."

Halona was dark skinned with high cheekbones; she was most likely Native American herself. "No wonder he knew where to find this magnificent creature." Smokey indicated the hawk who now seemed to be watching her. "But that doesn't account for the quality. What does he do, work for *National Geographic*?"

"Hardly, although I think he's good enough. He contracts some with BLM, the Bureau of Land Management, in addition to managing his own timber acreage."

Although she wanted to say something, for some reason she couldn't concentrate enough to put the words together. In her mind's eye, she clearly saw Mato slipping silently through the forest, a shadow among shadows, camera at the ready, senses acutely tuned to his surroundings. He saw the forest, not as a great unknown, but home, *his*.

Maybe the creatures who lived in the forest sensed that about him and shared their wilderness knowledge with him.

A man like that would be physically hard, primal, alive, real. If he saw a woman he desired, there'd be no playing games, no dance of attraction, no slowly getting to know her. Like the animals who shared the forest with him, he'd claim his mate, take her down, and fuck with her.

Struggling to ignore the heat chasing up the sides of her neck at the decidedly uncivilized thought, Smokey concentrated on swallowing. "What do you think?" she tried. "Any chance he'd sell me that picture? I notice it's not for sale."

"None of his work is, because he wants visitors to see and appreciate what exists around here."

"Around here" meant the Oregon coast, specifically the vast forest that extended to the seashore and was in danger of swallowing the little town of Storm Bay where she'd be spending the next few days.

"I'll tell you what," Halona continued. "I can give you directions to where he lives. Hopefully your vehicle's made for off-road travel because the road into his place can get pretty hairy depending on the weather."

"Mine's a four-wheel drive," she replied. Her gaze strayed to the one window and beyond it, the gray clouds and wind-whipped trees signaling an approaching storm. As if she didn't feel isolated enough. "He wouldn't be there this time of day, would he?"

"I doubt it. I don't know how pressed you are for time, but I'm sure where he'll be tonight."

A small alarm went off in her mind, but she kept her expression neutral. "Oh?"

"The meeting." Halona made it sound as if nothing else mattered. "The whole town's going to be there. There's even reporters hanging around, although maybe they're still here because that man's been missing about a week now."

Not breathing, Smokey waited to see if Halona would

ask if she was one of those reporters. Instead, Halona shrugged as if dismissing the AWOL human being.

Lying could come back to haunt her, and damn it, she wanted to be open and honest with this engaging young woman, but she had a job to do, one that wouldn't be easy and maybe impossible if she didn't keep certain things to herself, starting with her full name, Smokey Powers. Reconciling herself to deception, although she already knew the answer, she asked where the meeting was going to be held and when it would start.

"The school auditorium, seven o'clock. The school's the only place large enough to hold everyone."

"It sounds important."

"It is to us. What's at stake is whether the land our people have lived in harmony with for generations will remain unspoiled or if greed—I'm sorry, I'm sure you don't care. You're on vacation. You are, aren't you?"

Shrugging, Smokey divided her attention between Halona and the piercing yellow eyes that wouldn't leave her alone and seemed to have seen beneath deception and omission. "How will I know who Mato is?"

"He'll be speaking, I'm sure of that. And even if he doesn't—" Pressing her hand to her chest, Halona sighed. "He's the sexiest man alive. Early thirties and in his sexual prime. Unless you're dead from the neck down, you'll know."

"Oh."

"Okay." Halona grinned. "Maybe not the sexiest man alive but definitely the finest representative of his sex I've ever seen, not that I've observed that many in this one-horse town."

She hadn't come here to lust after a man. She'd driven down and west from Portland because what had happened in Storm Bay, not just recently but over a long period, had gotten her reporter's juices flowing. More that just flow, she'd been both fascinated and horrified by what her digging had turned up. When she'd told her editor at *North-*

west News about the story she wanted to do, his reaction had been exactly what she'd wanted.

"Hot damn, that's unbelievable. Fucking unbelievable! Go for it! Your instincts have yet to fail you, which is what makes you so damn good at what you do. Just be careful. There's something seriously weird going on there."

Well, *careful* didn't get the story researched and written. Probing, listening, watching, questioning, and sometimes taking chances did. And because she was who and what she was, she was willing to take those chances.

"I don't know about trying to approach him," she said, pretending a hesitation she didn't feel, or at least one she wasn't willing to admit. "If he's all involved in this meeting, he's not going to want to talk about selling a picture or giving me permission to paint it." Taking a deep breath, she looked at the photograph again. Yes, no denying it, the hawk was staring at her. How could she not paint something that intense? "But if I go, I'll at least get some idea of how my request will be received, don't you think?"

"When it comes to Mato, I don't make predictions. You know that saying about what you see is what you get? Well, there's a lot more to him than what shows on the surface, not that I have any objections to the physical package."

"He sounds interesting."

"Interesting?" Halona winked. "Let's talk after you've laid eyes on him, see if you still say the same thing. If I was ten years older—"

"Is he married?"

"No. Not sure why, maybe because he's so restless."

Like me. "Mato? Is that his first or last name?"

"First. Full name, Mato Hawk."

Against her better judgment, she again glanced at the photograph. "Same as the bird."

"There's nothing woo-woo about the connection, at least I don't think so. After all, he's taken thousands of wildlife pictures; you just happen to have zeroed in on this one of the red-tailed hawk."

In response to Smokey's question, Halona explained that the rich, russet-red coloring on the predator's broad, rounded tail identified it as the largest hawk species, this one weighing close to four pounds. What fascinated Smokey was that the wingspan could be as much at fifty-six inches, and its cry resembled a hoarse, rasping scream, two pieces of information Mato had told Halona.

"I'm sure he believes I'm nothing more than a curious kid." Halona sighed. "Little does he know that when I'm asking him about his photographs, it's because I can stand close to him. What is it about some men? They give off this electrical charge, this heat. Shit, Mato's heat is enough to set the woods on fire."

You have to be exaggerating. "Sounds fas—Ah, about the meeting, will there be fireworks? I'm thinking it must be about something important if so many people are going to be there."

The youthful eyes sobered. "Yes," she said slowly. "That's something everyone here feels passionately about. It might not matter to outsiders, but there's no reason for greed and money to jeopardize this precious land, none at all! Whatever it takes to protect it, we will, and no one is more committed than Mato."

Committed enough to kill?

Before she could come up with something to say, the gallery phone rang. Rolling her eyes, Halona headed toward the front counter. Alone again, Smokey deliberately avoided looking at the endlessly gliding hawk. Although the art gallery was small, the pieces on display were first class. Mato's photography was the star of the show, but apparently among Storm Bay's residents were a master wood carver, an oil painter specializing in ocean scenes, two spectacular free-form metal pieces that the overhead lighting reflected off, and excellent pottery in a subtle rainbow of colors.

This wasn't what she'd expected when she'd decided to

come to Storm Bay so she could dig into a number of mysterious deaths going back more than a hundred years. Small and isolated, the town had apparently come into existence as a fishing village, although Indians had lived here since before recorded history.

She'd learned that with fishing in decline and timber harvesting controlled by complex regulations, the town was losing its economic base. It had lost some population, but not as much as she'd expected, proof maybe that something beyond economics kept people here. Whatever that something was, it obviously fed some residents' creativity.

What fed Mato Hawk's creativity, his photographer's eye, his patience, his ability to find and capture what lived among the massive rain-fed trees? One picture was of a great bull elk nearly hidden among dense ferns, a thin ray of sunlight highlighting its antlers. Another, obviously taken with a powerful zoom lens, showed three young foxes, kits she thought they were called, wrestling while their exasperated looking mother watched. A third shot zeroed in on a white butterfly about to land on some dead pine needles sprinkled with either rain or dew. A close look revealed a spider clinging to one of the pine needles.

A man of contrasts? One willing to stand up for what he believed in and speak passionately about it, one capable of becoming part of his surroundings so he could identify and share its life force.

A sexy man.

She didn't know about the sexy part. After all Halona might not yet be twenty-one and filled with the romantic notions that came with youth and ignorance. Once she'd put a few more years behind her, Halona would learn there was more to a man than what lay between his legs. Broad shoulders and narrow hips might still get Smokey to occasionally, very occasionally, spread her legs, but it would take a hell of a lot more than that before she'd even consider hooking her life with some man.

And until or if she found the man with that nebulous something, she'd concentrate on a career she loved. And do a little painting on the side.

Glad she'd left her cell phone in her car because she didn't want anyone guessing the real reason for her being here if a work-related call came in, she continued her aimless wandering. She'd come into the art studio because she had time to kill until the meeting started. Oh, she could have stayed in the cabin she'd rented, but doing nothing always made her a little crazy. She didn't want to go into the one bar in town where she figured the other reporters would be killing time because she didn't want anything they said to influence her, or for them to know she was here before absolutely necessary. All too soon word would get around that the driving force behind the *Northwest News'* award-winning column "Just the Facts" was hot on a story.

Some fifteen minutes later, Smokey pushed open the door and stepped into a swirling wind. Lowering her head against flying pine needles and other debris, she made her way to her SUV and closed herself in. When she picked up her cell phone, she saw she had two messages, both from her editor. True to his nature, he had kept his messages brief: "Call me."

"You were supposed to check in," he snapped when she got through to him.

"I did. Called this morning to let you know I was almost there, remember."

"What have you been doing since then? This assignment you gave yourself's making me uneasy. If you're right about a series of deaths passing as accidents when they're really murders, that's serious shit. It's bad enough that no one's seen hide nor hair of what's his name in over a week, now you're there alone in enemy territory."

"His name was—is Flann Castetter and so far I don't have proof that this is enemy territory." *Feels a bit like it.*